Onesimus

A Novel of Christianity in the Roman Empire

Markus McDowell

RIVERSONG
BOOKS

An Imprint of Sulis International
Los Angeles | London

ONESIMUS:
A NOVEL OF CHRISTIANITY IN THE ROMAN EMPIRE

Join the author's Readers Group for a gift, news, and specials, at
https://www.markusmcdowell.com/send-gift/

Library of Congress Control Number: 2018940562
ISBN: 978-1-946849-22-9
eISBN: 978-1-946849-23-6

Riversong Books
An Imprint of Sulis International
Los Angeles | London

www.sulisinternational.com

To my Dad:

For your support and love in all my endeavors. In every place I went and dream I pursued—some a bit crazy—you were there, encouraging and helping me. I continue to be blessed by your life.

Requiescat in pace, pater.

Contents

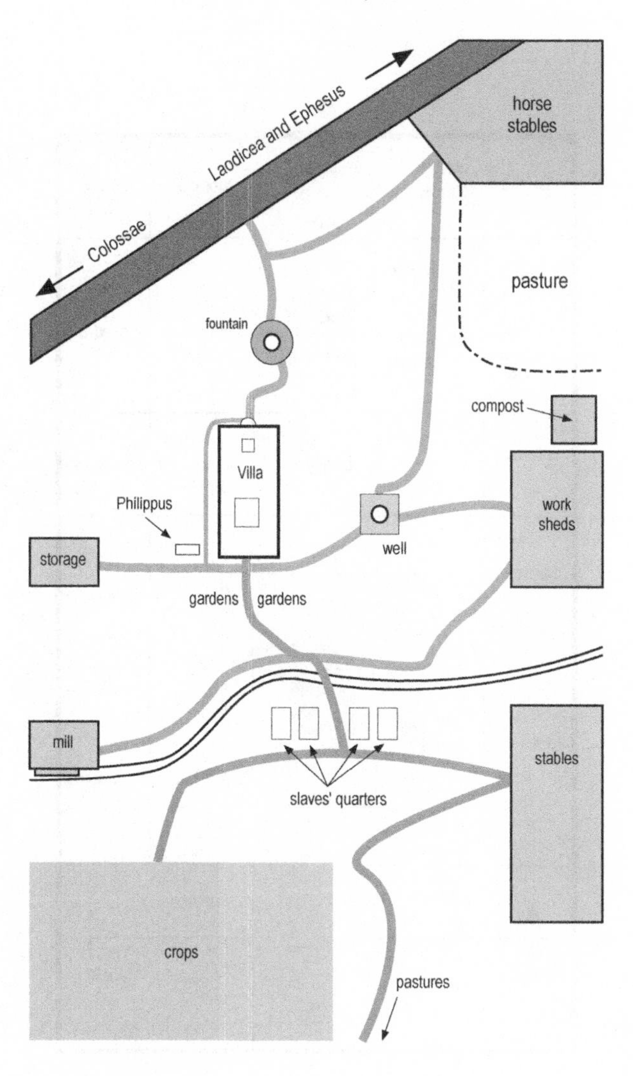
Philemon's Compound
Laodicea and Ephesus
Colossae
horse stables
pasture
fountain
compost
Villa
work sheds
Philippus
well
storage
gardens
gardens
mill
stables
slaves' quarters
crops
pastures

Philemon's Villa

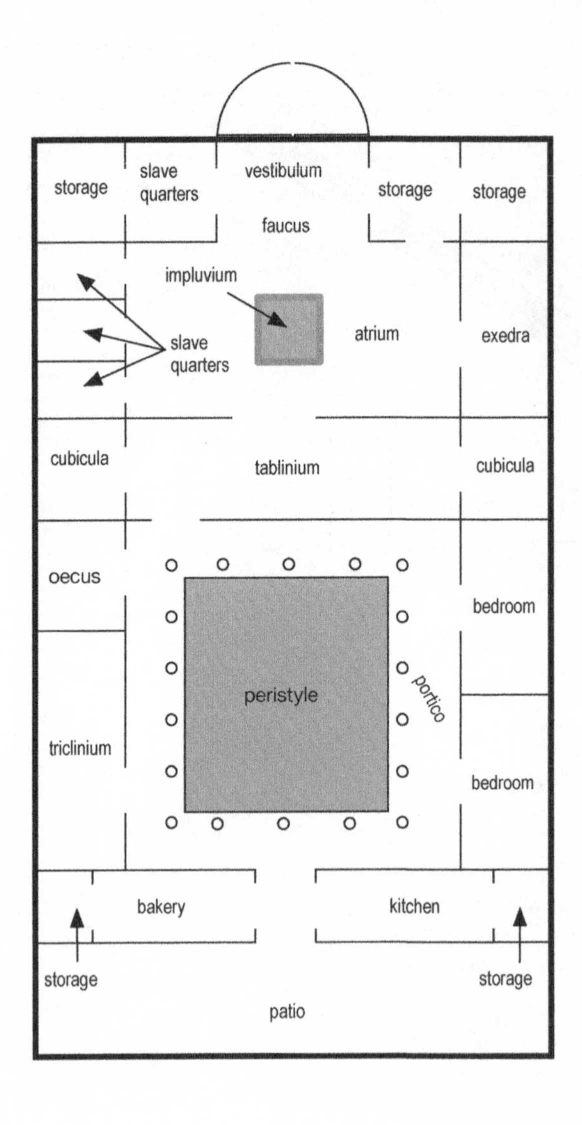

City of Corinth

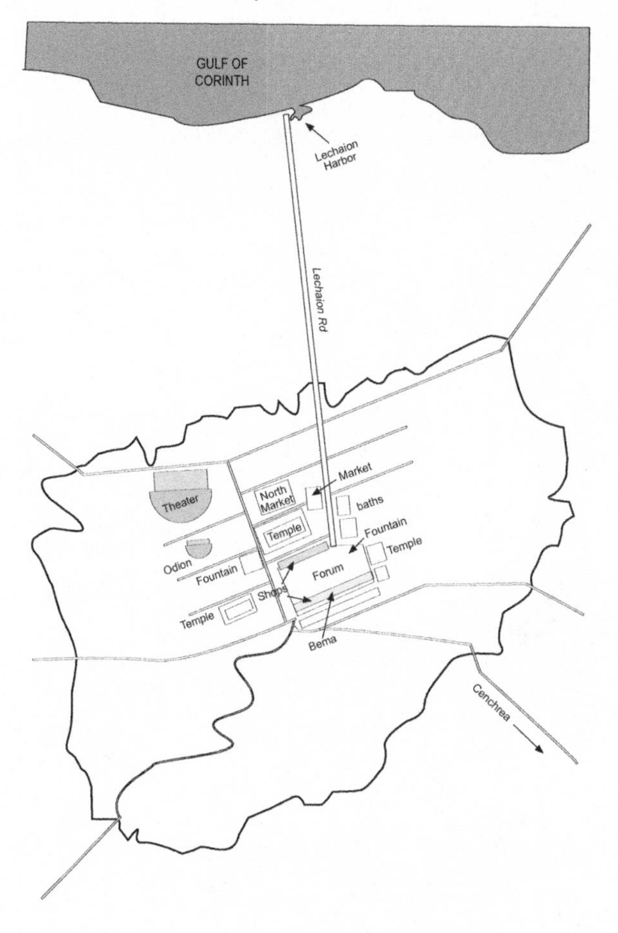

The City of Rome

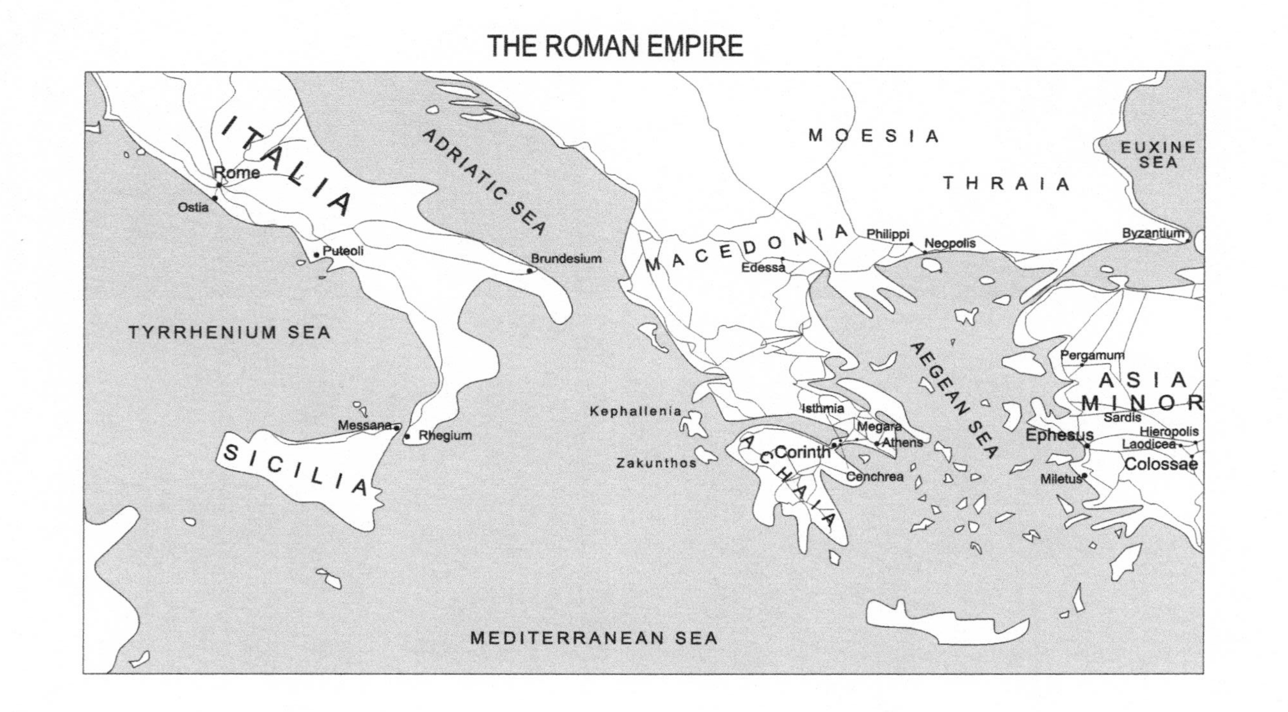
THE ROMAN EMPIRE
ITALIA
Rome
Ostia
Puteoli
ADRIATIC SEA
Brundesium
TYRRHENIUM SEA
Messana
Rhegium
SICILIA
MOESIA
THRAIA
EUXINE SEA
Byzantium
MACEDONIA
Edessa
Philippi
Neopolis
Kephallenia
Zakunthos
ACHAIA
Corinth
Isthmia
Megara
Athens
Cenchrea
AEGEAN SEA
Pergamum
ASIA MINOR
Sardis
Ephesus
Hieropolis
Laodicea
Colossae
Miletus
MEDITERRANEAN SEA

EPISTOLE ALPHA

To Giarri

I hope you are well. Thank you for your letter and for your faithful assistance all these many years. It encourages me in this damp, dark place.

I am happy to hear you are making progress on my collection of Paulus' letters. If you find any others, send me copies, and I will decide if they belong. And please keep trying to find a copy of the one to the Laocideans.

As for your question about including the letter that he wrote on my behalf—well, it is important to me, of course! My life would not have been the same without it. But I am not sure whether it is useful beyond that.

Which leads me to your next question about telling my story—I am not sure I want to tell it, Giarri. One thing I have learned in my long and unlikely journey is this: freedom comes from focusing beyond oneself.

Still, your argument is compelling, especially if the focus is on the work he did and how I was led to believe. So I will begin sending you my recollections in my next letter.

Finally, to your last question—no, I am afraid I will not survive this. The Roman officials are not happy with any of us. I suspect it is my time. But since the wheels of Roman bureaucracy turn slowly, I have many months, at least.

I must end this letter now. My writing ability is not what it used to be. Tychicus visited last week, and we recalled the memory of so many who are now dead.

Say hello to the whole household for me—especially Bacchus and little Terentia.

1. Inutilis

"Onesimus!"

The voice echoed through the window. A window with no glass or covering. The sound died quickly in the tiny room.

He sat on a wooden bench, head in hands. He was ignoring his name, though he knew that the owner of the voice would find him soon enough.

"Onesimus!" Closer now, and sounding more than a little irritated. He still didn't move.

Soon, footsteps sounded in the short hallway. The canvas flap over the doorway snapped open.

"O-*ne*-simus!"

Onesimus dropped his hands and looked up. The young man had his hands on hips, face red with frustration. On a more imposing figure, it might be intimidating. On Giton, it was just amusing. Onesimus let out a huff. Half amusement; half irritation.

"What are you doing *here* in our room? The domine sent me to fetch you thirty minutes ago. I have looked *everywhere*—even the latrines!"

Onesimus considered that Giton's large nose looked even more ridiculous when it was red with anger. They were almost the same age, but Onesimus thought of Giton as a child. No skills, no depth of thought, no education. Their only similarity was that they had the same master and the same status. The latter irked Onesimus.

"Well, if I *had* been in the latrine and you'd come in, you'd have gone out with a black eye."

Giton tightened his jaw. "I don't know why you are so rude. It'll be *you* that gets beaten if you don't get up to the villa. The master needs you *immediately*." He turned with great drama and stomped out. His voice came back down the hall: "Tell him your delay was not *my* fault—or I will!"

Onesimus still sat. He gazed up at the small window. The sky was clear and blue. Giton's sandals scuffed in the dirt as he made his way out of the slave compound. *It's an insult to send that cretin to "fetch" me. He's no match for my worth.*

He stood up. No matter. He and Turia had a plan. A good one. It would take a while. But it would solve all his problems.

Crossing to a small table, he splashed his face with water from a clay bowl, using a nearby rag to dry off. Taking a deep breath, he left the small cell—one among six in the hutment.

He blinked in the sunshine as he made his way between the four short slave buildings made of stone, wattle, and wood. Ahead was a gurgling stream spanned by a stone and wood footbridge. The path led up the hill and to his master's villa.

He smiled at the sound of the mill's wheel creaking in the distance. It made him recall last night with Turia. An iron hammer was striking metal somewhere off to his right. Probably the smith at the stables. Behind him, beyond a stand of trees, women were working the wheat fields at the back of the estate. An occasional laugh floated up the little valley.

He passed through Italian gardens on the slope—a feature that gave his master great pride. The domine had lived here for many decades, but he had grown up in Italia. He spoke of it a lot. Onesimus would love to visit Italia—especially Rome! That's where everything important happened.

But that was not where his plan led.

Reaching the top, Onesimus passed before the entrance to the covered patio which looked out over the gardens and beyond, in the distance, to the green and brown slopes of Mount Cadmus.

"Onesimus!"

He spun at the sound of Turia's voice, who had just come out of the patio entrance. She bounced down the steps, holding a basket of folded clothes against her hip. She kissed him on the cheek.

"Turia!" Onesimus hissed. He glanced left and right.

She laughed. It was a laugh that Onesimus found beautiful and free, though others might have thought it dismissive. Her voice had that effect on him on the day they met. Almost a year ago, when the master had purchased her in Ephesus.

"No one is around. It is mid-morning and everyone is at work, and the family is in their quarters. You should be at work, too. What are you doing up here?"

"Got tired of counting bolts of leather and decided to take a stroll." He smiled at her frown. "Actually, Giton came screaming for me. The master has an errand for me."

She tossed her head, the bundle of her luxurious brown hair shaking slightly. She tilted her head and fixed him with a stern look.

"Maybe he is going to reprimand you for missing the meeting last night." She raised her eyebrows.

Her large, white eyes and dark green-brown pupils made him care even less about meetings or Giton or anything. She was so alive and exotic. Someone had told him that her mother had come from the Far East—perhaps beyond the Indus River.

Onesimus shook his head. "The master doesn't require attendance."

"True, but *I* would like you to be there. A chance to be together, after all. And it wouldn't hurt to give lip service to the master's interests. Might put you in a better standing."

"Well, first, I don't believe in all that foreign philosophy. I follow the same gods as always. Besides, I don't want to hobnob with other slaves. There are *freedmen* less competent and intelligent than I am!"

She smiled and placed a delicate hand on his arm. "I know. You should be the vilici of the household."

He smiled. *She* saw his worth. "Well, someday, maybe I'll have my own vilici! And we'll be far from here."

She searched his eyes for a moment, then dropped her gaze. "Speaking of our plan…I don't like to keep the money in my room. Claudia is a suspicious one."

"Claudia is a mouse."

"I don't care. It's dangerous. Find a better place."

He sighed. She was so adamant sometimes. "I can't keep it in my room. Giton goes through my stuff all the time."

"If we are discovered, it won't matter whether it is by Giton or Claudia. Find somewhere else, okay?"

"Fine, fine. If it'll make you quit worrying."

"It will. Thank you." She laughed again. With a swish of her tunic, she shifted the basket to the other hip.

"Meet me at the mill again tonight?"

She leaned in and whispered, her lips barely touching his ear. "We'll see."

With that, she was gone, looking back with a playful glance before she turned the corner of the villa.

Onesimus basked in the afterglow of her presence. He had never known anyone like Turia. A lover. A *partner*. Sure, he wasn't that old. But she was the only thing that made living at the villa worthwhile. And their plan would lead to the fulfillment of all he hoped for.

He shook himself back to reality. The non-house servants were not supposed to enter the villa through the patio, but through the slave's entrance on the side near the front. But he was in a hurry, so he strode across the terrace and through the entrance framed by two marble columns. Still feeling a bit light on his feet because of his encounter with Turia, he detoured through the kitchen and grabbed a handful of olives from a bowl, eliciting a nasty hiss from a cook. He smiled at her over his shoulder as he passed into the peristyle. The arch at the far end led into Philemon's tablinum.

The peristyle was one of Onesimus' favorite parts of the villa. It was a typical feature of Roman villas, but the master had filled it with so many grasses, plants, flowers, and small trees that one could forget it was part of a home. The open roof made being inside feel like freedom. Only the portico with its stone columns lining the four sides gave it away as a building.

He went down the right-hand side. It would be a serious breach to pass by the private rooms which lined the opposite way. This side only held dining rooms—the oecus for small gatherings and the triclinium for banquets. As he walked, he savored the garlic-flavored flesh of the olives, tossing the pits into the flower and tree beds.

He drew near to the entrance of the tablinum. Philippus, the master's vilici, stepped out as he arrived.

"Ah, Onesimus, did Tempestus bring a mighty storm between here and there? Or perhaps barbarians from Germanica have attacked anew? Those would be good excuses for your tardiness."

He sounded stern, but Onesimus knew that Philippus was fond of him.

"Giton took his time in finding me, vilici."

"And why are you coming through the peristyle again?" Without waiting for an answer, he turned and spoke through the archway into the tablinum.

"Domine, Onesimus is here."

"Send him in!" came the commanding voice. Philippus stepped aside, and Onesimus entered.

He was in the tablinum more often than the peristyle, meeting with Philemon about business. Like the peristyle, it demonstrated his master's elegant, rich style: oak and cedar walls, carved moldings at the ceiling, and marble columns at the entrances and down the middle of the room. Italian pavers on the floor, much of them obscured by large vases filled with greenery. Candles on iron stands were all lit, lending an air of sacredness to the room. A massive wooden desk, made of imported oak and local terebinth, sat in the middle of the space. The master sat behind it, writing. He did not look up. Onesimus stood before the desk at attention.

Quintus Philemon Scaptius was a minor nobleman who oversaw a successful trading business. Many slaves would be proud to be a member of such a household. Not Onesimus. Many slaves would bubble over with sycophant servitude. Not Onesimus. By Roman standards, Philemon's villa was small, and located in a small town.

Onesimus looked to his right, through another archway into the atrium. The statue in the middle of the square pool was dripping water, making a pleasant and soothing background. The statute was made of beautiful marble in the likeness of Daphne. Onesimus knew that it was expensive; he also knew that Philemon was not a worshipper of that goddess, though he used to worship all the gods that mattered.

He turned his attention back to Philemon. Surrounded by parchments, candlesticks, a bowl of almond-stuffed olives, and a dish of ink, he was still writing. Onesimus squinted, but he could not read the words from this distance. After a few moments, still writing, Philemon spoke without looking up.

"Take this letter to Archippus, then go into town and pick up a pouch from Hymas. When you return, give it to Philippus. Make *sure* it gets into the treasury tonight."

The last words caused Onesimus a moment of panic. *Does he suspect?* He quickly realized the emphasis was on "tonight." Sometimes, if he was late returning from errands, Philemon told him to avoid waking Philippus and keep the money with him, to turn in the next day.

Philemon finished the letter with a flourish, laid the stilus down, and looked up. His deep-set blue eyes always intimidated Onesimus a little. And that irritated him.

Philemon rolled and sealed the letter and handed it to Onesimus.

"Make sure you give the letter to Archippus himself, not his vilici."

Onesimus bowed deferentially. "Yes, domine. Anything else?"

"No. You may go." He retrieved a scroll from a pile to the side and began reading, Onesimus already forgotten.

Onesimus took the letter and left—this time through the slave door located at the side the atrium.

Why was he to give the letter directly to Archippus? He always interacted with the vilici. Onesimus didn't like him —he was like an older and more crotchety Giton—trustworthy, faithful, and deferential—just what a master would want. Why bypass him? Something unusual was going on. He hoped it didn't concern him.

Oh, well. At least he'd be in the city soon—where he had more freedom to do as he wished.

2. ARCHIPPUS

Onesimus rounded the front of the villa and walked down the path, around the sizeable gurgling fountain, and to the front gate. Turning right, he followed the dirt road towards the nearby villa of Archippus.

Archippus was Philemon's oldest son. His lands sat adjacent to his father's more substantial estate. His parents had bequeathed it to him at his marriage, and he had built a fine villa upon it. Someday Archippus would own both villas and be quite wealthy. *The rich get richer and slaves stay the same*, Onesimus said to himself.

Of course, he knew that wasn't always true. There were three ways—three legal ways, that is—for a slave to gain freedom and become a plebeian citizen. Masters were known to have written into their wills that, upon their death, a loyal slave was to be manumitted—often with a sizable sum to start life on their own. Philemon would never do that, Onesimus thought—it was not a good use of your family's assets.

A slave could buy their freedom, too. That meant earning money, which was possible by being loaned out by the masters. The master would take a cut; the slave kept the rest. Philemon had allowed Onesimus to do so, occasionally, because of his education and skills as a scribe. But he could never make enough to buy his freedom.

The only other way a slave could be freed was through emancipation—a declaration by Rome or a local government. That had rarely happened in history, and probably never would again after Spartacus.

Of course, there were other methods, not sanctioned by law.

Onesimus arrived at Archippus' villa. He walked through the gates to the front door, tapping the bottom with his foot. It was opened immediately by the door slave—Onesimus could never remember his name. He told him of his need to deliver a letter from Philemon.

He stood in the atrium, waiting. He was almost never in this room—usually, he delivered messages to the vilici, Symbius, through the slave's door. The atrium was nice, but smaller than his father's, and the impluvium had a simple stone carving in its middle instead of a marble statue.

He heard footsteps approaching and turned to greet Archelaus properly, but the figure who came through the door was not the master of the villa. It was Symbius.

"Why must you deliver the letter to Archippus himself? Did you make that up to avoid seeing me? Or because you think you are better than a vilici?"

"Because my master told me to, Symbius."

"Why would he do that?"

Onesimus rolled his eyes. It was just like talking with Giton. "I don't know; I just do as I am told."

Symbius let out a guffaw. "Yes, that's *your* reputation. A sound and loyal slave."

He turned and stomped out before Onesimus could prepare an appropriate insult. He stood, fuming, until Archippus entered the room with the door slave in tow.

"From my father?"

"Yes, domine." Onesimus handed over the scroll.

Archippus broke the seal and unrolled the top to begin reading.

"Ah. Yes. As I thought." He looked off to the side, thinking, then took notice of Onesimus again. "You can go. And don't be so rude to my vilici next time."

Onesimus opened his mouth to argue but closed it again. It would only make matters worse. It was not the first time Symbius had invented a false accusation against

Onesimus. Once, after they had argued over a transaction they were working on between their masters, Symbius accused him of working against the family, and that he was going to make sure he was sold off, even if it took years. They had not had a civil conversation since.

Onesimus left the villa and turned down the road towards Colossae. It was true that Philemon was a demanding master, but Onesimus could admit that he was usually fair, and less harsh with his slaves than many others. He was a businessman at the core, and his understanding of finance, trade, and commerce made him much respected in Colossae. That caused Onesimus wonder if his master's attitude towards his slaves was more of "investment" than selfless virtue. You got more out of slaves if they think they owe you something.

Some of the household slaves believed Philemon had become more generous since he had been influenced by a new philosophy he had adopted a few years ago. (Or maybe it was a religion. He was not sure.) But Onesimus had seen no such change. Regardless, Philemon did not force his slaves to participate in the meetings. Other masters made their slaves follow whatever religion or philosophy they did—even forcing them to attend ceremonies and festivals in town, above and beyond the regular festivals that everyone went to in the city for the various gods and goddesses.

For the first mile of the brief journey, he walked along a doublewide cart path. This path met a wide, cobbled street that led directly into the center of Colossae.

He took in the fine, warm afternoon. The shadowy bulk of the mountain was behind him; forward and below lay the city. The road dipped down and leveled out, and Onesimus trudged ahead, breathing in the pine scene and fresh air. He enjoyed his frequent errands to the city, and even visited on his own when he had free time. He loved the bustle; he enjoyed walking out to the sparkling blue water of the Lycus River; he imagined taking a boat towards the sea.

Someday.

Soon he passed some small homes, stores, and farms—he was getting close. The road ended at the center of town at the forum and the agora, like almost every other city. Onesimus often wished he worked for a town merchant rather than a wealthy landowner. But his real yearning was to see a real city such as Athens, Corinth, Tarentum, Beneventum—or even Rome itself. That was where real life took place he was sure. People did things that mattered, discussed important ideas, and enjoyed the fruits of life. Sometimes he despaired of ever being anything more than a second-rate slave in this waning town. He had only been to Ephesus three times in his entire life, and it was only one hundred miles away! He had been to Miletus many more times, but it was not a big city like Ephesus.

It would be so much better when he was free. *When* I am free, he said to himself. Their plan was a good one. He and Turia and talked about it for months before putting anything into place. And it was not without danger. If caught, the law allowed a master free reign to determine punishment for a runaway. Statius had told him of a slave who had his tongue cut out and left hand cut off. Another, upon a second offense, was dipped in boiling oil—slowly lowered into the vat by his fellow slaves.

But Onesimus was smarter than those slaves—he and Turia would not get caught. And if they didn't get found out during the preparations, everything else would seem above-board. Legal and common. Then, out of this sad city, and on to a place where things happened. Where he could really use his skills and education as a freedman, with his own business, making money and making a difference.

Of course, Philemon could say no. That would create a problem. One for which he didn't have an answer yet. It would be unusual for a master to deny freedom when slaves had the redemption price in hand. Onesimus didn't think that Turia had thought of that—if she had, she hadn't mentioned it. And neither had he.

No matter. They had a couple of years to go before they'd have enough money for both of them.

He sighed as he topped a low ridge. The city gates lay about a quarter of a mile away. Open during the day, the city's interior beckoned. Other than being with Turia, a trip into the city was the only pleasure Onesimus enjoyed. True, it was a small, insignificant town. But the traffic through it made it seem a bit more cosmopolitan than it really was. When there, he was usually able to steal time for a little wine and maybe some gambling. It was illegal for slaves (except on Saturnalia), but Onesimus knew of a place where it could be had. Perhaps today he could buy some good food. And, if he could get his errands done quickly, he could visit Nanilia at the brothel. Onesimus smiled. She was cheap and not all that comely, but the owner allowed slaves to buy some time with her if no other citizens or freedpersons were expected. Onesimus' smile broadened. Wine, food, gambling, and sex—that was how to salve the burdens of life!

He turned a corner and there were the massive wood and iron gates of Colossae before him, open for the day.

EPISTOLE BETA

To Giarri

I hope your health is good. I am thankful for your frequent letters, and I am glad to hear you are receiving mine.

Your mention of Colossae in your last letter caused me a good bit of nostalgia. Despite the bitterness of my youth, I did love that city. I'm sorry you have never visited it. Old and full of history—perhaps the oldest in the Asian province. I wish I could have seen it in its prime, when it was known all over the Empire for its wool, figs, and olives. When I was born, it had been declining for some time. The earthquake in 61 left it as a ruin. I wonder if it will ever be rebuilt.

As a young man, I was unhappy to be in such a "backwater." I regret that I did not see the value of a peaceful life—even as a slave! The draw of a "cosmopolitan life"—even in a place as small as Colossae—seemed so important then. I thought bigger meant better and therefore more meaningful. I used to go down to the forum and pretend I was a freedman, visiting the tabernas and popinas, and—I am ashamed to say—the brothels.

But the city seemed so alive! The farmers selling produce to shop owners or renting their own stalls. I used to browse those little cubicles lining the forum, pretending I might buy something, much of it from all over the Empire: shoes, cutlery, baked goods, and leather goods, among other things. And the variety of food available at the little stands—usually just a window with sliding shutters. Sometimes I'd wander out of the forum and visit the full-service cauponas and tabernas. Of course, I also visited the temples—saying prayers and leaving votive offerings, always asking the gods to grant me freedom. There were so many in Colossae! Artemis, Zeus, Demeter, Helios, and even Athena. I avoided Isis and Serapis because back then, I thought foreign religions were ridiculous.

How full of myself I was! And how little I knew what the future held for me, a future that upended everything I believed.

Every day, I dreamt of being a freedman. I had a plan, as you have read in my last few letters.

I was so naïve, in so many ways. And not a very good person.

How I would love to see Colossae and the beautiful Lycus Valley again. I do not think that will happen. Eparch Tertillus is supposed to hear my case soon, and I imagine he mirrors the hatred that the Emperor holds for us.

Greet all that meet there, and give them my love. Stay strong, brother. Your letters refresh me.

3. Peculium

Onesimus entered the forum and went directly to the shop of Hymas, a dealer in leather goods and a steady customer for Philemon's Italian leather. At the moment, he was dealing with a customer, so Onesimus went across the way to wait, leaning against one of the marble columns that lined all four sides of the grass rectangle in the middle of the forum. It was crowded, though not as much as on market day.

He looked around. There was a crowd around a collection of the public buildings where citizens found services, judges, and the proconsul's office. Onesimus glanced down at the podium, located at one end of the rectangle. No one stood on or around it, which meant there were no trials or public business to be discussed or announcements to be made. Not unusual for late afternoon.

Onesimus looked back at the shop just as Hymas finished with his customer. He beckoned, and Onesimus strode to the counter.

"Greetings, domine, from Philemon."

Hymas reached under the counter and pulled out a small pouch.

"Send my greetings to your master as well, and thank him for supplying that special order last week. Here is the payment. Also—" he went to the other side of the stall and retrieved a scroll from a small desk, "—give him this order."

Onesimus took the pouch and the scroll, both neatly tied with a strip of leather. "Yes, domine."

Two women had come up behind Onesimus while they were talking, and Hymas dismissed him with another wave and turned his attention them. Hymas was laconic and all business. He was never rude, though, and Onesimus liked him because he didn't treat him with disdain like some of the other shopkeepers.

Now for some activities and fun of his own. He scanned the square and saw with dismay that many of the small food stands had already closed their shutters for the day. Still, one of his favorite places was always open late: a popina at one corner of the square, run by a freedman named Novius, who was kind to slaves. He offered wine, hot food, and simple snacks. He often met other slaves there, though it served freedpeople, too, of course.

He checked his money pouch and headed over. As he entered, Novius gave him a wave and pointed to a table, where he saw Statius, a slave of Veturius, a town magistrate. He made his way over and sat down.

"Statius, how's the day for you?"

He raised his head to show sleepy eyes. "Onesimus. Busy. The master had me running all over the square and half of the city today. Preparations for Robigalia are making me old before my time. And we just finished Parilia! There are too many festivals in the month of Aprilis." He lifted his cup and took a slow sip.

A female slave appeared and Onesimus ordered a cup of watered wine and a bowl of stuffed dates. "There are a lot. Robigalia is next week."

"Five days. Aren't you preparing for it?"

"Not really. Philemon follows that Syrian sect, remember? He recognizes the festivals, but we don't really celebrate like we used to."

"What does the family do on festival days?"

"Oh, they attend the public ceremonies, they just don't hold household sacrifices or ceremonies. And they didn't run in the Lupercalia last year. You'd almost think them atheists. We do get Saturnalia, though, thank the gods."

"It's true that some of these foreign religions are strange. Have you heard about what the Isis women do?!"

Onesimus grinned. "Yeah—now maybe *that* would be a religion worth examining!" They both laughed, and turned to talk about other doings of the slaves and masters of Colossae.

*

Much later, Onesimus realized it must be close to dusk. He excused himself, dropped a few coins on the table, and left. Shadows stretched across the forum. No time for dice or a romp with Nanilia at the brothel. He swore and hurried across the square and up the street.

Thirty minutes later, he stole through the gateway at the back of the compound, sweating in the chilly night. This way was longer than going through the front gate, but it also ensured that no one from the villa would see him. Still, he had to get the pouch to Philippus.

It was dark now. He wanted to see Turia, too, but if he waited too late, she would be asleep with the rest of the female servants in her hutment. He hurried down the path to the servants' quarters. He heard the creaking of the mill house to his left. The character of the sound told him that the gears were disengaged—which meant it was even later than he thought.

He neared Turia's hutment and crept underneath her window. Cupping his hands to his mouth, he whispered.

"Turia."

He waited a few moments. Then, a little louder: "Turia!"

A head appeared in the window.

"Shhh! I'll be right out."

Onesimus backtracked and waited below the pungent branches of a large spreading oak. A shadowy form emerged from the darkness. They embraced without a word, then she pulled away and looked into his face.

"What are you doing here so late?"

"I had to go into town to pick on an errand. I stayed longer than I intended."

"As usual. You're stupid to waste your time and risk punishment." She paused and tilted her head. "Money?"

"Yes, money," he replied. "Is that all you think about?"

Her eyes narrowed. "No. What I think about is you and I getting our freedom."

"I know, I know. Me, too." Onesimus gazed at her. She was so beautiful. "We could get married now, you know. We could ask. I'll bet Philemon would say yes. 'Married slaves means more slaves,' as the saying goes."

"We have discussed that. We're not getting married until we are free. Married slaves are worth much more, which gives us less chance of being granted the right to buy our freedom."

Onesimus sighed. "It's just taking so long. And I don't really like taking money from Philemon."

"What?! You, of all people, having a sudden attack of loyalty? What is wrong with you?"

"I don't know."

"Yes, you do," said Turia. "We have no other option. We could never earn enough for the redemption price. It isn't fair. But no one will miss a little here and there. We aren't hurting anyone. We get married after."

He looked up toward the villa up the hill.

"Onesimus—this was your idea. I just worked out the details. You want this as bad as I do."

He sighed. "Yes, I do. I don't know. I'm just impatient, I guess. But you're right.

"Yes, of course I am. So, how much today?"

"Not a lot." He pulled out the pouch and she snatched it from him and worked open the drawstring. "So how much?" she asked again.

"Ten silver drachmas."

"Let's take one this time."

"I wish Hymas used smaller denominations." She took a single coin out and handed the pouch back. He pulled it tight and tucked it away.

"Okay." He smiled at her again. "As much as I want to stay with you, I had better get this to Philippus. He will be frustrated with me as it is. Meet at the mill after second watch?"

She shook her head. "No, my dear. Claudia is getting suspicious."

"So? She's too much of a mouse to say anything."

"No," She said. "Maybe in a few days."

He grunted in frustration. "Okay. See you tomorrow."

She gave him a quick kiss on the lips and disappeared into the shadows.

She was the only person who had ever cared for him. He had never known his parents. Raised in the slave market, he was hired out periodically until Philemon bought him six years ago, at the age of thirteen. His life here was certainly better than it had been in the slave market. Yet he knew, in his bones, that he was destined for something more. But he had to have his freedom first. Slaves did not amount to anything, even if they were as educated as he was (thanks to the slave master back in Moesian). Educated slaves brought higher prices.

He crossed the footbridge, trudged up the hill, and stopped near the top. He saw no lit lamps or candles, nor could he hear any voices. Neither family nor slaves were on the patio. He turned left onto the walkway that led to the side of the house and Philippus' little shack.

The quarters of Philippus were nothing extravagant, but wonderful for a slave. Larger and better insulated than the slave quarters, it had its own fireplace, a wooden door, and actual windows with wooden shutters.

He knocked, and soon the door creaked open to reveal the head of Philippus. Beyond, Onesimus could see his wife, Phryne, sitting at a table. A door behind her showed darkness, but Onesimus could make out two small figures, eyes peering into the room, unmoving.

"Sorry to disturb you, Philippus. I have a pouch of money for the treasury from Hymas. He held it out.

"I expected you back over two hours ago."

"Yes, I, uh, got caught up in town talking to a slave of Hymas, and then—"

"There's always an excuse."

Onesimus was taken aback. Philippus often criticized him, but like a grandfather clucking over a mischievous but lovable grandchild. This was sharp and abrupt.

"Why so stern, Philippus?"

Philippus sighed and softened a bit. "Onesimus, I know your heart. But a slave must be responsible and punctual, or he may find himself demoted. Or punished. Or sold. And I do not need to tell you that most masters are not as kind or forgiving as Philemon. But even he has limits."

Onesimus had heard this before, though not this harshly. He had done as he was told, what was the problem?

"The money is here, Philippus, as required. It couldn't be needed before tomorrow. It's not even an inconvenience."

"You miss the point." Philippus sighed and looked firmly into his eyes. "Your job is to do the tasks as the master assigns—not to dally around like a freedperson. Moreover, your actions are an inconvenience to *me*. It's late and I have a family. I don't suppose that crossed your mind."

Anger grew in Onesimus. As if Philippus' life was inconvenient! What an overcompensated dullard! He has a lovely little place up on the hill—right beside the villa, no less!—not in a bug-infested hollow with the rest of the slaves!

But Onesimus knew that being repentant would get him farther than saying what he thought. "I'm sorry, Philippus. The truth is, the market was crowded, and I took a wrong turn coming back. I didn't want to tell you because I felt stupid."

Philippus sighed. Onesimus could barely see his eyes, so he could not read the emotions in them.

Finally, he spoke. "Very well, Onesimus. I know you mean no harm. But take more care. Please."

Onesimus was relieved. "I will. See you on the morrow!"

He turned and stepped off the small stone porch.

"Onesimus."

He stopped and looked back. "Yes?"

"The master wants to see you right after breakfast tomorrow. First thing. Don't be late."

Onesimus heart sank. Something in the tone of Philippus' voice told him it was not another errand. "About—what?"

"I don't know. He was irritated tonight on account of your delay."

Onesimus felt a moment of panic. Was it possible Philemon had discovered the missing money? They had been taking so little! And he *always* altered the account books kept in the shed to hide it. It *can't* be that.

But he wished they had not taken the single silver coin this time.

4. POENA

"Why should I not punish you? Or just sell you to a trader in town?"

Onesimus was standing once more in front of the large desk, behind which sat an irritated Philemon, elbows on the desk, fingers steepled together.

Onesimus was in a cold sweat because he still didn't know what his master was angry about. Philemon had been spouting anger about something without saying what it was. Intellectually, he could not see how his actions concerning the money could have been discovered. But he didn't know for sure. He waited, his mind feverishly working through all he had done in the last few days, trying to find some piece of information that would assure him it was something else.

"Well?!" Philemon dropped his hands to the desk with a thump. "Explain yourself."

He felt a drop of sweat trickle down his chest inside his tunic. "Well, domine, I do not know what to say. I am sorry, but I am a loyal slave and I would never—"

"Oh, cease with the platitudes!" Philemon sat back heavily in his chair and glared at him. "You are one of the brightest slaves I have ever owned. You learn so quickly. I watch you adapt to new tasks, new situations, to new challenges. If you were a freedperson, I've no doubt you could be successful—except, Onesimus—*except*...you have a fatal flaw! You insist on...on..." Philemon leaned forward again, looking even more intently. *Here it comes*, thought Onesimus. He braced himself. "...on....well, on just doing your own thing whenever you feel like it. You were *two hours* late last night—from a simple errand!"

Onesimus almost let out a sigh of relief. Philemon was still talking.

"Last week you did all the errands *on time*—except the most important one—delivering my offer to Quotinius! I could have lost that sale! I can list example after example! You are an infuriating mix of competence and irresponsibility. What am I to do?" He sat back in the chair, turning his head to stare at the pool in the atrium.

Onesimus began to relax in the silence. It was the same old song, new stanza. He felt his body cooling down. Everything was fine. He knew how to handle this.

"Domine, I—"

"Silence!" Philemon roared, without looking at him. Onesimus was taken aback. Philemon showed anger at times, but it was always channeled and firm. Outbursts were rare.

Better to wait and see how it goes before deciding how best to work this situation. He stood, eyes down, adopting the posture and expression of the humble and repentant servant.

The trickling water in the impluvium was the only sound in the almost suffocating morning. He thought about what his master had said. He hadn't *forgotten* to deliver the letter to Quotinius; he'd merely found something better to do and knew the letter could wait. Quotinius wouldn't have responded to Philemon's offer until his supply train returned from the Far East. Since Onesimus had some extra coins, he had visited the brothel. It was not often Onesimus had the time and money for such a luxury usually reserved for the freedmen, workers, and travelers. He probably should have saved those coins for the stash, but it was just too tempting. Turia was irritated, but she got over it. And the letter was delivered the next day, and Quotinius subsequently accepted the offer—*after* his supply train returned. No harm done.

Philemon sighed and turned back. "My boy, you must learn responsibility and obedience. I am not a harsh master. In fact—" he looked away again "—some say I am too easy." He stopped again, still looking off, as if lost in thought.

Onesimus shifted again. This was getting tiresome. *Get on with the lecture and let me go as usual.*

Philemon sat up straight.

"You need to learn a lesson. I will not have you beaten like other masters. For the next seven days, you will work in the stables. Go see Pallio."

Onesimus was stunned. The stables? That was slob work—*farm* slaves did that work. Uneducated. Stupid. He was a *household* slave—he could read, write, and speak Greek and Latin. He was as skilled as Philippus—more so in some ways. Why not just send him to the mines or the garbage dumps?!

"Domine, I am sorry. Truly I am. It will not happen again."

Philemon leaned back, and a glimmer came to his eye. He smiled. "Yes, my boy, I am sure you are sorry. For the moment. Maybe this will teach you to think *before* you act."

Onesimus prided himself on reading people, and it was clear that no amount of cajoling and arguing was going to change Philemon's mind. Usually, that worked—but not today.

"Yes, domine."

Philemon nodded, still seeming slightly amused. "We both know you are destined for better work than cleaning manure. Make the best of the situation and learn from it."

"Yes, domine." *There is nothing to learn from pitching manure.*

"Dismissed."

Onesimus bowed his head. As he reached the archway, Philemon called his name. He turned back.

"Yes, domine?"

"Another matter: you know that the ekklesia meets here in my home each Saturday evening. I know I have made it clear that all are invited, including slaves. But you have never attended. I want you to know that you *are* invited, too."

Onesimus nodded, confused. Slaves and forepersons did not mix socially, except at certain public events, like the city festivals. It was not proper. There was a reason why society was structured that way. Not that people couldn't move between stations in life. Yet Philemon had even invited others outside the household—a couple of nobles and freedman, but even outsider slaves and a couple of poor beggars! Onesimus was surprised the city elders had not talked to him about it yet. Maybe they had.

"Yes, domine, I will attend."

"No, no, Onesimus, you misunderstand: this is not an order." Philemon stood up and came around to the side of the desk. "It is an invitation, and only if you wish. I know it is not common for a master to invite a slave. I merely want you to know you are free to attend." Philemon seemed almost uncomfortable—it was almost more disconcerting than his anger. Onesimus was confused. He had no interest in this philosophy or whatever it was. He had always worshipped Artemis—like most slaves. Why would he risk angering her? Yet if he did not attend, would it affect Philemon's estimation of him? Why was Philemon even making such an invitation right after punishing him? Onesimus was not often at such a loss in judging the motivations of his master.

"Well, there it is," Philemon said, returning to his desk. "It is offered, and I will think no differently either way." He sat down. "You may go."

"Thank you, domine." Onesimus nodded and left the tablinum.

As he passed through the atrium and out the servants' entrance, he pondered the strange conversation. He'd been in trouble before, and even been punished before, though not beyond a day's confinement. But it was the personal invitation—free to reject, that puzzled him.

He didn't know what to make of it. Yet its connection with Philemon's adherence to the new philosophy may offer some clue. These behaviors had begun a few years ago when Philemon met someone named Epaphras, a sort of traveling teacher or philosopher, as Onesimus heard it. He had told Philemon about the beliefs of this group, and Philemon invited him to stay at the villa. Onesimus never met him, but for three or four days, various people were coming and going and holding meetings or discussions in the tablinum and the oecus. Not long after, Onesimus heard that the family and some of the household slaves had become followers of the philosophy. Onesimus heard that Philemon had also met with some man in Syria who was an important leader of the group.

The household slaves gossiped about it—especially at first. Some decried it as a foreign religion, and thus illegal. But Onesimus knew that not all foreign religions were unlawful. Others said it was a philosophy, much like Epicureanism. Which told Philemon that the gossipers didn't know anything, because philosophy and religion had nothing to do with each other.

Still, one could not deny it had changed Philemon, whether a religion or a philosophy. He stopped the beatings for anything more than the most severe wrongdoing. He sent money to some of the poorer sections of town for no apparent reason. Then a motley group began meeting at the villa regularly, consisting of a couple of nobles, some freedpersons, a few commoners, and some slaves. Men and women were equally present, along with a few children. Even in public festivals, those groups were segregated! But not at those meetings. It made Onesimus uncomfortable. He looked forward to being a freed person, but until then, it wasn't right to cross the lines. It seemed anti-Roman, inviting chaos.

Onesimus had reached the stream. He crossed the footbridge and passed by the slaves' quarters, then turned down the left-hand path that led to the stables. The wind was blowing in his direction, and the air was ripe with the pungent smell of manure. A surge of anger rose up in him. He was better than this. How could Philemon send *him* to such work?

Maybe he *would* attend the ekklesia! He was sure Philemon did not expect him to. And if he was joining his little social group, then Philemon might feel a bit guilty, and end the week of punishment.

Onesimus would play on Philemon's strange new behavior by appearing to surrender to it! He smiled as he trudged up the hill.

5. Stabula

The stables were located across the stream, past the slave quarters, and up over a small rise in Philemon's land. The rise sheltered the house from the stables and its aroma. Onesimus could not recall the last time he was at the stables, though he was sure he must have at *some* time during the previous six years. As he reached the top of the rise, he stopped to look at the paddock. It was a large, enclosed area of dirt and shoddy buildings, housing twenty-five head of cattle and thirty sheep. Another stable, for the horses, was located at the front of the property for easy access by the family. He did go there once in a while, when he required a horse for errands that took him further than Colossae.

He continued on to the gate, stopping again. It was a filthy, smelly place of sheep, cattle, and barns. A wooden fence enclosed the entire area with thick posts driven deep into the ground. The animals were at pasture at the moment, taken by the shepherds and beyond the back gate of the compound. He sneered at the open barn, the stacks of hay, and the tools of the trade.

He didn't deserve this.

He opened the gate and stepped inside. He wasn't sure he had ever talked to Pallio, the slave in charge of the stables. Or even met him. Clanking noises were coming from a small shed directly ahead, so he walk ed in that direction. Before he had taken three steps, the sounds stopped and a figure emerged: a small man, in a slave's tunic, belted and girded. The clothes were filthy, and so was the man in them. He was stooped and walked with a limp. As he drew closer, Onesimus saw grey hair sticking out in all directions. He was missing an eye but wore no eye patch. The codger was apparently not aware of Onesimus until he was almost upon him. He stopped with a surprised little jump, then nodded.

"Ah, you must be Onesimus," he cackled. "Good, good. I was told early this morn you'd be here."

"Yes, I—"

"Onesimus." The old man smacked his lips. "Good name, good name. I imagine you'll be able to help me out, with a name like that." He cackled, his head bobbing up and down. Onesimus rolled his eyes. He had heard every possible joke about his name. It was a common name given to those born into slavery: it meant "useful." How demeaning.

"Yes, well, I see you are already aware of my coming. How can I be of use?" Onesimus asked, wondering if the man was astute enough to catch his sarcasm.

Pallio squinted at him. "Well, you can clean the stables. That's what we do when the herders take the beasts out. Follow me…" He turned towards the covered stalls. On a post between two of them, a pitchfork hung from a single spike. The old man lifted and held it out to Onesimus. "I'll get the cart, young Onesimus." He headed back towards the shed, entered, then reappeared pushing a one-wheeled cart. *He's pretty spry for an old man with a limp*, Onesimus thought.

"Okay, young boy, here's the cart. Now scoop up all the skubalon and pile it in here. Then, take this over to the compost heap—you'll see where to dump it."

"Where is the compost heap?"

The old man squinted at him again. "You new around here?"

"No, I am not. I have been here for six years, but I am a messenger and business manager."

"Ah—so you are being punished? I thought as much when Philippus told me I'd have an extra hand for a week or so." He cackled again, grinding on Onesimus' nerves.

"And so you have soft hands, eh? But I imagine you can be useful to me." More cackling.

"Just tell me what to do, old man."

The man stopped his chuckling and frowned. "No need to get testy, young Onesimus. Just having a bit of fun."

Onesimus didn't reply.

The old man shrugged and pointed. "The compost heap is over there, between the work sheds and the stables."

Onesimus turned towards the stall with the pitchfork.

"Hey."

Onesimus turned.

"I am Pallio."

Onesimus nodded. "Yes, I know."

"You'll need a shovel, too. I'll fetch it, then I have to run some errands." He turned towards the shed.

"Pallio, who cleans the stables when I'm not here?" Onesimus called out.

A big smile lit up the man's face, revealing a number of missing teeth. "I do."

*

Onesimus spent the next two days hauling skubalon, pitching hay, loading feed trays, and helping move the animals in and out of their pens. It was filthy, exhausting work, especially in the heat of the end of Aprilis. It only fueled his anger at Philemon. *Punish me, fine; but make it something useful—this just makes me want to get away from here even sooner.*

Onesimus knew that Philemon would miss him when he was gone.

The only reprise was the slightly less dirty job of working with the horses, which he did for two hours each afternoon. His task was to haul grain from the storehouse on the north side of the compound and bring it to the forward stables. This was also exhausting because it took three trips. But he enjoyed the horses, and he liked the horse master, a middle-aged freedman named Titus, who knew all there was to know about horseflesh. Onesimus interacted with him on occasion before this, when he needed a horse. But now he got to spend a bit more time with him, and he found him intelligent and engaging. Titus was more than happy to share his knowledge and his passion, and Onesimus was keen to learn, having always had an interest in horses. Getting Titus to talk also had the added benefit of keeping him from his work, which the horsemaster did not seem to realize and Pallio was none the wiser.

Titus was responsible for eight horses, two of which belonged to Archippus. Onesimus learned that the best horse was named Ajax—the master's horse, naturally. Ajax was an elegant black Arabian steed: tall, strong, and proud. Philemon's wife, Apphia, had a smaller horse, befitting the domina of the villa, but still an excellent specimen, named Delicatus. Two of the remaining horses were serviceable as travel steeds or pack animals. Onesimus' favorite was Lampros, the horse that he rode during his occasional business trips to Miletus, Heiropolis, Laodicea and, rarely, to Ephesus. The other horses were bred for pulling carriages and wagons or for plowing. Despite his hatred for this punishment, he enjoyed being able to feed, clean, and exercise Lampros.

Onesimus learned that Titus had been a slave in one of the horse markets in Edessa as a young boy. Upon his master's death, Titus had been manumitted and given a small sum of money. It was enough for him to travel east, looking for work, where he eventually met Philemon in Sardis. Philemon hired him on the spot after a lengthy discussion of equestrian matters. Onesimus was tempted to share his own desires to be a freedman, but he refrained. Maybe someday.

By sundown on the fourth day of his punishment, Onesimus was exhausted as usual and considered skipping the ekklesia. Philemon had said it was optional. He hated how Philemon had chosen to treat him, but his options to turn the situation to his own end were limited. But *not* going would change nothing, and perhaps Philemon seeing him there would make him feel guilty about the punishment. He wouldn't even have to pretend to be drained of all physical and mental abilities. Who knew what other possibilities or chance meetings might arise that could further his plan?

He hurried down the hill towards the slaves' privy to clean up. As he headed along the bank near the slave compound, he met Turia walking in the opposite direction.

"Hello, Onesimus," she said as she drew near. She glanced around, then kissed him on the cheek.

"Hello, Turia, my love. Where are you headed?"

"Just finished work, and headed to my room to change for the ekklesia. And you? I've seen so little of you these past days." She smirked. "How are the stables?"

"Oh, quite lovely," he said. "I have to ensure this never happens again. I think I will smell of dung for weeks to come."

"I hope not," she replied, wrinkling her nose. "More importantly, when you are at the stables, you have no opportunity to handle money." She raised her eyebrows.

"Only four more days."

"Good. What are you doing now?"

"I'm going to clean up and go to Philemon's meeting."

"You are?! Why?"

"Well, Philemon invited me, and—"

"So? He invites everyone. It's not like you got a personal invitation."

Onesimus blinked. "Actually, I did. When he sent me to the stables."

"Oh!" She paused. "That's strange. I wonder if he saw it as further punishment."

"Maybe."

She pursed her lips. "No. That doesn't fit. These meetings are very important to him. He really believes that stuff."

"You've been. What's it like?"

"It's fine. I just go to keep in good graces with the domina. I don't pay a lot of attention."

"Well, I don't have any interest at all. But I thought it might do the same for me—get me back into his good graces."

She nodded, a smile spreading across her dark face. "Good. I'm glad you are thinking that way. You do us no good by being obstinate and willful. Maybe he'll eventually let you handle bigger tasks and more money."

Onesimus stopped walking. "Is that all you think about?"

"What?"

"The money."

She cocked her head and reached out to touch his arm lightly. "Oh, of course not! Money is a means to an end—you and I buying our freedom and getting married."

Onesimus nodded. "Sorry. Didn't mean to be critical. I am just so exhausted."

She brightened and took his hand in hers. "It's okay. I forgive you. Now, go get cleaned up. I'll see you there."

6. Ekklesia

Onesimus washed himself thoroughly. It would not do to enter the master's villa smelling like a cow. After changing into a fresh tunic and brushing off his sandals, he left the slave compound, crossed the footbridge, and headed up the path towards the villa. As he reached the gardens, Philippus was coming down the way from his quarters, with his wife and children a short distance behind.

"Onesimus, good evening. What are you doing up here?" he asked pleasantly, the events of four nights ago apparently forgotten.

"I am attending the ekklesia tonight." Onesimus nodded politely to his wife, Apphia, and smiled at the children hiding behind their mother's tunic.

"Really? So am I. Let's walk together."

They entered the servant's entrance and turned towards the peristyle. "Have you attended before?" Onesimus asked.

"Indeed. We attend every one unless my work prohibits it."

Onesimus was uncomfortable. He had been to plenty of religious ceremonies, of course, but never in someone's home—let alone his master's.

"What is it like? Like any other?"

"Ah, well, that is difficult to answer. Some parts are similar to the festivals of the gods. Other parts might remind you more a meeting of Epicureans or the Stoics, if you know of them. I think it best to just experience it."

"Okay."

Philippus' answer made him more apprehensive. Was this like some Egyptian mystery religion? Surely Philemon would not engage in something illegal.

They reached the peristyle and stopped in the archway, looking down the length of the open garden surrounded by the colonnades. About fifteen or twenty people were gathered in the sitting area in the center of the garden. A brazier burned brightly, holding off the slight chill of the evening. Chairs, couches, and pillows had been placed throughout, enough for thirty or forty.

"Let's sit," Philippus said. "Social status matters little here, but I always sit off to the side there."

Social status matters little? Again, Onesimus wondered if Philemon was engaging in something nefarious. It was improper, if nothing else.

They sat near a column along the left edge of the colonnade, and Philippus turned his attention to his children. Onesimus sat a little ways away to give the family some room.

He looked around for Turia, but she had not arrived yet. He spotted some other household slaves, plus three others he knew belonged to Archippus. There were males and two females he did not recognize, and five freedmen he had never seen. One of the latter wore a pilleus on his head, so he was a recently manumitted slave. Three noble couples were present, standing off by themselves and talking quietly. One of the men looked familiar. Onesimus may have seen him in town, perhaps speaking from the rostra.

A curtain drew aside from one of the rooms on the side of the portico and Philemon, Apphia, and Archippus stepped through. Onesimus moved a little closer to the pillar, involuntarily attempting to hide himself. With them was a man whom Onesimus did not recognize.

"Ah," Philippus said, "the domine and domina, with a traveling guest." He arose and went to them. Onesimus was surprised at the ease with which Philippus interacted with them—even with Apphia and the stranger—as if they were all old friends and all of the same status. It irritated him.

He scanned the room again for Turia, but she was still not present. He frowned and sat back feeling quite self-conscious. He looked closer at the man who was with Philemon and Apphia. He resembled the Jewish shopowners he knew in the forum, and those he saw when he passed by their synagogues on the other side of Colossae. Onesimus had no reason to distrust them, other than their bizarre diet and strange religious practices, which were a bit offensive. But why would a Jew be here?

Slaves, freedpersons, citizens, males and females—all socializing together in the peristyle of a country noble. It was improper. No wonder there was gossip about Philemon's new religion.

He was glad when Philippus returned.

"Who is the man with the domine and domina?"

"He is called Simon, a Jew from Smyrna; an important leader of The Way there."

"The Way?"

Philippus looked at him. "Yes, that is the name of the people of this faith. You had not heard?"

Onesimus shook his head. "No, I just always heard it was some Syrian mystery religion."

"It's not a mystery religion." They were interrupted by slaves bringing in bowls and plates of food, which they set down in front of each little group.

Surely they weren't all going to *eat* together?

Philemon, his wife, and Simon reclined on a set of couches near the center of the patio. Others were on couches, chairs, or the cushions strewn about. Lamps and candles had been lit, making the area a large, bright sphere in the midst of the garden beneath the starry sky. The smell of the juniper trees was strong and pleasant. The sound of the fountain at the far end of the peristyle provided a pleasing aural backdrop.

Soon, as if on a silent cue, the talking died down, and Philemon stood.

"Welcome, everyone," he said, spreading his arms in a gesture of hospitality. "I am happy to see you all again, and a few new faces as well. We have a guest with us tonight—this is Simon ben David from the ekklesia in Smyrna, here to give us a word and some news. But before that, let us offer thanks to our god and then eat."

Philemon's short prayer was similar to invocations Onesimus had heard other religious gatherings or festivals, except that Philemon spoke only of "a god"—he did not use the name of the god—which was strange. How did he expect the god to hear him? He closed the prayer by invoking the spirit of the god and a name which might have been the name, but Onesimus was not sure.

Everyone began eating and drinking. Philippus motioned for him to take from a nearby platter. It was awkward and uncomfortable. Philippus made small talk, alternating between his family and Onesimus and some of the others sitting nearby. If he noticed Onesimus' discomfort, he ignored it.

After a time, Philemon stood and, when the chattering and clacking quieted down, introduced the visitor. The Jew stood up and bowed. "It is a pleasure to be with you. I bring greetings from your brothers and sisters in Smyrna."

It seemed inappropriate to call this varied group "brothers and sisters." The term was reserved for countrymen and soldiers. And members of the Mysteries. But Philippus had said it was not a mystery religion?

The group engaged in some chants. Onesimus didn't know them, of course, but he listened carefully to the words. The language and the style were reminiscent of other religious chants he had heard and sang.

After a few chants and a short time of silence, Simon began speaking once more.

"We know that when our domine was here, he taught many things and did many miracles. We know also that he was arrested, crucified, and rose three days later."

Crucified? Philemon's god was a criminal? Or an insurrectionist? Ha! Not much of a god who could not prevent his own arrest and execution! As for coming back from the dead; well, that was common fare—Asklepius, Achilles, and Memnon had all returned from the grave. Onesimus never ceased to be amazed at how people could be taken in by these silly foreign superstitions.

As Simon continued, it became more confusing. It sounded like he was referring to two people: the god and another person. Perhaps the latter was a priest or holy man, and *he* was the one put to death for being a priest of this foreign god. That would make more sense. Except that it wasn't always clear if it was two different beings. The name was something like "Iesous," which was *not* a Greek name. Another sign of the foreign nature of this belief.

There was much more, but it began to bore him, and his mind wandered. He looked for Turia again, but she was still not here. It irritated him—she encouraged him to attend, then she doesn't show up.

His attention came back as Simon was telling a story. This was more like it! Everyone liked stories.

"One day, he was at a small, simple home, teaching a crowd. So crowded was the house that many had to stand outside, looking in the doors and windows, straining to hear. A group of men, having heard of the domine's ability to heal, brought a paralyzed friend on a stretcher. But they could not get close enough to the domine, so they climbed up on the roof, took apart some tiles, and lowered their friend, with ropes, right in front of the domine!"

Amusing! This is more like it, Onesimus thought, though it was more like a story an itinerant philosopher would tell than a priest.

"The domine was impressed with the faith and determination of the friends. He said to the paralyzed man: 'Your wrongdoing is pardoned.' Then, turning back to the crowd, he said, 'These men have shown faith.' Now," Simon open his arms as if to include all in the room, "this was a man who needed *healing.* Why did the domine tell him he was pardoned?"

That's easy, Onesimus thought. The paralyzed man had offended the god, and the god had punished him. So now he was pardoning him. Though it was strange to do so based on his friend's actions rather than a proper sacrifice. But interesting.

But who was this "domine" and how did it relate to the god? Was "Iesous" his cognomen or was it his nomen?

Simon was still talking, and Onesimus caught only the end of the explanation of the pardon.

"…and that the domine himself had authority to do so."

Ah. So this holy man must be the god's messenger.

"But that was not all of the story," Simon Simon. "Some Jewish leaders came to hear him speak, but they believed he taught against their god. They wanted to trap him."

What did the Jews have to do with it? Were they against this belief? Onesimus knew that the religion had come from the Province of Syria. That was a land of many Jews. And Simon was a Jew!

Simon continued, but it only made Onesimus' puzzlement more acute.

When Simon finished, the people murmured their approval. Good storytellers were highly prized in both Greek and Roman society. It was always a fine story if it involved a healing by a god or a divine man—especially if it included a rebuke of religious or political leaders. This was the standard stuff of good stories. Onesimus appreciated that.

Simon clasped his hands beneath his chin as if to implore the hearers to understand, but it sounded more like a philosophical exhortation on virtue, yet appealed to the God. This is a belief that makes no sense. It was typical of these religions and philosophies that sprung up in foreign lands—all the rage for a while, especially among the nobles—then dwindling out because of the lack of a decent and lengthy history.

Simon finished with some sort of exhortation to the crowd that Onesimus did not quite understand. The people responded with a single word that Onesimus had never heard.

Philemon stood and thanked Simon. "Would you share the disturbing news you shared with me earlier."

"Yes, yes." He took a breath. "I recently came back from a visit in Pisidia Antioch and Iconium. While there, I heard from some brothers who had just come from Caesarea. They told me Paulus had been imprisoned in Rome."

Someone in the crowd gasped. Onesimus looked and thought it was the nobleman's wife—she had her hand over her mouth.

"Simon?" It was the nobleman with the woman who had gasped. "Do you know why? And how? The last we heard, he was in Corinth."

"No, I don't have any other information, except that he is supposedly under house arrest in Rome, awaiting a hearing before Tiberius Claudius. I think he left Corinth many months ago, but I could be wrong."

Onesimus wondered who this "Paulus" was. The reaction of the gathering indicated he was an important priest or leader of this confused religion-philosophy. It did not surprise Onesimus that he had been arrested.

After another prayer, the people rose and began to mill about. Onesimus heard many talking about this Paulus.

Philippus approached. "What did you think?"

Onesimus didn't want to offend him. "Who is this Paulus?"

"Oh, I am surprised you do not know. Philemon often speaks of him. He is the reason that Philemon is a follower of the Way. The master met him through Epaphras, and after many days of learning, was initiated into the Way, along the rest of his family. Philemon often says he owes Paulus his life!"

Onesimus recalled that he *had* heard Philemon mention someone who he owed a great debt. Onesimus had assumed it was some nobleman in the past that helped him start his business here in Colossae. He was about to ask how he had saved the master's life, when he spotted Turia motioning to him from the far end of the peristyle. He thanked Philippus and hurried to her.

"Where were you? You told me to—" As he drew closer, he saw she was frantic.

"Turia, what's wrong?"

She grabbed his arm, pulling him past the bakery and kitchen onto the patio.

"Turia, what *is* it?!"

She looked back at him with panic. "Someone found our money."

7. IMPLICATIONES

"What do you mean? It's gone?"

"It's not gone." Turia replied. "Someone messed with it. I hid under a loose board beside my bed. I went to check it today when I got back. It was not in the same spot."

Onesimus sighed. "You probably just forgot how you placed it."

She gave him a withering look. "No. I am quite careful every time."

"Well, did you count it?"

"Yes, of course I did. It's all there."

"Well, then, you probably forgot this time. If someone found it, they would have taken at least—"

"Stop patronizing me. I *know* someone had moved it."

He sighed. "Ok. Well, when was the last time you checked it?"

"When you gave me the money from Hymas just before you went to work in the stables."

"Who would have moved it and not taken any of it?"

"I don't know! Claudia. Portia. *Anyone*. What difference does it make? Someone found it and we have to do something."

He didn't know what else to say. She sometimes displayed a paranoid nature about things, but Onesimus knew it was fruitless to try to dissuade her. She could be stubborn. It was the only characteristic that irritated him. He still thought she probably didn't remember.

"Well, it's still safe. It was not taken. All is well."

"No. It's not worth the risk. You have to take it and hide it. Maybe next time whoever it was will take it."

Onesimus blew air out of his mouth in exasperation. "Turia, they would have taken it the first time if—" She opened her mouth to argue, but he continued before she could speak. "—okay, okay. I'll find somewhere. But we can't exchange it now with all the slaves about down at the compound."

She looked at him triumphantly. "I already did." She reached into her cloak and brought out the bag. "Take it."

Onesimus sagged in defeat. "This isn't good. Giton is certainly back in our room by now. How am I possibly going to hide it?"

Turia smiled and, placing her hands on his shoulders, rose up on her toes and kissed his cheek. "You'll think of something."

Now it was Onesimus' turn to roll his eyes.

"And," she continued, "when you are done with the stables in a few days, you can get us more."

"I'll be happy to be done at the stables for more reasons that!"

"Don't do anything stupid and it won't happen again."

Onesimus was stung. "I didn't do anything wrong. Besides—" he added before she could admonish him further. "—if someone really did find this, we should lay off taking any for a while." He felt a bit triumphant at being able to use her own paranoia against her.

"Oh, *skata*," she replied, dismissing him with a wave. "First of all, it isn't stealing. Most slaves get some bonus coin for the kind of work you do. And if it's gone from the hiding place forever, our snooping friend will have no reason to question anything. Now,"—she placed her hand on his arm—"go and do what you must. We should be in the hutments by now."

He nodded and gave her a quick hug. He waited for few minute, so they would not arrive at the same time, then headed on down. He was uncomfortable having the money on his person. Where could he hide it? There was a small hiding place in his cell, behind a loose stone, but he had to move his cot to get at it.

When he arrived at his cell, Giton was there already, as he suspected, and already in bed. He'd wake him if he moved his cot. Not having another choice, he placed the bag under his blanket, shed his tunic, and, being careful not to jingle the coins, placed it between his body and the wall.

*

In the morning, he waited for Giton to leave for the privy before getting up. He had decided that it was not a good idea to hide the money in his cell. Better to hide it elsewhere, outside of the slave housing. That way, if anyone *did* find it, there would be no way to connect it to him.

But where? He thought of the storage shed where Philemon kept leather and other goods before selling it. Onesimus went there often, of course, so there would be no suspicion day or night if he visited. But Philippus and Philemon visited there often, too. If it were ever found, there would be no doubt that it belonged to Onesimus. Both Philippus and Philemon would know that Onesimus had not made that much money doing side jobs.

"Ah," he said aloud. The stables. There had to be a good place up there, that no one would ever look in. Perhaps behind the stable and compost shed. Perfect.

Except...he couldn't be going to the stables every time he obtained more money. If caught, *that* would be suspicious. He could do it at night, of course, but only if he limited the frequency.

He had a plan. He'd save the money from each trip—usually a small amount—in his own hiding place in his cell. If anyone found it—well, most slaves had a little stash somewhere. That wouldn't be suspicious. When the pouch got too full, he'd transfer it, at night, to the stable hiding place.

Foregoing the privy, he headed up to the stables and to work. He needed to get there before Pallio. He hurried down the path, across the footbridge, and turned right, following the stream. If someone saw him, they would surely question why he was going to work early—it was quite out of character. But he arrived without seeing anyone. The stalls and paddock were still closed up; Pallio was not here yet.

He passed in front of the stables. The sun was not up yet, but there was enough light to see and, he hoped, enough darkness to make him difficult to spot if Pallio did arrive before he finished. The smell of dirt, manure, hay, and animal was strong. He could hear some of the beasts moving and snorting inside their stalls. He must be careful not to spook them.

He came to the compost heap—a large, open shed with a canvas top and wooden sides, designed to create the conditions to enable the production of rich, moist fertilizer. As he recalled, there was space between the wall of the compost heap and the wall of the stalls. He moved into the shadows. Yes, there it was—smaller than he remembered, but enough room to squeeze between them.

He was surprised to find that the space between the back wall of the compost heap and the outer wall of the compound property was about six feet. Because of the high walls on either side, it was deep in shadow. He waited for a moment for his eyes to adjust. Soon, he could see that the ground was mostly dirt, as sunlight would not reach here during the day. In the far corner, there was a large a pile of rocks, probably left when the slaves had built the outer wall. He removed the stones from the top of the heap, placed the bag down inside, and then restacked the rocks on top. No one would ever find it here.

Satisfied, he crept back out. Emerging from the side of the compost structure, he saw Pallio just entering the paddock.

"Onesimus, my boy!" he cried out with a big smile. "Why are you hiding in the compost barn? Is it a comment on your character?" He laughed at his own joke.

"I was relieving myself. The privy was full up."

"Ah, well, why not add to the fertile pile? I have done so myself!" He laughed again. "Come on, let's get to it!"

Onesimus sighed in relief. If he'd seen him coming from behind the compost, he'd have been far more curious.

No matter. It was done, and the plan was now safer than ever.

*

Onesimus worked in the stables for the next few days, finishing out his punishment. At the end of each day, sweaty and stinking, he went to the small servant's bathhouse by the stream to clean up. By the time he finished, he was exhausted, and it was often too late to see Turia for more than a couple of minutes before returning to his room and fell exhausted into his bunk.

The next week, he returned to his regular duties as steward and messenger. He was determined to tow the line—or makes sure no one could find out if he didn't. He was *not* going back to the stables. Not because he'd "learned a lesson," but because it was a miserable and unfair way to treat a good slave who was just a little late and caused no harm.

His new hiding-place was working well. He didn't have to transfer the money to Turia. Once he turned in the money to Philippus, he would go back to his room with his secreted coins. If Giton were not there, he'd slide aside the bed, pull out the stone, place the new coins into the little pouch, then put everything back. If Giton were there; he'd simply wait until morning. Easy.

He became a little anxious when the pouch began to bulge a bit much, and he needed to transfer the contents to the hiding place at the stables. But, as if the gods were looking out for him, a perfect opportunity presented itself. One of the packhorses had come up lame and needed to be taken to the veterinarian. Normally, the horse master would perform this task, but he was busy in town. Since Onesimus was one of the few slaves who could ride, he was ordered to deliver the lame horse to Petilius at his villa to the northwest of Colossae, on the road to Laodicea. It was only a few miles, so Philemon asked him to walk the horse instead of riding another and leading the lame one. His instructions were to wait if the procedure would not take more than a few hours, but return on foot if Petilius needed to keep the horse overnight.

It was a perfect opportunity to move the money from his cell to the stables. If the horse needed to stay overnight—and it was the horse master's opinion that he would—Onesimus would return in the late afternoon. He knew that Pallio always went out to the pastures to help bring back the cattle and sheep in the later afternoon. So before he left for the horse stables, he retrieved the pouch from his room.

He collected the packhorse, an Arabian named Anemos, and was soon on the road to Petilius' villa. Upon arriving, the slaves took the horse around to the doctor's stables, while Onesimus relieved himself at the slave's privy. He sat by the villa's well to wait.

About thirty minutes later the veterinarian appeared, informing him that the horse would be fine, but he should not walk for a few days. He would send a slave with the horse to Philemon in two or three days, along with a bill.

Onesimus set off for home and, upon arrival, passed by the horse stables. As he drew near, he scanned the paddock: no one. He listened carefully, but heard no sounds that might indicate the herds were on their way back.

He ran to the wooden wall of the stables, along the back to the compost pile, crept to the corner and saw that everything was just as he had left it. Still, he breathed a sigh of relief upon removing the stones and finding the bag. He took it out, dumped the contents of the pouch into it, then scurried out.

As he reached the path that led down to the slave compound, he smiled to himself. Everything was working out perfectly.

8. Solitus

Three weeks later, things had settled back to normal. Onesimus took a trip to Heiropolis once and Laodicea twice, plus his regular trips into Colossae, to collect money and deliver goods for Philemon. He had extracted a few coins from those payments and easily concealed them in his hiding place in his room. His movements were more flexible than Giton's, so he could almost always find a time during the day to hide the money.

Meanwhile, he waited for opportunities to move the smaller stash to the main stash behind the stables. When he needed a horse for an errand, it was easy to sneak to the rock pile and add the money. The only real problem was getting coins out of his room, hidden on his person, and keeping them there until he could get to to the stables. It became a problem after a period of weeks where he had not needed a horse. The little space behind the stone in his room was not large at all—really just as a spot where the builder had forgotten to put any plaster to hold the stone.

One afternoon, before going up to see Philippus about an errand, he was replacing the pouch after adding three new coins. The stone would not go back into place without protruding. As he sat pondering, he heard the footsteps down the hall. Without putting the stone back, he shoved the bed back against the wall and sat down just as Giton entered.

"Giton," Onesimus said, trying to appear calm and normal. "What are you doing here?"

"One of the sheep fell into a ravine and I came back to get some help. I came here to—" He stopped. "Why are you here?"

"Oh, just taking a break before I run another errand." He hoped Giton could not see the loose stone under his bed.

"Well, anyway, Primus is collecting some help from the stable hands and told me to meet him at the animal gate in five minutes. I came back to get an extra cloak to use as a sling." He went to his trunk and took out a ragged cloak. Onesimus was not sure what to do. If he moved, Giton would see the pouch. If he just sat, Giton would wonder why he was not moving. He *could* explain it was his personal stash—it was small enough. But he didn't want Giton to know.

Giton went to the basin and began splashing water on his face. As quietly as he could, Onesimus set the bag behind the bed near the hiding place, then pushed the bed back and sat down.

Giton dried his face and looked around. "Why are you just sitting there?"

"I told you, just resting."

Giton continued staring at him as he dried his face.

"I'm tired……long trip into town." *Change the subject.* "How is the sheep? Is it injured?"

"Fine." He frowned. "She's fine." He walked to the door.

"Good. Well, good luck."

Giton nodded. Onesimus hoped Giton was preoccupied with the sheep and did not think the conversation was as awkward as Onesimus did.

"Thanks." Giton left.

Onesimus waited until he heard Giton's steps fade away. He took a deep breath. He needed to find another hiding place. He considered the storage shed. The next time he was there alone, he would explore the building and see what hiding places it might provide. For now, he could keep some of the coins on his person. Or maybe he should just take the entire pouch to the stables now. Or take it to the shed and hope he could find a place.

No. It would be just like Giton to wait outside and follow him. On the other hand, it would be just like Giton to come back later and search behind his bed.

Why did Turia have to be so paranoid? It was so much easier when she was hiding it under her wooden floor.

He thought for a few moments.

If he went to the shed now, Giton might follow him. That could lead to disaster. On the other hand, if he left the money here and Giton found it, it was a natural explanation that it was his private stash. Except it was a lot of money for a slave stash.

He pulled the bed out, took a few of the larger coins out of the little pouch and put them into the pocket of his tunic, stuffed the bag back into the opening, and put the stone back. This would have to do, though he didn't like carrying this much money on his person. Maybe he could figure something out tonight when he got back from his errand.

He pushed the bed back into place, left the room, walked across the bridge, and headed up to the villa. He quickly located Philippus in the exedra just off the atrium.

"You sent for me, Philippus?" The vilici was sitting at a table, melting wax to seal two scrolls.

"Yes. I need you to take these bills into town. This one to Lucas and this one to Simon's. " He handed the scrolls to him.

"Anything to pick up?"

"No, this is all, but the master wants these paid as soon as possible, so get them there quick." He handed the bills to Onesimus.

"Should I take a horse?" he asked, hoping for a chance to secrete the coins in his pocket.

"No. It's not that urgent."

"Very well. On my way."

He left the villa and headed on down. He was still worried about the coins in his pocket—it was not excessive, but more than a slave would normally carry about.

Of course, he could always spend some of it in town. He deserved it, after all the work he was having to do to secure the plan for the money. Better than getting caught with it. Surely Turia would agree, if she knew.

It was a cool, pleasant day, and the walk was pleasant. He quickly delivered the bills, then went to Navia's and ordered a full jar of wine and a pitcher of water. He drank it slowly, savoring every sip. He had splurged on a Falernian wine. He nodded to a few other slaves who passed by, and acknowledged a couple of freedpersons he knew.

Feeling relaxed, he dropped a coin on the table and headed out, across the forum, into a side street, and over to the brothel. It had been a long few weeks, with a lot of stress. Besides, it was better to get rid of this extra money. Safer. There would always be more. Things were going well.

Being late afternoon, the brothel was not crowded, and, as he hoped, Nanilia was available. Onesimus gave more of the coins to the proprietor, and went to Nanilia's small room, feeling quite good.

*

Onesimus washed in the small privy provided for customers and stepped outside. He felt warm, sated, and relaxed. Looking at the sky, he realized it was later than he thought, but it didn't matter. He had nothing to deliver to Philippus or the storage shed, and he should arrive at the villa just after sundown. He took his time walking back. It was a few days after the Ides of Maius, and the late afternoons were balmy and clear.

When he entered the front gate of the compound, he heard his name called. Philippus emerged from the shadows of the villa.

"Hello, Philippus, what are you doing out here?" he said.

Philippus said nothing until he was within a few feet of Onesimus. "Follow me. The domine wants to see you." He turned back towards the house. Onesimus walked behind, wondering what it could be. The master hardly ever had tasks for him after sundown. Maybe an urgent letter to write, or counting inventory after a shipment.

"What's going on?" he repeated as they walked up the path to the front door. Philippus neither answered nor looked back at him.

They entered the house and headed, not to the tablinum, but to one of the cubiculas off to the side that Philemon used as a private study when he did not want to be disturbed. Philippus entered first.

"Onesimus is here, domine."

Onesimus entered the room to see Philemon sitting behind the desk. He was not alone in the room. Three others stood, in a line, in front of the desk: Turia, Claudia, and Giton. Onesimus gave Turia a questioning look, but her eyes were focused on the lower portion of the wall opposite her.

Philemon cleared his throat, and Onesimus turned to him. Sitting on the desk, in front of Philemon, was the pouch of money from his room.

9. Oppono

Onesimus felt heat rising through his body.

"Well, Onesimus?"

"Domine, uh…yes…" His heart was pounding. What was going on? At worst, this was his private stash that had perhaps more money than might be expected.

"Let's do this in an orderly manner." Philemon took a deep breath. He glanced over at him as Philemon turned to Philippus. "Philippus, repeat what you told me about the accounting."

Philippus cleared his throat. Onesimus looked over at him, but Philippus was looking into the center of the room.

"Yes, domine. As you know, last week Pentius claimed that you shorted him a payment. I went back through the books, comparing them to the invoices and receipts, and discovered that we *had* paid Pentius properly. But in comparing the receipts to the accounting book, I discovered a discrepancy. So I checked all payments for the last three months against the treasury count for each of those months. It came up short for for each of those months, a different amount each time. Of course, mistakes have happened before—but not every month. When there is a problem, I have always been able to find it: a mistake in my counting or a mistake on a bill or payment. I have performed this task for over twenty years. On rare occasions, I was never able to find the problem. But an unaccountable shortage each month for three months is unusual."

Oh, no.

"When Claudia came to me—"

"Enough," interrupted Philemon. "Claudia, relate what you told Philippus earlier today."

Onesimus looked at Turia again. They should have come up with a story they could tell in case this ever happened. Why did she feel the need to move the hiding place?! Why had he never considered that Philippus might check the month's totals against the treasury?

"Yes, domine." Claudia's voice was shaky. What does she have to do with this? Onesimus thought, while frantically trying to come up with an excuse. Some way to disconnect it from the missing money from the treasury. Some way to save Turia and himself.

Claudia cleared her throat. "About a week ago, I…I was returning to the room and found Turia kneeling on the floor. She seemed embarrassed…nervous…She said she…she had dropped something, but I saw nothing. She left…after she left," she glanced at Turia, "I—I examined the floor and found a loose board. Underneath was a bag. I looked inside. There were…many coins."

"Did you count the coins?" asked Philemon.

Claudia flinched. "I tried, but I cannot count well. There were too many."

Onesimus glanced at Philemon. His face was red despite his controlled tone. His eyes were fixed on Claudia. "Continue. Why did this bother you?"

She glanced at Turia again, who continued to stare at the wall. "I did not…know where Turia got so much money. So I, I asked her. She—"

"Good." Philemon held up his hand. "Turia shall speak her own words in a moment. When did you speak to Philippus?"

"I didn't, domine…I mean, not directly. I clean…one of my duties is to clean Philippus' quarters. I heard Philippus tell his wife about the missing money. He…he was afraid you would punish him. I like…Philippus and his wife have always been kind to me…so…I did not—"

"Yes, yes," Philemon interrupted, "go on. What did you do?"

She ducked her head. "Sorry, domine…I told his wife what Turia had told me, and…and…"

"That is enough," Philemon said. "You have done well."

Claudia, with a little smile of relief, stepped back, looking down at the floor. Philemon took a breath. "Very well." He looked at Turia, who was now staring at her feet. He raised his eyebrows. "Turia?"

"Yes, domine." She took a deep breath and looked up at Philemon. She seemed more angry than nervous. Ah, thought Onesimus, she has a story! Something to explain all this.

"Domine," Turia said, "I do not wish to implicate anyone—"

"We have discussed that. The inquiry is over—we are just repeating it for Onesimus' sake."

They had spoken already? What had she said? He'd have to think quick on his feet as it unfolded.

"Yes, domine. As I told you—" now she was looking at the floor again, "—about six months ago, Onesimus asked me to hide a bag of money for him. He would not tell me where he got it—I assumed it was extra money he had earned."

What was she saying?

"But he brought me more and more over the next few months. I was suspicious but did not think it my place to question. When Claudia asked me about it, I got worried. I wanted nothing more to do with it, so I gave the money back to Onesimus and told him I could no longer hide it for him—it was his business."

Onesimus was stunned.

He stared at Turia, his vision narrowing like an iris closing. Her gaze did not waver. What was she saying? What was she doing?

Panic welled up in him. Why was she saying these things?! It sounded like she was trying to protect herself.

But, she wouldn't do that to him. They were in love. They were to be married. Something else was going on that he did not understand yet.

Giton was speaking now. Onesimus had missed some of the conversation.

"...so naturally, with his strange behavior, I investigated. Normally I would never go near another slave's bunk, of course, but knowing of the missing money, I felt it my duty..."

How did Giton know about the missing money?

"...so I hid behind one of the hutments. Once I saw him leave, I went back inside and searched behind his bed. I found it behind a loose stone in the wall." He pointed to the pouch sitting ominously on the wooden desk.

Onesimus felt sick. How stupid of him. Of course, another slave would not search another slaves' belongings—unless he had reason to think the slave was doing something improper. But how did Giton know?

Giton lifted his chin slightly. "I felt it was my duty to you, master."

Onesimus hated Giton's thin, arrogant voice.

His mind was reeling. This cannot be happening. What could he say? He looked at Turia again, but she continued to stare ahead as if she were one of Alexander Magnus' soldiers. He tried to read her face, but it was impassive, though the fingers of her right hand, at her side, were trembling ever so slightly.

Philemon took another deep breath. "Very well. You are all dismissed—except you," the latter was barked at Onesimus with a withering look. "Philippus, take this pouch and count the money. I want to know how closely it matches the amount I am missing."

Philippus took the pouch from the desk and bowed. The four slaves filed out the door past Onesimus. No one looked at him. Onesimus followed Turia with his eyes, hoping for a look, a glance—something to explain or acknowledge that everything was going to be okay. But she kept her eyes on the ground before her. Soon Onesimus and Philemon were alone in the room. Now it was Onesimus' turn to stare at the floor.

The bang of Philemon's fist on the desk made him jump. Philemon was on his feet, staring fiercely at Onesimus.

"Do I deserve this, Onesimus? Have I been such a harsh master? Ah!" He turned away and began pacing. Onesimus' only choice was to argue that it was merely his private stash, earned properly. But the accounting of Philemon and the lies of Turia made it look bad. Still, he had to try.

"Domine, the money was—"

"Silence!" He fixed his gaze again at Onesimus. "You dare steal from me? I am not a harsh master. Even my punishment of you last month was a…a trifle."

Philemon turned away and faced the scroll case along the wall, his hands clasped behind his back. Onesimus' heart was pounding, his vision blurry.

"Domine, that was my private—"

"Don't compound this by lying, Onesimus. I know how much your extra work brings. And the testimony of your *fellow* slaves condemns you. Even…even Philippus and Turia, who seem to have a fondness for you!"

He didn't know what to say. His mind raced in a panic.

Finally, Philemon turned around. "Maybe this is my doing…Maybe I am too kind." He sighed. Onesimus looked at him. Some of the anger had changed into disappointment. Maybe this was an opening.

"I had such hope for you, Onesimus. You are smart. You took to the training I gave you like a fish to water." Philemon shook his head. Some of the anger returned. "The training *I* paid for! Others told me, 'Don't waste money on a Moesian slave.' But I thought I saw promise. And you have betrayed me!"

Maybe you paid for my training, Onesimus thought. *But you never recognized my talents, never gave me any special jobs for extra money like you do for Philippus and others. Now you talk like you have been so good to me.*

Philemon put his hands on the desk and leaned over towards him. "Why, Onesimus, why? You could have come and asked for money if you needed it. I might not have given it—but I well might have! Better than… this…" He shook his head again.

Onesimus did not believe for a moment that Philemon would have given him money. Or helped him make money.

Philemon stared off through the archway. "Twelve more years and a ring for you…"

Onesimus frowned. Twelve years? A ring? What was he babbling about?

Philemon turned again, staring at the desk. The silence stretched out. Onesimus could hear the snuffling of the candles in the room. Somewhere, in another part of the villa, a woman was speaking. Strange how, at moments like this, one's senses become acute.

Philemon sat down and sighed. Almost to himself, he said, "Maybe the Lex Alia Sentia didn't go far enough." He looked up. "Go back to your room. Do not leave until I send for you. I won't beat you like some would. I should probably sell you—but another master would not want you if he knew of this. Maybe you should go back to the slave market. I'll lose a lot of money, of course."

It's always about the money, isn't it, old man? Onesimus thought.

"I need to consult with my son and my wife. I want to make the proper decision. Now get out of my sight." Philemon picked up a paperweight that was sitting on his desk and began to turn it in his hand. Onesimus wondered if he might throw it at him. Onesimus turned and left the room, through the peristyle, out into the public rooms, and through the back garden, in a daze. His heart was pounding and his mind was racing.

What had Turia done?

Part of him thought she would come find him, and apologize, and tell him of her plan to deal with it all. But another voice, a sinister voice, said that she'd been using him all along, and now she had betrayed him to save herself.

Now what?

10. Fuga

He would *not* go back to the slave market. The memories of that place were packed away, never to be taken out and examined. Just a fleeting thought of it was enough to make his heart pound.

He needed to find Turia. Maybe she'd just been scared and reacted without thinking. Perhaps someone forced her into it? Giton, perhaps.

He stopped in his tracks just before the footbridge.

Don't be naïve, Onesimus . She betrayed you to save her own skin. She could easily have taken the blame together. Or stuck to the story of it being their legitimate stash. But she *lied*. She made up a story to make him look bad and portray herself as an unwitting and ignorant accomplice.

He was furious. How could he have been so blind?! What was he to do? Come morning…

He didn't have much time. He'd like to find her—and Giton—and beat them both to death. But he needed to put those emotions aside at the moment. A slave accused of stealing was in terrible trouble. A defective piece of property, good only for the mines or a galley. Or death.

He would not let that happen—not to him.

He crossed the footbridge and turned left, up towards the stables. No one would be out this late, but he still moved quickly and quietly. The space between the stable wall and the compost shed was pitch dark, as was the hidden space behind. He groped his way to the stone pile, and, like a blind man, removed stones until he felt the bag of money.

With one hand on the wooden wall, he crept back out and stopped. He scanned the space between him and the horse stables. No movement. No lanterns. He heard a faint snort from one of the horses.

His absence from the room would not be noticed for some time—probably not until morning. Giton would assume that Philemon had put him in the small slave-lockup. Onesimus was pretty sure it would not cross Philemon's mind that he would not go to his room. Owners might be smart, but being an unquestioned authority sometimes made them blind to the fact that one of their own might not obey.

He stole over to the stable gate and into the stables. He took some apples and carrots from a storage bin and stuffed them into a saddlebag, then put the money bag in. He went to the stalls, quietly so as not to spook the horses, and located Lampros. She would know him and give him no trouble. He untied her and led her from the stall. He stroked her to keep her calm.

"It's okay, just a little night ride." He lifted a saddle and blanket from the storage and threw them over her back, but did not fasten the saddle just yet. He put a bridle loosely over her snout and the bit into her mouth.

Should he go out the front gate, which would be faster, or around the back of the villa and out through the fields and pastures? The former would get him on the road faster, but he would have to open the gate at the front of the villa. The back way would allow him to stay mostly hidden, but he would have to pass near the slave quarters.

He squinted at the main entrance of the villa. He could see a dim lamp burning at the front door. Lentulus, the old door servant, might still be sitting beside it, inside the archway. Or he might have already gone inside to his little room, having forgotten to put out the lamp. Either way, he was probably sleeping, as usual. His hearing was terrible, so it was unlikely he'd hear anything. The faster way was safer.

He cinched the saddle, took the reins, and paused to think. Once he was outside the gate and on his way, he will have crossed his Rubicon. If caught, he was a runaway slave, and everyone knew what that meant.

That thought made him waver. What if he went back and waited until morning? Threw himself at the mercy of Philemon? He still wanted to confront Turia, the lying lupatria!

He shook his head. No. She had time to think before she spoke in front of Philemon. Her story had sounded rehearsed, hadn't it? It was no unthinking reaction. It was his story against that of her, Giton, and Philippus.

How could he have been so gullible?

He was doomed here. He would become a stable servant at best, or sold to the slave market at worst. No master would ever give him a chance at a better life—even as a slave!—after this.

He had money. He had a horse. And he knew where to go. He was educated; he knew maps; he could read and write. He had money. All he had to do was get out of the Asian Province and he'd be home free.

If he chose this path, would Artemis protect him? Guide him? It would be dangerous—perhaps almost as dangerous as staying.

"Artemis, help me. I don't have much time."

He stood in the dark stable, hand on Lampros, waiting for a sign.

11. Lycus

It was deathly quiet now. Suddenly, Lampros lifted a front hoof and pawed the ground.

Onesimus took a breath and nodded. "Very well."

Emboldened, he led Lampros out of the stable and alongside the outer wall. A calm and tame horse, she obeyed and stayed quiet. Looking back at the front of the villa again, he detected no movement or sound. Resolved, slid the bolt back, and opened the gate just wide enough for Lampros. He led her through and shut the gate with care. As he pushed the bolt back into place it clanked. He froze.

He could hear a few sheep bleating in the distance, the murmuring of the stream, and the gentle breeze blowing in the trees above. No sound came from the door of the villa.

He cinched the saddle, mounted up, and headed down the road.

Now that he was on his way, he wanted to move with speed, but he had to be patient. The sound of galloping hooves might be audible in the still night. His heart was still pounding. He focused on the horse and the road to try to keep himself from thinking about the enormity of what he was doing.

It seemed to take forever, but he finally topped a short rise. Once on the opposite slope, he nudged Lampros to a canter. Soon, the path curved up and over a more substantial rise, meeting the main road down into the Lycus river valley and towards Laodicea. He halted Lampros at the crest and looked around. The moon was high enough for him to see the ribbon of the road as it fell away below him into the distance. It was nine miles to Laodicea, then another 25 or 30 to the Meander River. In spite of his fear and urgency, he knew he had to take a break and water Lampros at some point. There was enough moonlight to gallop, and he knew the road reasonably well since he traveled it every couple of months or so. It should be late enough not to have to worry about bandits. He slapped the reins, and soon they were flying through the moonlit night, a dark shadow passing swiftly down into the Lycus Valley. He knew he was riding Lampros hard, and he felt a bit of guilty about it.

He leaned down close to the horse's ears. "Sorry, friend. I'm going to ask a lot of you right now."

It would do him no good if she collapsed. She was a good horse. But he needed to put as many miles between him and the villa as possible. If he could make Miletus just before daybreak, he could rest, eat, and care for Lampros there. His absence would not be discovered until morning, he was sure. They would search the villa and then Colossae first, so he would have time to plan the next stage of his journey.

They made a good, steady, rapid pace. Laodicea was larger than Colossae, and it lay directly on the road to the port cities. Because of all the commerce which passed through (including Philemon's goods), it had become major banking center. This made it a wealthy city, boasting a large theater, a gymnasium, a stadium, numerous temples, and even its own aqueduct. He liked it better than Heiropolis, and spent extra time there when on errands, enjoying the more cosmopolitan culture.

The gates would be closed, of course, so he would have to go around the city. This was no problem, because Laodicea had a paved, colonnaded road around the city as well as through it—another testament to its wealth. Reaching the fork in the road just before the city gates, he spurred Lampros to the left. He placed his hand down upon her side. She was wet with lather. But he had to keep going.

He passed along the city walls, came to the opposite gate, and soon left the town behind. He felt a bit wistful because he was sure he would never see Laodicea again. *That's okay,* he said to himself, *you are bound for something even better.*

The road passed through small hills and trees, headed to where the Lycus River joined the Meander River. He slowed a bit, feeling somewhat safer now that he had the city behind him, and it also allowed Lampros to rest a bit. The horse was a good trotter: strong, with a good set of lungs. He should be able to make it to the Meander river before she needed more water, but he didn't want to abuse her. He leaned down, putting his head beside her neck, listening to her breathe.

"That's a good girl. Bit of as rest now, but we can't stop yet."

His mind turned to the future. He would love to stop in Miletus, but it was much too close. He and Turia had planned on heading northwest beyond Moesia, maybe as far as Raetia or even Belgica, near the borders of the barbarian lands. But he couldn't go there now—she might suspect that is where he'd go and tell Philemon. While he was not sure Philemon would send someone to search for him, he was taking no chances.

How could he have been so wrong about her? He was so good at reading people. He began to get angry. She was a clever one. He wanted revenge on her. And Giton, but mostly her.

He wondered, too, how love could turn so rapidly to a desire for revenge. Well, she had brought it on. But he wouldn't forget. He had allowed Turia's scheme to lull him into complacency. Never again.

It came to him that their plan had all been a pipe dream, anyway. How much would he and Turia need to save so that Philemon would accept the redemption price and give them their freedom? Onesimus had imagined, many times, going to Philemon, Turia by his side, and placing a bag of money on his desk. "This is our redemption price." Everyone had heard stories of slaves who did that—but in every case, the master was *pleased* to give a long-tenured and beloved house slave their freedom. Turia and Onesimus were young, at the beginning of their prime as slaves. Philemon would refuse. What would he have to gain? Unless they could pay him so much that he could not refuse—but squirreling away a coin here and a coin there would never be enough.

How naïve they were. Their only hope for freedom had always been to run. Just like Onesimus was doing now. Or to work until they were old and feeble, and maybe, if they remained loyal and subservient, Philemon would find it in his heart. *Ha!* Onesimus thought. *Not that skinflint.*

Philemon had said *something* about twelve more years and he might have released him. Was he planning on selling him anyway? Why in twelve years? He had mentioned some law—Alisentia or something. He was probably just trying to scare Onesimus.

"Ha!" He said to Lampros. "No matter! I have taken things into my own hand and acted boldly for the first time in my life. I am in control now, right, girl?!"

A little over an hour later, the road turned and he began a slow climb, which crested and then descended to the river. A tiny village lay beside the darkly flowing water. It consisted of a few domii, a taberna, and some outlying farms. He rode on past. The road turned west, following the river through its broad valley until it turned south, while his road continued straight on through low foothills towards Ephesus and the other coastal cities.

After putting a few more miles between him and the last village, he looked for a place to stop by the river. The moon had already reached its zenith and was on its way down. It was clear and visibility was good. Seeing an opportune beach on the bank to his right, he guided Lampros over and dismounted. He let her drink from the water while he took off the saddle. He wiped her down with the blanket, and, when she seemed to have cooled off enough, he fed her an apple and a few carrots from the bag. He helped himself to an apple as well. After a long, refreshing drink, he sat down with his back against a boulder to rest and to think.

He considered his plan to head to Miletus.

"What do you think, Lampros? Miletus is the coastal city you and I have visited more than any other. But if your owner sends anyone to search for us, that will be the next place after Laodicea and Heiropolis." Lampros snorted. "You agree? Okay, then, we'll head to Ephesus. Have you been there? It's a much larger city, which should allow us a better chance of going unnoticed."

After that? Moesia was a start. Would Philemon send someone that far to seek a runaway slave? He wasn't sure. But he should probably avoid anywhere with which he had a connection. Moesia was just the geographic accident of his birth. For that matter, he mused, my birth was an accident of the gods. Or a joke.

"Hey, girl, maybe after that I could pose as a slave on a journey for his master, riding the master's horse. No one would be suspicious of that. We've probably got enough money for more than half a year, if we stay frugal."

He also had an advantage that many slaves did not: Philemon had made sure Onesimus was educated. He had a good picture in his mind of the Empire and geography. He knew if he went far enough north, he would come to Bithynia, and even further still, across to Byzantium. From there, he could go through Thrace and Moesia and onward to the edge of the Empire. Or, he could go east, through Cappadocia to Armenia, lose his slave's tunic, and become a day laborer among the Barbarians.

In any case, Ephesus was the first step. From there, he could take the road north to Pergamum and eventually cross the gulf separating the Aegean and the Euxine Sea. Or he could take a ship from Ephesus to southern Thraia—maybe disembarking at Neopolis. A ship's journey would be faster—and no one would expect he would take to sea.

*

He woke with a start. He had not intended to sleep. In a panic, he jumped up and looked for Lampros. She was farther up the slope, dozing under a tree. He searched the sky: the moon was low, he estimated he had been here for perhaps two hours. Ephesus was still sixty miles away.

He retrieved Lampros, allowed her to drink some water briefly, then tossed the saddle on and cinched it.

"Ah, what an idiot I am, Lampros! We've given them hours to catch up to us. Why didn't you wake me?" The horse looked at him mournfully.

"It's okay girl. Not your fault."

He lead her slowly up to the road. Stopping at the edge, he looked both wasps and listened carefully. Only silence. He mounted and urged Lampros on at a steady pace.

He passed the sleeping towns of Nysa and Tralles. Not long after the latter, the Meander River took a turn to the left and south, on its way to the sea. Twenty miles further on he reached the crossroads. To the left, over thirty miles away, was Miletus. To the right lay Ephesus, a mere two miles. The road was now broad and smooth.

"Okay, here we go. On to Ephesus! And our destiny!"

Villas and farms began to appear on both sides of the road, which curved up and between two peaks. The sky behind him was starting to turn a deep blue. He urged Lampros on. The road was paved now, Roman style. As he climbed the rise, he passed a couple of farmer's carts, loaded with goods, making their way slowly towards Ephesus.

He capped a rise and pulled Lampros to a stop. There below, about a half a mile away, lay the port city of Ephesus, just coming to life in the dawn of the new day.

Now what?

EPISTOLE GAMMA

To Giarri

I hope your health is good. I am thankful for your recent letters and your prayers. I am overjoyed to hear of the good news coming to the Maecilius family.

As for your problems with the Ephesian city fathers: they always were a bit full of themselves. Like their ancestors, they are quite proud of their history, believing the city was founded by an Amazon tribe. I don't know about that, but it is quite a pedigree to have been a significant city for the Persian Empire, then the Greek, the Sparta League, Alexander's Empire, and now, finally a jewel of the Roman Empire. I suppose it is enough to make one prideful.

As a young man, I had been fascinated by Ephesus. I visited rarely, and only on business, so its mystery grew in my mind. A city of a quarter of a million people!

Did I tell you that I visited the temple of Artemis in Ephesus on my way to meet him? It was so beautiful—I had never seen such elaborate marble-work. I walked about like a fool, with no idea of what lay ahead of me. If I had, I might have turned around and gone right back to Colossae, tail between my legs.

It is interesting how things that loom so large in our young minds later shrink to proper proportion. What seemed so alluring loses its appeal. You and I have worked in that city for so long that I could walk past the amphitheater, the State Agora, or the stadium, and never even glance at them. Even the renowned medical school seemed unimportant. But, of course, our work far exceeded the importance of any of those things.

As you can probably tell from the telling of my story, as a youth, I acted so confident, but I could not admit—even to myself—how terrified I was to be out on my own. That young man had no idea that he was about to take a path that would define him forever. All from a chance meeting at that same temple, and three little Latin words.

Of course, I know now that it was not mere chance.

I have still not been called before Eparch Tertillus, though I did hear—through one of the guards who is one of us—that he is considering exile, but his advisors believe that stoning or beheading would make him look better in the eyes of the Emperor.

I am ready for whatever may come.

It is quite cold here, as you can imagine, with no fire, and the single blanket I am allowed is sparse and worn. I will keep writing my story to you, though I am less and less sure of its interest to anyone except you and I. Please keep your letters coming, for they are a comfort to me, and I will answer your questions as best I can. Greet everyone for me.

12. Proposita

Onesimus was struck by how stunningly beautiful the city of Ephesus appeared. It had been some time since he last visited—this was only his third time here. Even though the memories of previous visits had loomed large in his mind, a recollection is no match for the glory of reality. A long, white, marble road leading from the gate into the forum, the agora, temples, and even a massive theater. It was so beautiful, so *modern.* He lifted his gaze and could see, beyond the forum, a long road which led to the docks, and beyond that, the bay itself, now sparkling in the early morning sun. Sounds of a city coming to life reached his ears. He sat upon Lampros for a moment, enjoying the sights and sounds, almost forgetting his plight.

After a few moments, he started down to the entrance of the city. He approached the massive gates, thrown open to greet the new day. He dismounted, leading Lampros, just one of many hundreds of people, animals, and carts streaming in and out of the city on the marble street, lined by tall columns and surrounded by ornate buildings, all resting between two low hills.

Just outside the city walls, he found a taberna with a stable. He tied Lampros to a hitching post and entered through the low door. It was cool and dark inside. As his eyes adjusted, he saw a number of tables scattered around an empty room. He was the first customer of the day. A fireplace, newly lit, popped and crackled. At the back of the room was a counter behind which stood a slave.

"Good day, can I help you?" The slave was a young, well-groomed, well-dressed servant. This was no cheap, dirty hovel. This was a real city.

"Good day. Yes, I need my horse stabled and some breakfast. Do you have rooms for rent?"

"Have a seat. I'll have someone go out and care of your horse. We do have rooms."

Onesimus found a table near the fire. It felt good to sit on a bench after riding almost all night. The heat of the fire began to warm his body, still cold from the long ride in the night.

Soon, a young girl entered and began rolling up the window shades. The light revealed the details of the room. It was a well-worn establishment: clean, old, but well-kept. Onesimus could see that the girl was a freed-woman by her dress; probably the proprietor's daughter. She disappeared behind the counter and through a door —the kitchen, from the sounds Onesimus could hear coming through it.

He perused the menu painted on the wall above the bar. After a short time, the slave returned, bringing with him a jug of water and a board heaped with bread and a bowl of honey.

"What would you like? We have fine breakfast foods. I recommend the millet porridge with raisins and honey."

"That sounds fine," Onesimus replied. "I will have a bowl, along with some warm honeyed wine."

The slave nodded and disappeared into the kitchen, leaving Onesimus to enjoy the fresh bread and honey. It tasted like nobleman's fare to his famished body. It felt right: on his own, master of his own destiny.

Onesimus heard the door open behind him. Two men entered, about the same age as Onesimus, taking a table across the room. Both were well-dressed, but Onesimus noticed that the smaller man had a pilleus—a cap made of felt which marked the wearer as a freed slave.

"Well," the larger man said, "how did your first day of freedom feel?" His voice was strong and confident. Onesimus was reminded of Philemon.

"To tell you the truth, Sollus, it did not seem that different from all the days before! I am doing the same work, in the same surroundings, with the same family!" He laughed.

"Yes, that is true. But just wait…" the man leaned closer, "…when you get paid for that work. And more important still, when you begin to know the other advantages of being a citizen. *Citizen* Panurgus."

Onesimus perked up. The slave had not only been manumitted, but granted Roman citizenship! Without being too obvious, Onesimus tried to spot the iron ring that would be on his finger.

"It will take a while to sink in, I suppose," Panurgus said. "I waited long enough."

"Oh, by Jupiter, you just reached thirty years!"

"True, but my grandfather was manumitted with citizenship when he was twenty, and I think my service has been more exemplary than his."

"Indeed it has, Panurgus—especially that deal with Demetrius when you discovered that cheater's plan! Oh, how proud the master was of you! If our lord Emperor had not passed the Lex Alia Sentia, I would wager you would have been granted citizenship right then."

Was that the same law that Philemon had mentioned? Onesimus thought. Three more men entered the taberna, and he had to strain to hear the conversation.

"…wait until thirty! An accident of history!"

Onesimus' breakfast arrived, and the serving slave extolled the virtues of the meal he had just delivered. When he left, more patrons and entered and the room became too noisy for him to hear much of any conversation.

What had Philemon said? Something like "…twelve more years and I might have released you…" and then some law. At the time, he assumed Philemon was just trying to get his goat, like a parent saying, "look what you might have had if you weren't so bad!" But why had he said "twelve years"? Onesimus would be thirty years of age in twelve more years, just like the ex-slave over at the other table. A coincidence?

Well, he thought. *It doesn't matter now.*

He finished the porridge—which was quite good—and sat sipping the last of his wine, staring into the fire, thinking about his next move. First, he must buy some supplies and then find a northbound caravan that he could join. He decided to make for Pergamum. From there, he could either go northeast over to Byzantium and then on to Lesser Moesia; or he could catch a ship to Neopolis from Byzantium and then head north towards Greater Moesia. Either would be a long journey. He needed to preserve his money. Not knowing anything about the nature of those routes, he should find someone at the agora who could offer some advice.

Onesimus caught the attention of the slave and called him over.

"I wish to buy some supplies in town, and I need information about travel routes. Do you have any suggestions?"

The slave thought for a moment. "At the forum you'll find plenty of markets. But for travel information, go to the docks and find a merchant known as Decimus Secundus. He has a warehouse there—large; you can't miss it. His company trades goods across land and sea, all along the Ignatian Way to Rome and beyond. If anyone has the information you need, it will be him."

The slave paused. "Oh, by the way...you said you had a horse?"

"Yes, out front."

The slave blanched. "There's no horse."

13. TEMPLUM

He was right. Lampros was gone. The slave explained that the posts were not for the inn—they were public posts, and no one ever left horses there without someone to watch them. Too easy to steal.

Onesimus was angry, first taking it out on the slave, then on himself. He ran to the building next door—a caupana, then to a domus on the other side of the taberna, and then to two buildings directly across the street. No one had seen a horse or anyone taking one.

Dejected, and feeling like a rustic rube in a big city, he trudged back inside the taberna.

"No luck?" the slave asked.

Onesimus nodded. He settled the day's bill, gave him a deposit for a room, and told him he would in the afternoon to pay the rest and take a place for the night.

What an idiot.

He left the *popina* and stepped out into the rapidly warming day. Heading towards the center of town, he made his way down Curates Street. The crowds grew increasingly larger and louder, until he was part of a teeming throng, moving up and down and in and out of this thriving seaport city.

By losing Lampros, he'd also lost a good amount of money. On the other hand, it was not money he had been counting on anyway, before he made his plans. And he didn't need Lampros. It was fine. Just a good lesson as he began his new life.

As the walked, he soon forgot about Lampros. The sounds were a cacophony: merchants shouting to customers and potential customers, children laughing and squealing, and the creek of wagon wheels as they wound their way through the city. His mind was reeling. All the people, the marble buildings, the pillars, and the domii up on the hillside—he had not remembered the overwhelming magnificence of this city. He had to apologize a few times for running up on the back of someone, or suddenly coming inches from a face as he ogled something at the right or left as he walked. Ephesus was indeed a prosperous place and its citizens wealthy beyond understanding. It was so vibrant and alive. He loved it.

Soon he spotted a sizeable public latrine and went inside to relieve himself. The sloped floor was cool beneath his sandals, and, though the room smelled of urine and excrement, it offered some shade from the sun. He nodded to the city slave who periodically sloshed a bucket of water across the floor and the stone benches.

As he received himself, he considered might have ended up with a job like that! Or worse. He was fortunate indeed. Pulling his cloak back around him, he spun quickly to speed his way out of the steamy and pungent place.

He collided with someone, and both fell to the ground. He scrambled to his feet and began to offer an apology.

The other was a large man, a slave by his dress. But he was big and muscular—a bodyguard or a door slave, perhaps.

"What in Zeus's name, boy! Look at this!" Standing, he indicated his soiled and soaked cloak.

"I…I'm sorry. I did not see you in the dim—"

"Should have known! A foreigner—barbarian by the look of you!" He spun around towards the latrine slave.

Onesimus frowned. He may be a foreigner, but he was no barbarian!

The slave turned back towards him and threw a bucket of tepid water over him. Onesimus gasped and ran out of the latrines.

He shook himself and walked quickly away, down the street and around a corner. He stopped, out of sight, back against a wall. He didn't think the oaf followed him, but he didn't want to take any chances.

The big city was not as friendly as he had hoped. He needed to be a lot more careful.

He stuck his head around the corner and looked back up at the latrine. As he did so, he saw the slave walking past him in the crowd. His heart lept into his throat, but the man was looking straight ahead, off on an errand.

Onesimus waited a few more minutes, then went back outside and continued toward the harbor.

He could hear the buzzing of many voices growing louder as he approached the Forum. When he arrived, he experienced again the failure of memory to capture the spectacular scene before him. Much larger than those of Colossae and Laodicea, this massive rectangle in the middle of the city thrived and pulsed with activity. Shops lined the four sides—all apparently doing brisk business. In a far corner, he saw that a court case was being held at the bema, where a bored but wise-looking old judge sat high up on the bench. Nearby, at the podium of the Forum, was a man giving a speech to a crowd. From the snatches of oratory he could hear, it was some sort of political speech.

He made his way through the crowds and around the perimeter, taking note of a bakery, a cheese-seller, and a butcher. He would come back later and buy a few supplies for his journey. For now, he left the forum and headed down the paved street towards the harbor. Soon he passed beyond the hills and the crowded part of the city, arriving at a long flat slope which led down to the bay. The Amphitheater appeared to his right, on the slope of the hill he had just passed. He stopped and stared at the marvel of architecture, built up the entire back of the hill. It was mostly empty now, which meant no plays or speeches were going on. He felt the smallness of his previous life: this theater, with its finely built ledges, finished in marble, held about 25,000 people—the entire population of Heiropolis could fit inside!

He turned back towards the bay and saw some symbols carved and painted at his feet—a footstep with an arrow. He recognized the universal symbol that denoted the way to a brothel. He was tempted—the last twenty-four hours had been quite eventful! After Turia's terrible betrayal, he felt the need for companionship. Even a lupatria would be better than her! But his money was limited, and he should not tarry too long.

Turia! If he had been mystified and confused before, he was now just angry. He wanted to make her suffer. If only he could go back and turn the tables on her. She had manipulated the situation so perfectly that it left him no choice but to run. He daydreamed that someday, when he was a wealthy landowner, he would come back and buy her—and then he would make her pay!

He had reached the storehouses, food stalls, brothels, and warehouses that crowded the docks. It was not difficult to find the establishment of Decimus Secundus. He went boldly into the main entrance—he had to remember that his alibi was a slave on business for his master.

A number of people were at work in the large main room—mostly slaves, though he spotted a few freedpersons or freeborn. Most of the latter were giving directions and instructions. Much of the work appeared to be bookwork—scrolls, parchments, charts, and wax tablets were everywhere.

He made his way over to a counter behind which a freedperson stood reading a scroll. He was tall and wore a fine purple cloak with a silver broach clasp at the neck. Silver rings bedecked his fingers. A Greek by his looks, middle-aged with a weathered face and deep blue eyes. As Onesimus approached, he looked up.

"Good morning. I'm on business for my master, a certain Philemon of Colossae. To whom do I have the pleasure of speaking?"

"I am Titus Stephanos, the steward of Decimus Secundus. How may I help you?"

"I'm ordered to deliver a package to a client of my master in Moesia. Do you have a caravan that I could join?"

The man nodded. "We do not serve Moesia directly, but we have a wagon train leaving in three mornings for Byzantium in Thraia, a journey of about twenty days. We also have a ship sailing to Neopolis—tomorrow, I believe—which is quite a bit faster to Thraia. Let's see..." He turned behind him and called out, "Porcius, when does the *Astron* sail for Neapolis—tomorrow?"

A slave, standing at a table covered with parchments, turned toward the two. "No, *domine*, in two days. It is the *Hespera* that sails tomorrow, but bound for Cenchreae."

"Ah, yes. Still room on board the *Astron*?"

"Yes, *domine*."

The man turned back to Onesimus. "Of course, traveling with the caravan is cheaper. Pay the fee, contribute supplies in the equivalent, or a combination of the two." Merchant caravans were happy to have other travelers join them; there was safety in numbers. "The fare for a ship's berth varies depending on whether you can lend a skill during the voyage. Fare alone is three drachmas."

Onesimus nodded, thinking. He needed to leave as soon as he could. Waiting three days for the caravan seemed risky. Besides, he had money for the ship's fare, and it would get him to Moesia sooner.

"Where in Moesia are you bound?" Titus asked.

"I...well...I would rather not say." He cursed himself for being caught off-guard. He should have anticipated such a question from a travel and trade merchant!

The man raised his eyebrows. "No?" The last thing Onesimus needed was to raise suspicions as a slave. His mind raced.

"Well, it would probably be fine to tell you, but the message and the matter are personal between my master and a former partner. He told me to keep it to myself. He probably did not mean someone like you, but I follow my master's orders diligently." A bit wordy, but plausible.

"Ah, well, no matter. Do you want to book the ship's passage or join the caravan?"

"The ship, please."

"Very well, let me find out what skills we can use on that particular voyage. Come this way…" He motioned Onesimus towards a large desk.

Onesimus and Titus spent twenty minutes looking over documents for the voyage and discussing Onesimus' training and skills. Soon, they found that the ship's navigator needed a scribe to keep a logbook. They decided on a discount and Onesimus paid half the fare due, as was customary. Titus instructed him to be at the dock, at dawn, in two days. The Astron's quartermaster, a slave named Stachys, would be dockside to settle accounts and get him aboard.

Having taken care of this business, Onesimus headed back to the forum for a bite to eat. Walking back down the harbor road, he felt quite pleased with himself. Staying two days should not be a problem, though it nagged him a bit. As he passed through the forum, he saw the temple dedicated to Artemis. He paused. Making an offering might be wise.

He crossed over, mounted the marble steps, and entered a small sanctuary. He stood for a moment, allowing his eyes to adjust to the dark interior, lit only by candles. Upon the altar stood a human-sized bronze statue of Artemis.

Two other supplicants were nearby, kneeling and murmuring prayers. Onesimus approached, took a gold coin out of his bag, and laid it on the altar. He lit a taper using another candle, then joined the other two supplicants, also slaves.

He whispered, "Oh, Artemis, hear me now. Bless me and protect me on my journey as I set out. Bring harm to those who would harm your servant; give prosperity to those who would help me. In return, I offer this gold coin to you."

He arose and exited the temple, stopping at the top of the steps to allow his eyes to re-adjust to the bright sun and dazzling marble.

"Yes, next week! I will become thirty years of age, and on that same day, I will gain my freedom!" said a woman's voice. He glanced over to see a middle-aged female slave, sitting on the steps next to a male slave.

Another discussion of a slave being freed at thirty years of age? Was this some special time for freeing slaves in Ephesus?

"It is wonderful news," the male was saying, "though not unexpected. You have been a valuable and loyal servant to our master. And it is a custom."

Onesimus looked away so as not to be seen staring. He pursed his lips and sat down.

"Well," the female replied, "I knew it would happen, as you say. The domina has hinted of it the last year or so, as I told you. But I did not know she would choose my birth date as the manumission date!"

"So what will you do? I know you mentioned before that you would like to continue working for her as a freedperson…"

Onesimus stood and stepped down onto the street, then stopped. Here he was, in front of the temple Artemis, in a city of Artemis—a goddess *known* to listen to slaves—hearing almost the same discussion he had listened to this morning. The same topic Philemon mentioned last night. Was the goddess speaking to him? But why should Artemis, or any other deity, care about him? They certainly had not before!

It is said that there are no coincidences when it comes to the gods. And it was hard to ignore these repeated events in light of the past two days.

He turned around and cleared his throat. The two stopped talking and looked up.

"Excuse me, fellow slaves, but I could not help but overhear your words about some custom of manumitting slaves in the thirtieth year and granting citizenship? Did I hear correctly?"

The man spoke "Yes, brother. My friend here, Rhoda, is to be the recipient of that custom."

Onesimus nodded. "Is it a widespread custom? What is it all about?"

"Well, it is quite common in Italia," the man replied, "but perhaps less so here. Our domina is from Italia, but I have heard even some Ephesian families practice the custom." He cocked his head to the side. "Have you not heard of it, or the Lex Alia Sentia?"

"Uh, no, I have not. I am on a long journey for my master from…from the east."

The woman spoke up. "My domina says that many of the masters in the Provinces adopt it, and used to be done whenever the domine or domina wanted to reward a good and loyal slave. But years ago there were so many slaves being granted citizenship that Emperor Augustus passed a law that no slave could be granted citizenship until they had attained thirty years of age and the master must be at least twenty. I do not know if that law is binding on the Provinces, but my domina is following it."

Onesimus nodded, thanked them, and stumbled away down the stairs.

Philemon had grown up in Italia. His brother still lived there. He followed Roman laws and customs.

"Twelve more years and a ring..."

A ring of citizenship.

"...Lex Alia Sentia didn't go far enough..."

The law to limit manumission.

"...custom..."

The Italian custom of manumitting hardworking and loyal slaves.

Everything he wanted had been his all along. And he had thrown it away.

14. PATEFACTIO

His mind was reeling. Three times in one morning he is chastened: a stolen horse, an embarrassing encounter with a local in a latrine, and now it was revealed that his ignorance about slave laws had led him to make a terrible mistake. A life-altering mistake.

He sat, staring at the ground. Had he made a mistake? Was Artemis *not* leading him, but, in fact, punishing him? Or perhaps it was another god that, unknowingly, he had offended.

What now?

His head snapped up. Wait a minute. Everyone knows that when something happens three times, it is an omen. Three times today, he had been chastened. But also, a law he did not know had been mentioned in his presence three times the last twenty-four hours—more clearly defined each time. And the third time was the same occurrence as the third chastening! Three bad omens and three mentions of the law converged in the last occurrence of each! This *meant* something. He had to figure it out.

Had Philemon really planned on freeing him on his thirtieth year, following the custom of Italia and within the confines of the Roman law? Philemon *had* always praised Onesimus for his abilities, for his quick learning, and for his intelligence. The master had often said he had "high hopes" for him. Onesimus had always assumed that meant in service to Philemon. But what if he'd meant that he had high hopes that he would be a successful freedman and citizen, and that he would continue to work for Philemon as a freedperson, with even more opportunity to learn and grow and benefit them both?

Here, on the steps of the temple of Artemis—the goddess who listens to slaves—it had all been revealed to him, right after he made an offering and prayed for guidance.

It was a sign from the goddess.

But could he believe it? The gods were sometimes known to play tricks on humans.

No. Not this time. Here, on the steps of the temple of Artemis—the goddess who listens to slaves—it had all been revealed to him, right after he made an offering and prayed for guidance.

It was a sign from the goddess. But what should he *do?*

He sat down on a nearby curb and leaned against a stone wall. He wanted to go back and throw himself on the mercy of Philemon. To explain his error. But he knew Philemon would not listen. He had stolen money. He had stolen a horse (and lost it). He was a runaway slave. A runaway slave was considered dangerous in the Empire, especially since the uprising led by Spartokos over a century ago. Theft only compounded that crime.

It would be the word of the others against his. He would not be believed. No master, no matter how kind, could withhold punishment for such a betrayal. Manumission would now be out of the question. Masters had the right to put their slaves to death for such actions, though Philemon had never been a vindictive or brutal taskmaster. Still, Onesimus would likely face torture or maiming, and would surely be sold for mining or galley work, being found unfit for anything that requires integrity.

So why was Artemis showing him all this if it changed nothing? He could plead his case, but so what? He'd run away, and whether he understood the law or not made little difference. And Philemon would certainly not believe he'd turned over a new leaf—he'd think he only came back when he realized it was in his best interest.

If only he had someone who could plead his case. Someone who had gravitas with Philemon, who could argue that he was young, influenced by puppy love, been betrayed, and panicked. It was not uncommon—a slave who had a disagreement or complaint with his master could go to an advocate and ask that person to serve as an intercessor. In fact, for a slave to run away to seek an advocate was not viewed as an escape.

Ideally, the advocate should have a good relationship with the master so the master would take the plea seriously. It could not be another slave. But the only people in that position that Onesimus knew was Archippus and some shopkeepers—and they would not agree to do it.

He sat, thinking of all the people he had met in his work for Philemon. Was there really no one?

He stood bolt upright. A name came to his mind.

It would be bold. Daring. The man might not even agree to do it. Onesimus was not sure he'd ever met him, though he knew of him visiting the villa. But he would have tremendous influence over Philemon. And Onesimus knew precisely where to find him. He was the one who introduced Philemon to his new religion, and, by Philemon's own words, had "saved his life."

Paulus.

The problem was that Onesimus could see no reason why the man would agree to serve as an advocate for a slave he did not know—unless Onesimus could convince him that doing so would benefit his friend and patron Philemon. That might be a tall order, but it was his only chance to set things right.

He could argue that this was in Philemon's best interest, because Onesimus was a good slave that benefitted the household. He would explain his error; confess his wrongdoing, and express remorse. He would ask Paulus to intervene on his behalf for Philemon to take him back and give him a second chance.

Onesimus began to warm to the plan. Second chances seemed to be part of the religion Philemon followed. It was perfectly legal: since he was now seeking an advocate, he was no longer a runaway slave under Roman law; he was on a mission to be reconciled to his master. And even if he could not convince this Paulus, he would be far away from Colossae. Once in Rome, he could go anywhere.

He would go to find this Paulus who was imprisoned there, and convince him to act as his advocate to return him to Philemon for a second chance. And then, in twelve years, he would be a freed person *and* a Roman citizen. If not, well, he was no worse off than he was right now.

"Artemis, continue to guide me," he said aloud to his patron goddess, who, for the first time in his life, seemed to be listening to him.

*

Onesimus set off, weaving his way through the throngs of people until he arrived back at Decimus Secundus' place of business. Inside, he attracted the attention of Titus once again. Foregoing any greeting, Onesimus spoke.

"I have just received a message sent after me from my master that the——the package—that I am to deliver must now go to Rome. That is, the recipient is no longer in Moesia, but in Rome. Can I change passage?"

"Ah, well, I do not think we have a ship headed to Rome anytime soon."

Onesimus' heart sank. Secundus went to a nearby desk and began searching through piles of scrolls, parchments, and wax tablets. He pulled a parchment from the pile. "The *Noros* will leave for Rome from here on the Nones of Junius."

"That's two weeks! Are there other options? By land?"

"The land route is quite lengthy—far more so than waiting for the *Noros*. The caravan leaves in three days—up the Bosphorus, through Byzantium, Thraia, and Macedonia along the Via Ignatia, across the Adria and down to Brundisium. The entire journey takes forty-five days."

Exasperated, Onesimus threw up his hands. "Is there no faster option? Another merchant?"

Titus tapped his fingers on the desk, looking up into the rafters as he thought.

"Well, you could take the *Hespera*, which leaves tomorrow for Corinth. From there, ships constantly leave for all parts of Italia. I do not know if there would be a ship leaving for Rome when you want, but it is likely that there would be one within a day or two. That would make your entire trip only two or three weeks, perhaps."

"That's fine, let's do it!"

"Understand, boy, I cannot offer you any guarantee that you—"

"It's fine, I understand. My master will not hold you accountable."

Within twenty minutes, Onesimus had booked passage on the *Hespera*, which left in the morning for the Corinthian Isthmus in Greece, making land at the port city of Cenchreae. After receiving a chit that authorized him as a valid passenger, and instructing him to find the steward Stachys at the docks at dawn, Onesimus left. He walked back through the city in a bit of a daze. A whirlwind of trauma, decisions, travel, and changed plans in the space of thirty-six hours!

Back at the *taberna*, he inquired about the availability of lodging and was led to a small room on the second floor. He received a meager meal as part of the deal.

As he lay in the small bed that night, Onesimus found it difficult to sleep, despite the fact that he had hardly slept the night before. Was this the right thing to do? Would it work? What was happening back at the villa? What was Turia thinking right now? How would he go about finding Paulus in Rome? What would it be like to sail the ocean?

Finally, physically and mentally exhausted, he fell asleep.

*

The next morning Onesimus arose early and washed his face. After a quick breakfast of honey and bread, he found the proprietor and sold him Lampros at a low price. He hated doing it, but he had no other choice, and it did give him some extra money.

At the docks, he had no trouble finding the slave named Stachys—a tall, thin slave with a self-important air. Onesimus showed him the chit. After checking the manifest, Stachys pointed to a small boat docked nearby. "There."

"That's the *Hespera*?"

Stachys roared with laughter. "No, my land-dwelling friend! That dinghy will row you out to the *Hespera*!" He pointed toward the middle of the bay, where a large ship lay at anchor.

Onesimus shrugged off his embarrassment and made his way over to the boat. Crewmen were loading crates and barrels into the vessel. A man and his wife, freedpersons, were already sitting on one of the benches aboard, clutching at the gunwales and looking alarmed as the small boat rocked with the activity of the sailors.

"Is this the boat which goes to the *Hespera*?" Onesimus asked of one of the men. A jerk of the head was his only answer. Onesimus climbed aboard to share the bench with the couple. He felt entirely out of his element.

It was not long before the crewman finished the loading, climbed aboard, cast off, and began rowing in sync with practiced efficiency. The dock was left behind, and the *Hespera* drew closer—looking much larger than it had from shore. How could something so substantial float upon the water?

Drawing up alongside the starboard side, the passengers were directed to climb a wood and rope ladder to the deck. Once on the high deck, Onesimus was amazed at how solid it seemed, though it was in the middle of a harbor with water on all sides!

The passengers were directed to an aft section of the ship and down some stairs to a common room lined with bunks secured to the walls. He found an empty one, stowed what little he had, and went back up on deck. The mass of activity fascinated him, a sort of strange choreography as the slaves belowdecks rowed the ship toward the mouth of the harbor, crewmembers swarmed all over the triple masts unfurling the sails, and a man below barked orders using terminology that Onesimus had never heard. Still other crewmen on deck were working the lines that were attached to the sails and the masts, moving them to and fro and securing them to cleats and posts on the masts and the deck. It seemed far more complicated than Onesimus had assumed. It was like a dance of marionettes being directed by a shouting master. Eventually, however, the great sails were unfurled in the manner and placement required, and began to billow and stretch themselves taut in the wind.

Onesimus felt the ship catch the wind and lurch. Grasping a railing, he was both scared and exhilarated. Though it had been windy when rowing and setting the sails, after the wind caught the sails and the ship began to glide across the sea, it was as if the wind had stopped. He marveled at the smoothness of the ship's movement as it floated across the Aegean Sea. The sunlight sparkled off the waves, and a stream of churning foam made a long "v" shape behind them, marking their path out of the harbor.

Onesimus watched as the coastline—the land that had been his home for his entire life—become less distinct, until, finally, it disappeared beyond the horizon. He turned to look in the other direction, out to sea. Somewhere out there lay Greece, and beyond that, the great city of Rome itself.

And his destiny.

Epistole Delta

To Giarri

I pray that you have recovered from your illness. Your letters continue to encourage me, and I am thankful for you, as I have been all these decades.

As for your request for more of my memories of Corinth—I do not think I can capture the excitement I felt upon my first visit. I did not know then that it had been destroyed by the Romans two centuries earlier and then rebuilt only twenty years before I arrived, though perhaps the brightness of the marble should have been a clue. I just assumed that all large cities looked like that! Did you know the city was named after the currant fruit, abundant in the region? I had my fill while I was there!

I was thrilled to be in such a famous place, of course. I couldn't imagine that Rome would be any more beautiful or overwhelming—my naïvety showing again! You asked about the temples—I did not visit any of them, primarily because of what happened to me and who I met. But I saw them, and they were stunning— vast and opulent. I wanted badly to visit the temple of Aphrodite that sat 2,000 feet up on the summit of Acrocorinth—and especially the temple to Artemis in order to thank her—but, as I said, events kept me from it. In hindsight, it was no loss.

Ephesus was nothing compared to Corinth. Situated as it was between the narrow isthmus between the Gulf of Corinth and the Saronic Gulf, it held more people than Athens! It was a melting pot like I had never seen: people from everywhere—even barbarians!—and every form of art, science, architecture, philosophy, religion, crime, and every decadence a Roman, Greek, or Egyptian could devise. I assume you know the origin of the phrase, "to go out corinthianizing!"

It is interesting that there, in that huge, teeming, busy, happy, dirty, cosmopolitan city, my life would take another step toward its destiny—but not the one I thought. Of that encounter, of course, I have told you plenty in my other letters.

The cold has gotten worse, but the guard who is a member of the Way gave me another blanket. His rank is the lowest, but to me, he is a saint. You ask about my courage—well, it is faith alone that sustains me. Writing to you is a wonderful distraction.

Greet everyone there for me, and tell them they are always in my heart.

15. Adpulsus

Four days later, on the thirtieth of Maius, Onesimus stood at the port railing of the *Hespera*, contemplating all that he had heard and learned about Corinth. As the ship sailed into the small port town of Cenchrea, he wondered how this peaceful little bay was the eastern gateway to such notoriety.

As they drew close to the docks, he saw many ships of various sizes anchored in the bay and a beehive of activity ashore. Soon he could see the small boats ferrying people and supplies between ships and shore, just as they had in Ephesus.

Corinth would be the largest city he had ever been in, supposedly around 200,000 people! He had heard that the slave population was even larger, maybe twice as large as the freedpeople population—which should make it easy for him to remain inconspicuous.

The ship's crew began their elaborate dance once again, and soon they had dropped anchor and lowered the sails. Once all was secured, the crew began hauling up the goods from the hold and the passengers were directed to the ships' boats which would ferry them to the docks. Onesimus climbed aboard when it was his turn, and clutched the gunwale tightly as waves from other boats crossing the harbor sent his small boat rocking back and forth. It was so much busier than Ephesus. He tried to keep his mind on the sunny day and the refreshing spray of water. The Grecian land ahead looked beautiful with its mottled green, yellow, and tan rolling hills. In spite of all the activity in the bay, the port of Cenchrea looked like a small, sleepy town that could be any Roman town.

They drew up alongside a pier and, once moored, Onesimus clambered out awkwardly. He marveled at how his short time at sea made the terra firma seem like it was swaying. He smiled a bit at himself: Onesimus, the seafaring traveler, having to adjust from his sea legs!

Following signs, he headed up the Cenchrean Road toward Corinth, and it was not long until the huge city walls came into view. A freedman aboard the ship had told him that it was six miles long and enclosed the entire city! As he approached the main gates, they were even more stunning than the wall: massive, made of bronze, gleaming so brightly in the sun it hurt his eyes to look directly at them. Onesimus avoided the temptation to stand and stare. He followed the crowd along the main road into the center of the city and soon arrived at the agora. There's he could not help but stop. He had stood in awe at the architectural feats of Ephesus, but Corinth outshone it by a factor of ten. Rich marble, gold trimmings, and the sheer number of people made his mind reel.

A colossal temple rose up from behind a row of shops on the opposite side of the forum. He wondered to which god or goddess it belonged. Towering columns—he could count twenty-eight from where he was standing, each five times as tall as a man—upheld an ornate pediment that defined the slope of the gold-plated roof. The giant steps leading up to the sanctuary were like nothing he had ever seen or imagined. He would have to visit there and make an offering. The large grass rectangle in the middle was large enough to fit six or seven Colossian agoras—with all of its shops! There was a marble speaker's rostrum that looked like the dais of a throne. At the west end sat another massive platform with yet another temple, behind another long row of shops. Onesimus could see the name of the Emperor chiseled onto the pediment. The practice of dedicating temples to the imperials was becoming more and more common. Onesimus did not know much about politics, though he heard the scuttlebutt. It made sense to him that a great emperor—such as Gaius Julius—would become a minor deity upon his death. Maybe even Octavian. But the more recent practice of an emperor taking on divine honors while still alive did not seem proper. And rumor had it that some Roman governors built temples to actually offer *sacrifices* to the living emperor. Sheer sycophancy to Onesimus' way of thinking.

To his right was a third row of shops which stretched the length of the forum, ending with a small building which appeared to be a basilica—one of the many set up all over the Empire following the murder of Gaius Julius. On the opposite corner, a large and ornate public fountain was spouting water impossibly high in the air—a testament to Roman engineers' use of gravity. Just beyond the fountain was a set of marble-paved steps; another major road coming into the forum.

He decided to walk the perimeter of the forum and find something to eat. He the must find out where to book passage to Rome and a place to sleep, unless Artemis granted him a ship leaving today.

Onesimus was feeling pretty good. Here he was, in one of the largest cities in all the Roman Empire, with money, freedom, and plans. He had just sailed across the Aegean Sea and was preparing to sail to Rome. He would make a good freedman, he told himself.

*

Feeling confident, he stepped out into the busy agora and walked along the row of shops. He was amazed at the variety of pottery, leather, cutlery, produce, meats, clothing, money exchange, bankers, stone artisans—he even saw two of the same kind! How large must the population be to support *two* butchers in the same agora?!

In the middle of the long line of shops, a large crowd had gathered in the walkway. Standing among them were some Roman soldiers and other officials—important Corinthians as shown by their togas. As he made his way around the edge of the crowd, he saw a Roman official sitting on a raised platform, attended on either side by two slaves who were writing furiously. Below the platform stood a man, chained to a short pillar. It was the bema—far larger and more ostentatious than any he had ever seen. He wondered what crime the man was accused of, but he did not care enough to join the crowd. It would be over quickly—a fine, a punishment, or prison to await further hearings. The Romans knew how to administer justice, Onesimus thought. Roman punishment was usually swift and came in the form of fines, whippings, exile, or execution. Prison was not punishment, like in some cultures—why should the State pay for it? No, prison was a place to wait briefly for your trial or decision. Quick judgments and sound penalties were just one kind of order that Rome had brought to the world.

He spotted a small shop with an open counter and a sign above listing various foods and drinks. The counter had a six or seven amphorai sunk into the countertops around the three walls of the shop, full of white and green olives, roasted chestnuts, dates, bread, apples, and almonds. A back door led out to a small patio where he could see smoke coming from a small grill. He smelled the pungent aroma of roasted meat. A placard next to a large covered pot announced that it contained hot barley, cabbage, and lentil soup. Pure wine, honeyed wine, and goat milk were also available. Onesimus' mouth began watering. He joined the short line and ordered a bowl of soup and some watered wine. As he stood nearby eating the hot meal, he wondered whether Corinthian fare was particularly good, or only in comparison to the sea rations he had been eating.

A full belly added to the confidence he now had about himself. After returning the bowl and cup to the proprietor, he decided it was appropriate to reward himself for a safe journey and a good plan. Heading out of the forum down the northbound road (which was called the Lechaion Road). It was not long before he spotted the phallic symbol beside an outline of a foot, with an arrow, on the paving stones: the universal symbol for a brothel. Similar symbols, every hundred feet or so, led him past another basilica, alongside an Athena temple, and past the second, smaller agora. He found himself in another large plaza, looking new with its unworn paving and sharply defined curbs and appurtenances. A public fountain stood at the center. The square served as a primary entranceway to an enormous amphitheater, also looking remarkably new—or at least recently renovated. Looking through the multiple entranceways to the theater, he guessed it held at least 15,000 people! After gawking a bit, he resumed his search for the brothel symbols. He found an inscription for the square itself—some rich man had financed the building of it upon his appointment to the office of city treasurer.

The symbols led him out of the square to the northwest, and, not far beyond, the symbol pointed to a rather plain three-story building, its back against the city way. The only decoration was a large, fancified wooden phallus hanging over the door. Onesimus stepped inside. The room stood in contrast to the simple exterior, boasting ostentatious decorations, plush chairs, deep couches, wall hangings, plants, rugs, and marble statues.

A richly dressed man appeared from behind a doorway covered by silk curtains. He was large—the business clearly provided him with ample food. He reminded Onesimus of the stock figure found in many popular Greek plays: the obese and jolly bumbler. Onesimus smiled inwardly.

"Good day, good day, my dear slave. Are you here to procure for your master, or for your own pleasure?" He seemed friendly, and the fact that Onesimus was a slave seemed to matter little.

"For myself, domine."

"Ah, fine, fine, my boy." His forehead was perspiring in the warm Corinthian day; he dabbed at his brow with a cloth. "Prices are on the wall," he said as he waved towards a board listing various services and options. "You are welcome to all except the top category: those are for patrons, who, ah…order out." He laughed at his little joke.

Onesimus decided on a standard thirty-minute session from the lower tier—and the proprietor disappeared behind the curtain and returned shortly with three females in tow. They lined up dutifully for Onesimus' examination. As soon as they saw he was a slave, their faces fell. It was the dream of every prostitute to find a patron—the richer, the better—who might take a special liking to them and purchase them, where they could live a life of relative ease in a domus or even a villa outside of town. Or perhaps some noble would fall in love with them and, despite the shame, free the woman and marry her. It rarely happened—but the fact that it did happen sometimes kept the dream alive.

The proprietor stuck his head back inside the curtain and yelled "Megallis! Get out here!" He stepped back to the front, sweating all the more for the exertion and muttering to himself.

"Sorry, my boy, here are three choices for you. Another is on her way—a beauty, but slow." He smiled sardonically and continued. "Here are Livia, Chloe, and—" at that moment he was interrupted by voices and movement behind him. The curtains parted, and the third girl shuffled into the room and took her place beside the others.

Turia! Onesimus caught his breath and stumbled back. His mind reeled as he tried to make sense of her presence here in Corinth.

16. Synagogos

Of course, it was not Turia. But she had the same dark hair, the same cut, the same round white eyes, even the same facial shape and complexion. He could not stop staring at her in a panic. The emotions welling up in Onesimus were almost overwhelming.

"Boy? Boy? Are you okay?"

"I...uh, I...yes..." His whole body had heated up, and his hands were sweating. "I...I need some air—I'm not feeling well." He turned and fled through the door.

As he hurried down the street, his composure returned. He was stunned at his own reaction at Turia's doppelgänger. He had not thought of Turia that day at all, though there were days when he thought of her many times—usually with great anger and a renewed vow for revenge.

He was loath to admit he missed her—and angry at himself for it. He struggled for some way to make sense of her actions. To find *some* reason that would show she did not mean to betray him. Perhaps someone had coerced her! Or Philemon had threatened her with severe punishment if she didn't turn on him! Maybe Giton had blackmailed her!

At times he almost convinced himself, only to realize that he was grasping at straws. She had either been using him all along to get her freedom, or her love was so shallow that she would betray him to save herself. They'd been lovers for two years, and he had thought their love was deep. Onesimus prided himself on being smart, observant, and careful. How had he been so blind?

All of his confidence was gone. The event at the brothel made him think that he was no man on a hero's journey, he was an easily manipulated castrata led around by a pair of beautiful eyes to his own destruction.

Were the situation reversed, he would have protected her in any way necessary. He would have confessed to the crime and told them that it was all him, and taken the punishment alone to save her. He loved her. Or rather, used to love her.

No more. He knew her for what she was now. A selfish, betraying lupatria! If he could only talk to her, he'd tell her—

"Hey! Are you deaf? I said, 'What do you want?'" Onesimus looked up and saw he was standing before the door of a small building. A slave was standing beside the door, staring at him. "What is your business here?"

Onesimus glanced around. He had been paying no attention to where he had been walking. He looked back at the plain building in front of him. The only markings were carved in the lintel of the door: "Synagogue of the Jews." This was a place where Jews met for their strange worship. There was one in Colossae. They were not temples—they had no altar, not sacrifices, and no statues of their god. Yet they called it a "place of worship." Strange, but foreign religions could be bizarre.

Onesimus realized he needed to speak. "Uh, yes, sorry, I guess I'm lost."

At that moment, another man appeared at the door, a man wearing the toga of a citizen. A fringe of gray hair ringed his head; he was small and slightly bent with age. Onesimus saw the fringed shawl about his shoulders, the same style that he had seen Colossian Jews wearing.

"Who is it, Elunas?"

"I am not sure, sir. He seems confused."

The old man turned to Onesimus. "May I help you?"

"Yes, perhaps, domine. I am on my way to Rome—an errand for my master—to see Paulus of Tarsus. I believe he is an important Jew. Do you know of him?"

The man stiffened. "*Paulus?*" he said. "Is this a joke? You seek my neighbor, next door." He sneered at Onesimus in an unsettling manner.

"Oh, yes—my pardon. Next door?" He looked to the domus to the right of where he stood.

The man gave a dismissive wave and turned to his slave. "Come, Elunas." Then he stopped and spoke again. "Paulus of Tarsus may be a Jew by blood, slave, but he is no Jew in heart, soul, or mind, no matter what Gaius Titius Justus might think!" The door slammed.

Onesimus frowned at the closed door. What was he so mad at? Who was Gaius Titius Justus? And surely a Jew was a Jew? Onesimus didn't know much about these people—the synagogue in Colossae was small and outside the city walls. But he knew they were a strange people, and this encounter only emphasized the notion.

Still, what a stroke of divine luck! Artemis was still leading him, because next door was someone who knew Paulus. Onesimus should be able to gain more information to help him with his plan, and clarify whether Paulus could help him, or if he should just head on farther north.

He walked over to the adjacent building. It was a large, fine-looking domus. The façade was an expertly stuccoed wall, rising two levels and extending for some way on either side. The entrance was a massive, wooden, iron-reinforced two-piece door, ornately carved. This was the home of a wealthy Corinthian. The guidance of Artemis was looking better and better. If he could get this noble on his side, that would give him some leverage with Paulus, perhaps, as well as speeding him on his way.

He stepped up to the door and tapped it with his foot. The door creaked open. Standing before him was a large, imposing slave, dressed in a simple tunic with no sleeves—perhaps to display his massive muscles to any visitors who might not have the best of intentions. Onesimus wondered if the man had been a gladiator—those who survived the arena were often sold as bodyguards or door slaves.

"Good day," Onesimus said. "Is your master at home?"

"What is your business?" growled the slave, in an accent that Onesimus did not recognize.

"My master, who lives in the Asian Province near Colossae, has sent me to Rome to see Paulus. I am a lost, and I have reason to believe your master might have some information about Paulus, and would be willing to help me on behalf of my master."

"Wait here." The door closed, and Onesimus heard the bolt slide shut. He was left standing in the warm afternoon. "Justus" was a Greek name, which meant he was probably native to Corinth. Onesimus had hoped he might be a transplanted Roman noble.

The door opened, and the door guard spoke. "Follow me."

They passed through the vestibulum. It was far more ornate than the one at Philemon's villa. It was a sure sign of wealth for someone to spend so much money on a mere entryway. They passed through a short faucus and into a medium-sized atrium. A fountain was spilling water into the impluvium, which was constructed of marble and tile and surrounded by statues and potted plants. The walls were painted with frescoes of seascapes and ocean gods and goddesses. The slave led him through and into a connecting tablinum. Inside, a man reclined on a couch, reading a scroll and a holding a cup. A slight breeze was blowing through the room, probably from the peristyle, which must have been beyond the far archway covered with expensive curtains.

The slave bowed to the man. "The visitor, domine. A slave from Asia Minor." The man looked up from his scroll. In concert with his surroundings, he was richly dressed, wearing the toga, rings, and necklaces of a wealthy landowner or shop-owner. Onesimus guessed that he was middle-aged, noting his wild crop of brown-gray hair, thick around his pate. A pair of deep-set dark eyes, within a friendly but strong countenance, greeted Onesimus. The man stood and smiled. "So, you are on your way to see Paulus?! And you are from Colossae! Your name?"

"I am Onesimus, domine. You do not know my master, who is named Hermas Filius. I am on my way to see Paulus." He had decided it was best not to mention Philemon, instead using the name of a small shop owner in Colossae.

"Hermas Filius?" Justus frowned. "I do not know that name. I thought perhaps you had come from my brother Philemon of Colossae."

17. Justus

"Br…Brother?" stammered Onesimus.

Justus laughed. "Well, I have never met him. And 'brother' is merely an affectation of those of us of the Way. But I *do* know Paulus, and he has talked to me about the ekklesia that meets in Colossae. So naturally, I thought…"

Onesimus was no longer listening. This man was a follower of the Way? Onesimus frantically tried to make sense of what he was hearing. He remembered that the people of the Way called each other "brother" and "sister," even though they were not related by blood or ethnicity.

He tried to quiet his pounding heart. Maybe this was good. If Justus was a follower of the Way, it could work to his advantage. He calmed his beating heart. He had to trust Artemis.

"I know Paulus quite well," the man was saying, apparently reading Onesimus' reaction as confusion rather than panic. "He spent over a year living here, and has been back numerous times since. Last I heard, he was headed to Rome."

"Yes, domine. He is there. In prison."

Justus sighed. "Ah. That is no surprise, unfortunately. I warned him." He sighed again. "And your mission?"

"My master has a message for me to deliver, and, and… some money for him."

"Good, ah, yes, good. I am sure Paul will appreciate that. He lives simply, but often needs money from those of us who support him." He stopped. "So, your master sent you to help Paulus—what was his name?"

"Hermas Filius. domine."

"And he and his household are members of the Way, too?"

Onesimus affected a bashful look and lowered his eyes. "Yes, my master is a follower. But I have only recently attended my first ekklesia."

The man nodded. "Well, well, no shame in that. We all began somewhere on the journey." He laughed. "Who knows what God shall make of you? Look at me, after all!" He spread his arms wide. "I did not come from a family of nobility."

They sat in silence for a moment. Justus spoke again. "How does your master know me? Why did he send you to me?"

"Well, domine, perhaps he knows you through Philemon. Or perhaps from Paulus himself. He merely asked me to check in with you on my way to Rome if possible, to give you greetings and well wishes from his ekklesia. I do not know more than that."

He sat lost in some thought for a moment, then continued. "Where does the ekklesia of your master meet?"

Onesimus worried that he was making this story too complicated. He briefly considered telling him the truth —he was a slave of Philemon, in need of an advocate. But he didn't know this man and didn't know if he could trust him. Besides, he couldn't change his story now. His thoughts raced. "My master's villa is actually not in Colossae, but at a nearby a small town known as Hierapolis." Onesimus hoped he had never heard of Hierapolis.

"I do not know the place." He made a *harumph* sound. "While I prefer to know my visitors before they come calling, any follower of the Way is welcome here—or his slave. My questioning of you is not without purpose. Many here know my name—Gaius Titius Justus—and some are none too happy to hear that name in this city!" He smiled, as if it were a joke, but it was clear there was some pain associated with his words. "Come, let us sit."

He motioned for Onesimus to sit on some cushions near the couch. "So, you bring me greetings and well-wishes from my brothers and sisters in Asia Minor and news of Paulus. What would you have from me?"

Onesimus breathed an inward sigh of relief. "Nothing more, domine." He thought it was best to play this carefully, and see where it might lead. "I am also a bit unsure has to how to make arrangements for passage to Rome and find a place to stay. This is my first trip to Corinth or Rome."

Justus nodded. "Well, boy, I extend my hospitality to you as a token of graciousness to your master—I suspect he hoped I would do just that! And I am happy to do so for a brother. I imagine your sea journey was none too pleasant—they usually aren't." He turned and shouted through an open archway, "Plotia!" He turned back to Onesimus. "There are extra rooms in my slave's quarters. You are welcome to stay. I dare say it will be much better than anything you will find in town—and safer."

At that moment a young woman entered. She appeared to be an Egyptian slave. Onesimus had heard they were popular in Greece and Italia. She was reasonably tall, full-figured, with dark hair, dark complexion, and large white eyes. Exotic-looking.

"Yes, domine?" She had a slight accent that Onesimus found both peculiar and intriguing.

"Plotia, show our guest…" he glanced at Onesimus, "…to the slave quarters and get him settled. Show him where he can wash up, and bring some food back here. He will join me after."

"Yes, domine. She bowed and turned her exotic eyes on Onesimus. "If you please."

Onesimus stood and followed her through the arch, wondering at the hospitality of this Gaius Titius Justus towards a slave. He even called him a "guest," though he had hesitated a bit at the words. Yet he didn't even *know* the master that Onesimus had invented. These followers of the Way appeared to share a bond much like the followers of Mithras or the Epicureans.

Plotia led him through a large and beautiful *peristyle* garden, through another decorous archway and into a hallway with many rooms off to the sides. The lack of decoration and detail betrayed the fact that this was the slave quarters.

The girl took him to the last room on the right and pulled aside a curtain. It was a small cell with a table, chair, and bed—with serviceable cushions and blankets. It was better than what he had at Philemon's villa. He set his bag on the small table.

"There is a wash basin in the back," Plotia said, waving towards the end of the hall, "and the privy is beyond that. You can find your way back to the tablinum?"

Onesimus nodded. "Yes, thank you." She was gone with a swish of the curtain, leaving only a bit of mystery and a faint scent of sandalwood.

Onesimus sat on the bed, took an extra tunic from the bag, then found the privy. He cleaned himself using the bucket sitting beside a large reservoir that was full of fresh and cool water. He thought through his story with care, trying to anticipate what questions Justus might ask of him. One element in his favor was that a slave could plead ignorance of matters and issues relating to his master—he was only a messenger, after all.

He returned to the room and donned his tunic. Back in the tablinum, a platter of bread, green olives stuffed with almonds, and figs sat on a small table before Justus, along with two cups—one of which was in the master's hand.

Justus indicated a chair across from him. "Sit, boy, and eat. I wish to hear of your home, your master, and the ekklesia."

He was ready for that question. Onesimus sat, picked up the cup and took a sip of the full, flavorful wine. Justus did not seem to know much about Asia Minor, other than what Paulus had told him. So he described Philemon's place as if it were the villa and ekklesia of "Filius."

Justus continued. "You say you only attended the ekklesia once. How large is it? I have heard that some of the ekklesia is Asia Minor are quite large."

"Well, domine, that may be. I never visited any. The one in Heiropolis has about fifteen in attendance. Mostly free or freedpersons attend, but some slaves as well."

"Well, it is good to here the existence of ekklesiai, regardless of size. I have only heard of the one—rather large—at Ephesus and the one in Colossae. I have traveled extensively, but never to Asia Minor, surprisingly." He took a bite of bread and chewed for a moment. "So, Onesimus, what did you say your master's name was?"

"Hermas Filius, domine," Onesimus said, wondering why he asked again. "He has a small villa on the outskirts of town."

"It must not be too small; considering he owns an educated slave such as you that he can spare to send off to Rome." Justus raised his eyebrows.

Was he suspicious? "I am not that educated," he lied. "I am being trained to replace his vilici someday."

Justus slowly nodded as he examined an olive he had picked up. "Seeing as your master and I have a common friend in Paulus, can you tell me the nature of your errand with Paulus? As a fellow supporter, I am concerned."

Onesimus was prepared for this question, too. "I don't have details. I have a sealed letter; its contents are unknown to me. All I know is that he is in prison in Rome, and I am to deliver the letter and the money."

Justus sat up. "Do you know how long he has been imprisoned? Or the charges?" His brow was creased with concern. This Paulus was quite important to many in the Way. All the better for Onesimus if he could get him to act as his advocate.

"I cannot say, domine. My master did not share anything further."

"Hm, yes." Justus sat for a few moments, lost in thought. "I shall send a message to Prisca. Perhaps she knows something more," he said, apparently speaking to himself. Onesimus sat quietly, drinking the wine.

Finally, Justus stood up and smiled. "Well, my boy, if your master sent you to support Paulus, we'd better make sure you get there! I will send one of my slaves up the Lechaion to book passage for you. It will be faster if you sail all the way to Ostia. You have the funds?"

Onesimus hesitated. He had no idea where any of those places were located. "Yes. My master directed me to sail to Corinth, and then take a ship to Rome. I have about 150 sesterces."

"Well, then, passage to Ostia it is! Or, if there is not a ship there the next couple of days, we could book you into Puteoli." He turned to the archway. "Plotia!"

She appeared within moments. "Tell Marius I need him immediately. He should be in the library." He turned back to Onesimus. "Never been to Rome, eh? You are in for an experience."

"Thank you, domine. An enjoyable one?"

Justus laughed. "Well, perhaps. But that is not the adjective that first comes to mind. Astounding. Overwhelming. Disgusting. After it is over, and you have had time to digest it all…yes, you might see it as having been enjoyable." He laughed again.

Onesimus was not sure what to say.

"Rome can be a dangerous place, and it can be overwhelming. Stay out of the worst parts of the city, and do not go out after dark. And be prepared: Rome will change you."

With that dire warning, Justus dismissed him.

18. MARIUS

Onesimus slept well, woke at dawn and refreshed himself, then made his way through the domus—keeping to the public rooms, as was proper. He found Plotia in the atrium, scrubbing the tile floor.

"Hello, Plotia."

She looked up. "Good day. My master told me to send you to the library when you awoke." She stood and brushed a strand of hair back from her face. "Go through the tablinum and take the hall on the right. The library is near the end."

Onesimus would have preferred to spend more time talking to her, but she immediately knelt back down and began cleaning. He thanked her awkwardly and followed the directions. After the tablinum, he thought he was lost. The passageway appeared to be part of the private quarters. Ahead was an archway covered by finely woven curtains, which were partially open. As he drew near, he saw through into a room of cubbyholes filled with scrolls. He peered through and spotted a young slave, sitting at a desk surrounded by piles of scrolls, writing on a parchment. He was about Onesimus' age, but with a larger build and blond, thick hair. As he stepped through the curtains, the slave looked up, revealing a light coloring to his complexion.

"You must be Onesimus," he said, with fine Greek diction. "I am Marius, the vilici. How was your sleep?"

"Quite good, thank you. Your master's hospitality towards the slave of a master he has never met is unusual."

Marius chuckled. "Many in Corinth would have a harsher assessment, but yes, to those who he deems deserving, he is a kind and generous man. His status keeps his critics from doing more than murmuring behind his back. Speaking of which—" Marius picked up a scrap of parchment and read from it "—he had me check on accommodations for you. There is a ship to Puteoli that leaves tomorrow morning. There is a second ship that sails directly to Ostia, but it does not leave for five days. My master said you were in a hurry to help Paulus, so I booked passage on the one to Puteoli." He looked up. "Is that acceptable?"

"Yes, yes," Onesimus said, "more than acceptable. I am thankful for your master's help. Puteoli—where is that? Will it be difficult for me to find passage to Rome from there?"

"Not at all. There are many small ships that sail between there and Ostia, or even to the Roman docks themselves, depending on how much you can spend. In fact, Puteoli is the busiest port in all of Italia—maybe in all of the Empire. A little-known fact." Marius seemed pleased to share his knowledge. "Have you never been to Rome?"

"No." Onesimus felt at ease with this self-assured slave. "In fact, the more I learn about the Caput Mundi, the more anxious I become."

Marius laughed. "That is understandable. I have been to Rome six times—always traveling with my master. The first time I felt like a child at lost at the Isthmian Games. It is a monstrously large city."

"I think Corinth is overwhelming, and I always considered Ephesus to be a large city."

"I have never been to Ephesus. But Corinth *is* a large city—one of the largest and busiest in the Empire. Yet it is like a tiny hamlet compared to Rome! Hills covered with massive buildings and monuments! Temples! The Forum itself is as large as most towns in the Empire! And the winding streets—there seem to be thousands of them. The domii, shops, and the tenement buildings, one after the other, row and after row, stretching upon either side of the narrow streets. Old, rickety buildings about to fall down, standing in contrast with fancy, expensive domii of the rich with the marble- and gold-covered edifices. Overwhelming!" His eyes were shining as he became lost in memories.

His smile faded. "But it has a seamy side. There are no Roman soldiers or police: they are not allowed in the city. The foot traffic is constantly crawling through at the streets, like ants on a dead beast. Murders and robberies take place in daylight. Every sort of illegality and immorality you can imagine is occurring at all times day and night." He shook his head. "Still, one should never pass up an opportunity to visit the center of the world."

Onesimus smiled Marius. He smiled back a bit self-consciously. "You can see it had quite an effect on me—as it does on everyone who visits there. You are never the same afterwards."

Onesimus wondered what Rome would have in store for him. Would meeting Paulus turn out to be a dead end? Would he go on to a new life in the north, free but as a fugitive? Or would Paulus be the catalyst for a restored life with Philemon, which could eventually lead him to legitimate freedom?

"In the meantime," Marius continued, "you may simply relax here for the day, or, if you are interested, you can accompany me on my errands and take in a bit of Corinth."

"I'd be pleased to see some of the city, if you don't mind."

"Not at all. Let me gather up a few things, and we'll be off." He turned to a credenza behind the desk and began sorting through some parchments.

Onesimus smiled to himself. Rome is where everything started and ended. How fitting that his fate would be decided there. *May Artemis and Fortuna smile on me*, he whispered.

19. Hodos

Onesimus and Marius visited some shopkeepers. Both agoras were busy, and Onesimus could hardly keep from staring at the number of people who, by their dress and looks, were from far away lands. Later, they left the center of the city and visited a few homes—mostly of nobles, but a few that belonged to those from the professional class. Much of the home visits had to do with the ekklesia that met in Justus' domus.

At dusk, Marius and Onesimus returned to the domus, washed up, and sat together on some benches in the slaves' area. Onesimus had been hoping to see Plotia again, but was disappointed. They had been resting only a few moments when a gong sounded in another part of the domus.

"Ah," Marius said, "the household dinner is ready. Come, let's eat." Standing, he took Onesimus' arm and led him through the doorway.

"The household dinner? Do slaves eat with the master?"

"Oh, yes. He is quite kind to his slaves. It was not always so. I have been with him for almost fifteen years, and he used to be quite harsh and critical of masters who showed any kindness to slaves. But that changed when he became a follower of the Way."

"Really? Why is that?"

Marius looked at him. "I thought your master was a follower of the Way? Is it not the same with him?"

"Well, yes, there was a change. But we do not eat together. And I…I am not a follower of the Way."

"Ah. I did not know."

"And still," Onesimus said, feeling a bit awkward, "my master is new to this religion. I only recently heard it called 'the Way.'"

"The earliest adherents called themselves 'the Way,' I am told, in the Palestine province. Some call us *christianous*, and—" he leaned into to Onesimus, "I don't think they mean it as a compliment. A bit derogatory, don't you think?"

"And you are an adherent?"

"Indeed. For a few years now." They had arrived at a medium-sized triclinium. "Here we are. We do all eat together, though the kitchen maids still serve. When they are finished bringing the food, they join us." Marius indicated a spot for Onesimus, next to an older female slave. "Justus' wife and daughter usually join us, but they are visiting her family at Megara."

Onesimus settled down on the cushions and bowed to the female. Marius sat on his other side. Plotia and another, younger girl, entered carrying food in pots and on trays. Wine pitchers were set in the center of the table. When they finished, they took places at the table just as the master entered and took his place at the head of the table. He looked around.

"Welcome, all. Tonight we welcome a guest from an ekklesia in Asia Minor. Meet Onesimus." He indicated Onesimus, and the others nodded at him. "Where is Cario?"

One of the serving girls spoke up. "He said he would be along shortly. He is finishing the desserts."

"Very well," Justus said. "Let us begin." He looked up, raising his arms before him with palms upturned in the universal gesture of prayer. "God the father, bless this food which you brought forth from the earth. Bless this wine which you brought forth from the vine. We bless your name, King of the Universe."

It was a pretty standard prayer, Onesimus thought. It could have been to any god or goddess, except the epithet "King of the Universe" and the use of "father" sounded like a title for Zeus.

The meal was lavish compared with Philemon's fare, though not significantly so. But Onesimus had never eaten at Philemon's table (though Turia had brought him some leftovers once or twice.). The promulsis consisted of carrots with tuna and egg, followed by a prima mensa of roast chicken basted with pepper, coriander, dates, nuts, vinegar, and a garum-based cabbage and leek soup. Onesimus thought it was excellent. Cario, the cook, joined them during that primary course, then left with one of the girls to bring dessert: poached pears with roasted chestnuts. Onesimus felt like he was in a palace of the gods. A typical dinner for the slaves at the villa in Colossae was almost always porridge soup, an everyday meat dish (with garum) or a fish soup, and bread. The drink was posca, the same wine and vinegar mixture that the poor drank. This, by contrast, was a fantastic feast, and the wine was rich and full.

As they were all finishing the secula mensa , Justus called out to him. "Onesimus, I am curious. Since I do not know your master, how did you find my domus? Which shopkeeper in the agora told you of my residence?"

"No shopkeeper, domine, but the Jewish man next door."

Justus seemed surprised, and all the others looked back and forth between Onesimus and their master. "You spoke with *Quintus*?"

"He never gave me his name."

"And was he his usual cordial self?" The sarcasm was obvious.

"He *did* seem put out. I told him I was on my way to see Paulus in Rome and needed directions. He told me you were next door, that Paulus was no Jew, and then slammed the door in my face."

Justus laughed. "You got off easy!"

Onesimus was still confused. "I thought Paulus was a Jew."

"He most certainly is. You have never met him?"

"No, domine, though my master came to believe in the…the Way through him. I saw him while he was at my master's compound." With a start, Onesimus realized that he was speaking of Philemon's conversion and Paulus visit there. *It's okay*, he thought. Justus did not know anyone in Asia Minor, and Paulus could have converted many people in Asia Minor, for all he knew.

Justus smiled. "Well, you will enjoy the meeting. Paulus has a powerful presence, a brilliant mind, and is a passionate orator. He also loves his people like his own children." Justus leaned forward. "And, like a good Roman father, he can discipline them with withering words. He is quite the rhetorician." He picked up his wine cup, taking a long draught. "But Jewish he is. In fact, his name is 'Shu'el' in the Jewish language. My neighbor's problem with Paulus—and me—is that we proclaim that Iesous—another Jew, by the way—is the one foretold by Jewish prophecy. Quintus thinks such ideas are blasphemy."

Onesimus had no idea that the "Way" was part of the Jewish religion. But there were Greeks and Romans who practiced it! He almost shook his head at the ridiculousness of it, but remembered he was in the presence of people who took it seriously.

"Why would Quintus think his own people's prophecies were blasphemy?"

"Well, it is complicated. The Jews have a long a varied history. As for Paulus, he was here, in Corinth, teaching in the synagogue that Quintus now leads. Back then, the leader was Crispus, and he stood and debated Paulus and his friends, Silas and Timotheos. The Jews love to debate their laws and religion! Crispus was convinced and became a follower of the Way, but many of the other Jewish leaders became irate—Quintus was one of them.

"So how did you, domine, become a follower of the Way?"

"I was a member of that synagogue next door."

"But you aren't Jewish!" Onesimus blurted out.

Justus laughed. "True. Not many know it, but Jews welcome non-Jews into their faith. Of course, we can never fully be a part of the community, but we are taught their writings, go through a ceremony, and we keep the laws and commandments just as those who are born Jewish. They call us 'god-fearers.' I was there when Paulus came. I also was convinced, and offered my home as the meeting place for all Jews and Gentiles of the Way."

"So you know Paulus well?"

"Oh, yes. He stayed with us over a year, working and teaching anyone who would listen."

"So Quintus was so upset because Paulus took adherents away?"

"That…and more. He and the others had Paulus brought before the bema in the forum! A ridiculous move, as they had broken no Roman laws. Which is exactly what the proconsul ruled. Then he told Quintus and the others to get out of his sight and quit wasting his time." Justus chuckled. "So, you can see why he is not happy. It does not help matters that my domus is right next to his synagogue."

Onesimus wondered how he could use Justus' closeness to Paulus to his advantage. But since Justus did not know the true reason for his voyage, he could not see a way. Still, he could use Justus' name with Paulus.

Justus drained his wine cup. "Excellent as usual, Cario." He got up from his reclining position. "Onesimus, join me out in the peristyle in ten or fifteen minutes. Plotia, bring us wine."

The household slaves talked amongst themselves, making some polite attempts to include Onesimus. Though the interaction between the slaves and the master was quite free in contrast to most households, it was obvious that the slaves felt more free to talk now. Social distinctions are not broken down so easily.

When the first few began to leave, Onesimus excused himself and made his way to the *peristyle*, where he found Justus reclining on a pile of cushions before coal fire burning warmly in a brazier.

"Take the seat across from me." Onesimus obeyed and reclined on a set of cushions nearby.

"You leave early in the morning. Marius has an errand to run at Lechaion harbor, so he will accompany you and show you to the ship. I wish you a good journey. I also have a favor to ask of you."

Onesimus nodded. "Anything, domine. I am in your debt."

Justus smiled, almost condescendingly, Onesimus thought. "Nothing like it, my boy. I simply wish you to give Paulus a message for me."

"Of course."

Justus looked at him intently, as if taking stock of him. "Tell him this: 'Gaius Titius Justus sends his heartfelt greeting. I daily mention you in my prayers. Please send word if we can help you in any way.'"

"I will give him that message, domine."

"One more thing." Justus raised his eyebrows. "I assume you will come back this way when you finish this errand for your master? If so, I would also request you deliver his response to me, and I will be glad to pay you for it, and once again extend my hospitality to you."

Onesimus hesitated. While he usually had no trouble fabricating the stories necessary to achieve his goals, this man had gone far beyond what was conventional or even proper to show him kindness. He felt a small pang of guilt for deceiving him. Yet he had to protect his plan. "Certainly, domine, I will be happy to. And thank you for the offer to return to your gracious home."

Justus leaned back on his cushions and fixed Onesimus with a steady, slightly amused look. Onesimus began to become uncomfortable. What was he thinking?

Finally, he spoke. "Onesimus, you are a fine slave, I can tell. But I did not attain my position and status without being insightful. And my insight tells me you are hiding something significant. Tell me: what is the truth about your journey?"

20. Causidicus

Onesimus felt his stomach drop. The thick cushions underneath him became uncomfortable. He squirmed.

"Whatever do you mean, domine?"

"I mean what I said." His voice was steady and emotionless. " I have been a most gracious host. I know Paulus and his mission. I want to know what you are not telling me."

His mind raced. "Well, sir, I...I cannot tell you what I do not know. My master did not tell me the nature of the message I am carrying." A terrible thought came to him. What if Justus had his belongings searched and found no message cylinder. Maybe he suspected he was a runaway.

"I am not asking for information you don't have. Nor am I asking for information that is privileged. But I know you are holding something back."

He was almost tempted to tell him the truth. Yet he feared that temptation was prompted by Justus' kindness. He had been lulled into feeling safe—just like he had with Turia.

An idea began to form. The best lie was sometimes to tell the truth—just not all of it.

He affected a sigh. "Yes, domine. It is...a delicate matter. It is true I am delivering a message for my master for Paulus, but there is something else. My master and I had a serious dispute for which I was punished, and my position was taken away. My master thinks it resolved, but I do not. So I am also going to ask Paulus to act as an advocate for me with...my master." He almost said "Philemon" he realized with horror. He looked up.

Justus was still looking intently at him. "Does your master know that you have this second, personal mission?"

"He does not. I'd like to think he will be in favor of it, seeing how much he respects Paulus." Onesimus felt a bit of calm within. This was good. Really good. Almost the complete truth, without the bad parts.

"Well!" He laughed. "I was hoping for something more scandalous than that. A dispute between master and slave. Not very exciting or unusual." He leaned forward and poured some wine into a cup, then added a bit of water and leaned back again, motioning for Onesimus to join him.

As Onesimus poured himself some wine, Justus spoke again. "That does explain some of your strange behavior."

Onesimus was astounded at the insight of Justus, and a little scared. Was Justus an unusual man with finely honed skills of observation, or was Onesimus not as clever as he fancied?

"How did you know? I am on a mission to Paulus for my master—my personal mission is secondary." He was relaxing into his new story.

Justus smiled, but with a note of smugness. "I pride myself on keen observation and evaluating facts. I was the top of my class in forensic oratory when I studied at the Stoa in Athens."

Onesimus was impressed, and it must have showed, for Justus smiled broadly. "Yes, I have been educated by the best! And it has helped me in all I have done in business and politics. Alas…" he pursed his lips and looked down into his cup, "…becoming a god-fearer was a setback, and becoming a follower of the Way only exacerbated it." He looked up at Onesimus. "Not that I would have it any other way. To be called by god is far more important than money or gravitas. But don't let a Roman aristocrat—or even an Equestrian—hear me say that!" He laughed and took a large swallow of wine.

Onesimus took a tentative sip. It was excellent. "My master, too, talks of it being difficult sometimes."

"Yes, almost like being a follower of the Egyptian mysteries. It was a big problem here in Corinth, in the beginning—mainly because of the uproar caused by the Jewish community—which is substantial. It has settled down a good bit, and thanks to Paulus' lengthy work here, there are many followers of the Way here, in all areas of community life and status. Still, the Jews undermine us in every way publicly, and many of the Greeks agree with the Jews—for once!" He laughed.

He was not sure what to make of this Greek nobleman who had taken on public shame *willingly*, and who treated a visiting slave as if he were a patron freedperson. It seemed…weak, though Justus was no weak man and no coward.

"So, Onesimus, the slave with a complaint, indulge me. I am proud of my little household here. My wife and daughter are away, so it is not at its usual form. What do you think? I enjoy hearing an outsiders' view—be it from a citizen, freedperson, or slave."

Another strange request. It was not a slave's place to speak of such things. He must tread carefully. "I cannot say enough about your hospitality, domine. The welcome you have extended to me, in the name of my…my master, is…I guess...appropriate—"

"Yes, yes, yes. All things I would expect any houseguest to say. A typical Roman or Greek guest buttering up the host." He leaned forward again, as he seemed to do when he was making an important point or getting to the crux of a matter. "But what do you think of it *as a slave*? It is a point of view I do not—and cannot—have. You may speak at ease." He sat back, waiting, with a slightly amused look.

Onesimus did not feel at ease at all. It was a most inappropriate question—why would a master care what a slave thought?

Yet Justus did not seem like the type to posture or manipulate. It was a refreshing change from the attitudes of most free men and women, who constantly played the games of client and patron, honor and shame, and who's up and who's down. Slaves were not immune. They schemed and manipulated, always with the goal of gaining more honor or gravitas. Here was a man who had all of that but did not seem to care too much about it.

"I would say, domine, that you seem to treat me, and your slaves, as if we were freedpeople working for you rather than slaves owned by you. It makes me think of the Stoics with their reputations of being kinder to their slaves than most."

Justus nodded. "Yes, an astute observation. Yet it is not Greek philosophy but my belief in the Way that leads me to behave as I do. Unlike modern religions, the Way connects ethics with religion."

Another strangeness of the Way. Ethics were the subject of the philosophies, not religions. The gods don't care how people live unless it affects them.

"I see from your expression, Onesimus, that is confusing to you. It was for me, too—especially for my Athens-trained philosophical mind. Yet it has always been so for Jews, and as I learned more, it began to make more sense of the world to me. I began to apply my beliefs to how I lived. So the similarity to the Stoics is understandable, but derives from a different view of the cosmos. More wine?"

Onesimus shook his head. He had had enough tonight, and he would be up quite early tomorrow.

"Well, I do. Plotia! Wine!" He set his cup on the low table. "The Stoics believe that Fate decides the location of each person. A free man is free by Fate; a slave is a slave by Fate. Therefore, a free man who is a Stoic knows that he might well have been born a slave—therefore, take care how you treat slaves! Those of the Way believe that god, blessed be his name, has appointed each of us to the place in life. Yet it is more than that—and it was Paulus himself who taught me this. I am a slave of my god, and he is my master. So, I look to the god to see how I should act towards *my* servants, since I am likewise his servant."

Onesimus was taken aback again. It was not unusual for a follower to describe themselves as a servant of their god or goddess, but applying that idea to others made no sense. Why should a freedman treat their slaves like the god treats him?

It did make sense of Justus' behavior, however. He wondered if those who followed the Stoic way were more understanding of the Way.

Plotia returned with the wine, flowing in and out like an apparition. *Surely*, Onesimus thought, *I have had too much wine by now*. He breathed in the faint fragrance she had left behind. How exotic. How beautiful. But those thoughts brought the memory of Turia, and those images turned his mood sour. He stared at the fire burning itself out in the brazier. She would pay. After all, look at him now! Sitting in a wealthy man's house in Corinth, drinking wine and talking with him as if he was already a freedperson. He was no dumb slave, no uncouth barbarian or Scythian. If Fortuna had assigned to him a slave life, he could just have easily been fated to be a noble, or an Equestrian, or maybe even a Senator! It was not beneath him. Justus found him smart and educated. He would find his way to Rome, find Paulus, and all would be put right. He could return with a new standing with Philemon, raising him above all the other slaves of the household (except maybe Philippus). Then, whether free or slave, he would get his revenge on Turia. And Giton, too, the self-righteous bucco!

"Onesimus?"

He looked up. "Yes?"

"You best retire. You are falling asleep. I imagine your journey thus far has been quite hectic, with little rest."

"Yes, domine. Thank you again for your hospitality. May the gods bless you."

Justus smiled, the low firelight playing off his face in the dark. The air in the peristyle was considerably cooler now. "May god be with you, and may he bless your mission. Both of them."

Onesimus felt himself blush. Such a strange master! He nodded, bowed, and made his way carefully out of the peristyle and towards the slave quarters. As he approached his room, Plotia was coming out. She turned and saw him. "Onesimus, I have just put a skin of hot water and a basin inside for you. Marius said he would come for you just after dawn." She made to move past him in the plain hallway.

"Thank you, Plotia." He had an urge to laugh—he was feeling quite good. "You don't have to run off so soon, do you?"

She twitched her head and looked at him with no expression. "I have duties to attend."

Onesimus wanted to keep looking in her eyes, those dark brown pools in wide saucers of white. Mysterious and exciting. "Well, why don't you come back here when you are done?"

Her eyes narrowed slightly. "I think not, slave boy." She brushed past him and was gone.

Onesimus went into the room and fell on the bed. Slave boy?! As if she were a freedperson! He had heard that Egyptian slaves were often haughty beyond their station.

No matter. He was on his way to a *better* station, far better than she would ever have.

Epistole Epsilon

To Giarri

I was especially grateful to receive your last letter. Some dark times are ahead, I fear, and the knowledge that you are doing well and continuing our work heartens me. I give thanks for you often.

Tertillus called for me last week, and it did not go well. He sent me to Puteoli, and I doubt I will leave here alive. An interesting thought, for it was at Puteoli that first landed after leaving Corinth. I was a bit chastened when I arrived. As I told you in my last letter, I had left Corinth feeling quite good about myself.

I can still remember the Lechaion Road in the bright Grecian sun before I left Corinth—my ship floating in the harbor. Giarri, it was a trireme, and I could not believe something so massive could float upon the sea! I still remember her name—the Tutilina—and the colorful flag she flew high on a mast. I imagined it was the family emblem of some famous nobleman of Rome, but it could have easily been the flag of a merchant company.

You remember Marius of Corinth? He is the one who was killed many years ago in the skirmish between Roman troops and Jews outside of the city. He saw me off that day to Puteoli and warned me to be careful. I took it seriously, but not seriously enough. The ship alone overwhelmed me as I approached it. The main deck was at least three stories higher than the level of the water! Halfway up the ladder to the deck, a feeling of being small and frail overcame me. I was like a tiny insect crawling on the side of a log in the middle of a vast lake.

I remember finding my bunk—much like the ones you and I shared when we sailed to Philippi just after we began our work in Ephesus. I met another young slave on a journey for his master, too. It was nice to have some company, but his actions during a storm came back to haunt me later, as you know from my letters. I must say that I am sorry I never saw him again.

That trip was another turning point, I suppose, or, rather, a precursor. The first days were wonderful. I felt free, accomplished—like a freedman already! I had no idea I was going to be shaken to my core in so many ways.

The guard has just brought me my single meal of the day, and it has steam coming from it for once! More later, my brother. Greet everyone there for me, and give a special greeting to Bacchus, for I hear he has had a rough time of it.

21. Tempestas

Onesimus was surprised to find that it took almost two days before they would sail out into the Adriatic Sea. It took that long to traverse the long firth. Onesimus made sure he was up on deck for the moment they left the firth, but the event proved anticlimactic. The land on either side slowly faded away. The swaying of the ship increased slightly due to the swells of the greater body of water, but not much—the firth was quite broad and affected by wind and sea swells. In front of the ship was not open sea, but more land. He asked about it one of the slave crew, who told him that the landmasses were two islands, quite large, named Kephallenia and Zakunthos. A few other smaller islands also dotted the seas here and there, mostly to the north. Onesimus watched over the next few hours as the ship made their way between the two islands.

*

By the next morning, they had passed the islands and were sailing in an east-southeast direction. The seas were bit rough: the swells came slow but large, causing the ship to rise bow-first, and then drop down, stern up, throwing a spray of water high in the air. It was a bit alarming the first time it happened, but no one else seemed to pay it any attention, so Onesimus assumed it was normal. He did have to watch his balance, though.

The next couple of days found shipboard life becoming routine. Onesimus passed much of the time by trying to sleep in his bunk. It was not an easy task with so many others at such close quarters—and many snored. Most were freedpersons on some mission, but they did not speak with him. There were a few wealthy patrons on board, too, but they were in the more lavish quarters in the bow, and rarely showed themselves on deck. Onesimus once caught sight of an older woman and a young girl standing on the foredeck with a finely uniformed man he presumed to be the captain.

He met another slave who was also traveling alone. He introduced himself as "Mouse," which was not his real name, of course, but a fitting nickname, considering his diminutive size and delicate, tiny features. He was also on a mission to Rome for his master, who was from Megara. While it was nice to have another of his own station aboard, they did not talk much except during meals.

*

He awoke in a blind panic. It was dark, and the ship was pitching deeply bow to stern, and occasionally rolling sharply side to side—sometimes both at the same time. He gripped the sides of the bunk, experiencing, with great fear, the three directions a ship could move in addition to forward and astern. The sounds were terrifying as well: a dull constant roar punctuated by occasional booms, along with the creaking and moaning of the ship itself. Thinking he'd feel better on deck, he jumped down, threw on his cloak, and stumbled to the door. He felt his way carefully up the stairs. The motion was violent enough to throw him against the bulkheads two or three times.

He emerged onto the deck to see that it had been cleared of all items that had been loosely stored. The sails were furled, flaked, tied, and covered. The crewmen were stationed at various places around the decks, though it seemed they were only watching the storm. A heavy spray occasionally crashed over the railings and drenched the deck and anyone who was standing there. The sailors would duck down and grab a handhold and ride it out. He saw one lose his footing, but he soon recovered with movements that demonstrated experience.

Onesimus felt his way along the bulkhead below the quarterdeck, finally reaching a spot where he could grasp a deck post.

"Onesimus! Quite a sight, yes?!"

Startled, Onesimus saw a small figure crouching on the other side of the bulkhead. A flash of lightning illuminated the world, followed by a crack of thunder that caused Onesimus to jump. The illumination was bright enough to reveal that the voice came from Mouse.

"Mouse! What are you doing here? What is happening?"

Onesimus' eyes slowly adjusted to the dark. The sky was covered with a low, dark cloud cover. The sea was a black inky pool, with whitecaps and wind waves appearing and disappearing. The wind howled, making the sail ties and halyards whip and snap. Rain was falling—or not so much falling as being blown in all directions.

"I might ask you the same!" Mouse shouted. "It's a storm, as you can see!"

"Yes! I thought storms were rare during this season?!" He had to shout to be heard.

Mouse yelled, "One of the sailors told me this was not a storm—just a summer squall! Hate to see a real storm!"

A squall? How would the crew survive on deck in anything worse than this?

"They aren't worried?!" Onesimus could feel his heart pounding.

As Mouse opened his mouth to answer, a lightning flash erupted followed by another boom, obliterating his voice. Onesimus saw a frozen scene in that brief flash: Mouse, crouching and drenched, with his mouth open and his eyes wide; the deck of the ship slanted crazily; men stationed at the various positions, frozen in this act or that; and, behind it all, an angry sea and sky of green and black and white.

Onesimus blinked. The afterimage caused him to be more afraid—blindness and fear were not a good combination. "What?!" he yelled.

Mouse tried again. "I said, 'they said squalls don't last long.' We ride it out and go on…I don't know if it's better up here or down below!"

Mouse rose to a standing position, gripping the post with both hands.

"Are you going back down?!"

"Yes! I was trying to get up the courage when you appeared! You?!" It sounded more like a plea than a question.

"Yes!"

Mouse glanced around, then let go of the post and made a quick dash for the door that led belowdecks. Onesimus turned, watching him. At that moment, the ship lurched and jerked up and sideways, stronger than any jolt so far. Simultaneously, another blinding flash of lightning lit up the scene. As Onesimus cowered, a massive wave of water crashed into him, knocking him back. He gripped the pylon with both arms as the force tried to pull him away. A high scream sounded as the ship rolled back in the opposite direction. Water streamed past him as the ship righted itself, threatening to pull him away again.

"Mouse!" He yelped. There was no answer, and he could not see much because the lightning had temporarily blinded him again. Was he washed overboard? He stayed down, hugging the post, looking this way and that. He had never been so afraid. If he had not been holding on, that wave could have washed him overboard.

The swaying and rolling had resumed its previous ferocity. He had to get back below. He could do it, as long and there was not another violent lurch. He thought of what Mouse had said: this was just a minor squall and nothing to be worried about. He calmed his heart by telling himself that it was only twenty feet, and he would be safe to ride out it.

He prayed, "Oh, Artemis, if you can hear me, please rescue me from this danger. Please save this ship. If so, I will offer a sacrifice to you when we reach land. Hear me, Artemis, for I have always been your faithful servant."

Another crash of thunder and lightning ended his prayer, and in the flash of light, he thought he saw a dark shape against the far railing. Was it the crumpled body of Mouse? Slammed to the deck, bloodied and unconscious? If he had tried to get below when Mouse had…

Maybe he should pray to Poseidon. "Oh, god of the sea, Poseidon, hear the plea of this simple servant. Spare this ship from your depths. I beg of you. Though I am nothing, I have money. I will find your temple in Rome and donate ten sesterces to you if you will only let me live. And if you will spare us—"

There came another jolt, as mighty as the one that sent Mouse flying. He was jerked sideways. As the ship lurched back, another wash of water pulled his feet out from under him. His grip slipped but held. A dark shape went flying past, crashing into the bulkhead and then sliding off into the darkness towards to port railing. A barrel, come unmoored? A body?

He attempted to gather his courage and prayed again. "God…of…of the Way…" Should he add Iesous, too? "God of the Way and Iesous, please hear me. The god of Philemon and Justus…hear me, deliver me…and…if so, I will make things right with my master, and I will give to you whatever he tells me."

He took a deep breath, let go of the post and crawled like a crab to the wall. He slid his hands along until he felt the railing, then, carefully, made his way to the bulkhead, pulling himself inside the hatchway.

"Onesimus! There you are! Thank the gods; I thought you were washed away!" It was Mouse, crouching inside the doorway, hanging on to the inside railing.

Onesimus crouched down beside him.

They sat, resting and shivering as the ship rolled.

"Hey," Mouse said after a while. "I think the noise and motion are waning! Guess that sailor was right!"

The ship *was* rolling at less of an angle, and more regularly. The wind seemed less forceful. When there had been no booming thunder for some time, they arose and made their way toward their cabin.

"Ah, that was quite a thrill," Mouse said.

"I don't know about that. I thought you were dead, smashed against the bulkhead or rails!"

Mouse stopped and looked at him. "Did you? No, I got inside before those big ones. I was preparing to go out and look for you when you showed up. I'm ashamed to say it was taking me a while to get the courage up!"

Onesimus blinked and followed him into the cabin, slowly. He was coming to find him? They hardly knew each other. He'd had no thought of helping Mouse.

22. Italia

Except for that summer squall, the rest of the trip was uneventful. The shared experience made Onesimus feel like more of a compatriot of Mouse. Perhaps he felt some guilt about his actions, but that never seemed to occur to Mouse. They fell into a habit of going up on deck after meals, though there was often not much to see. The seas and weather remained relatively constant. But one day, they were standing at the rails when they sailed within sight of land: a misty apparition off to starboard.

"That's your first view of Italia, Onesimus! And soon, we'll be able to see Sicilia."

Mouse had traveled between Corinth and Rome many times on errands for his master. Much like Philemon, Mouse's master dealt in goods, though at a much higher volume.

Onesimus liked Mouse. He was a comfortable travel companion who didn't feel the need to talk a lot or intrude on Onesimus' space. Because he was familiar with Rome, they spent time talking about the city as they sat on deck. He described the layout of the city for Onesimus and told him of the cultural and social customs that might be different from those of Asia Minor. He also shared many of the delights of the famous city, as well as the dangers and things to avoid. He echoed the advice of Marius—never stay out at night—at least not alone.

They sat in silence as the ship made a wide, slow turn to starboard and began to sail between the mainland of Italia and Sicilia. Mouse pointed out the city of Rhegium to starboard and, a little while later, the town of Messana appeared, nestled in a small island harbor to port. Onesimus' heart pounded as he viewed these sights. Italia!

"Now," Mouse said, "once we leave this narrow channel, we'll be sailing the Tyrrhenian Sea along the east coast. Far to the northwest will be the islands of Sardinia and Corsica, though we won't be able to see them." All of these were names Onesimus had heard as if in legends. Now he was sailing among them! He was in the lands where important things happened. He was being led by Artemis. And he had options—all of which led to freedom.

*

Two days later they came within sight of land. As the dark coast began to resolve into detail, Onesimus could see that they were headed for a large bay. Mouse told him it was known as "the Cup." Rolling green hills and a few cliffs surrounded the bay, but the most prominent feature was a tall, snow-capped, pyramid-shaped mountain rising behind it all called Mount Vesuvius. Onesimus was astonished that a peak could be so lofty!

"Stunning!" He exclaimed to Mouse. "How does the earth keep from collapsing below it?"

"It's actually farther inland that it looks—many miles. But its massive size makes it look like it *must* be closer."

"I've never seen anything like it."

"They say it is a dormant volcano. The last eruption was over a hundred years ago."

They were soon distracted from the view as the crew swarmed up the masts, loosening, lowering, and flaking the massive canvas sails. The rowers' drumbeat from belowdecks began, and the ship rowed into the harbor that was officially known as the Bay of Neopolis. Mouse, pointing at each city at the water's edge around the bay, named each one."

"Puteoli, Baiae, Herculaneum, and Pompeii. A lot of wealthy families in Rome and elsewhere have vacation homes in every one of them."

The ship headed to the port of Puteoli on the north side of the bay. They watched from the railing as the details of the active seaport resolved.

"How are you getting to Rome?" Mouse asked.

"I don't know yet. I was told I could either find a ship or take the Appian Way up the coast."

Mouse blinked in the bright sun reflecting off the bay waters. "Take a ship. Faster, safer, and not too expensive. There is a man from Baiae who runs two ships back and forth daily. I know his vilici, who runs the business. I can take you to him."

"That would be great. You're not going on to Rome?"

"Not yet. I must take care of some business here for my master. A few days. Then I will take a ship up to Rome. I also want to find a shrine to Artemis; I need to offer a sacrifice." Mouse looked sheepishly at Onesimus, "I made some vows during that storm. Guess I am a cowardly landlubber." He laughed.

Onesimus didn't respond. He had made vows, too, but none of them seemed like a big deal now. A short little storm at sea, over within a few hours.

Puteoli had docks large enough and long enough (and water deep enough) for the ship to dock. Onesimus was relieved not to have to ride another tender into shore. They stood out of the way and watched the crews on the pier and on board working together to maneuver the vessel into position. They cast lines, and those on the pier secured it to large cleats and posts. Eventually, all was made fast, and the crews began unloading the cargo.

Onesimus and Mouse retrieved their belongings from the cabin.

"Hey, Onesimus, some advice. I don't know how much money you are carrying from your master, but take some out and put it inside a pocket of your cloak. If you have a pouch, put some in that, too."

"Okay. Why?"

"Never keep all your money in one place," Mouse said. "Something I learned the hard way from traveling so much."

Onesimus nodded and followed his advice. Mouse stepped politely away as he did so, offering privacy as he handled the money.

When he finished, they disembarked and walked down the pier to the shoreside docks of Puteoli. Onesimus found himself again amazed at the sheer numbers of people and goods.

"I can see this all fascinates you, Onesimus, but we need to find and book passage for you right away. Being early afternoon, there won't be many more ships sailing that day."

Onesimus, a bit abashed, followed the small man as he weaved through the crowd. He amused himself at the thought that Mouse really was like a mouse, darting here and there between larger creatures and obstacles.

They arrived at a small dockside building, and, in a short time, he was booked aboard a ship leaving in an hour for Ostia, the port city of Rome. Boarding receipt in hand, Onesimus turned back to Mouse.

"Thank you for assisting me with this."

"Oh," Mouse waved a hand. "I remember my first lengthy trip for my master! Happy to help a fellow slave. I'm sure you'll do the same someday for another young man."

"Much thanks anyway, and also for your companionship on the voyage."

"I'll thank you for that, too! Made it much more enjoyable. Gods be with you, brother! I must be off! When I get to Rome, let's get in touch if we can!"

Not sure that he would stay too long in Rome, he agreed without saying much else. They parted, and Onesimus watched as Mouse darted off to his own tasks.

Alone, Onesimus felt a bit unsure of himself momentarily. Still, he reminded himself, it was probably no bigger than Ephesus, even though it was foreign. He was fine.

He bought a few provisions from a nearby stand and stayed close to the dock, sitting near the water and out of the way. Looking out over the bay, which was bristling with masts of ships, he could see across to the opposite shore where the town of Sorentia lay. It was so clear that he could even make out the dim outline of the island of Capreae just off the southern tip of the bay.

His thoughts turned back to Philemon, his old home, and, as they inevitably did, Turia. He felt a momentary twinge of tenderness, but he quashed it. She had betrayed him, and someday she would pay. Any positive feelings he had came from the fact that he had been manipulated to feel that way. He had loved her, but she had never loved him. He said a small prayer to Artemis to help him obtain revenge. He wondered if the god of the Way helped his followers with retribution. Undoubtedly so—every other god did. But the god of the Way was strange, or at least his followers were, and Onesimus was a bit nervous at engaging him.

After he deemed that the hour was drawing near, he made his way over to the boat that was to take him to Ostia. It was much smaller than either the *Tutilina* and the *Hespera*. As a result, the cabins were smaller. Once aboard, it was not long before the ship cast off, and twenty oarsmen (ten to each side) powered the boat out into the bay and beyond until they neared the point of land at the northeast corner of the Bay. Onesimus could see some fancy villas and domii along the cliffs of Baiae. He marveled at the amount of money such nobles must have.

Each would have a domus in Rome, too—probably even more extravagant. He could not conceive of such wealth.

Soon the ship turned north. There was not much wind so it appeared that the rowers would continue to row until that changed. Onesimus once again thanked Fortuna that he was not born an oarsman.

Because they were not under sail, they would not arrive until the morning of the second day. Onesimus retired below and slept as much as possible. It made the trip seem shorter.

*

When they docked, Onesimus had expected another bustling port, more so than any of the others. After all, it was the port city for Rome. Yet it was not so. Ostia seemed smaller and less busy than Puteoli. Strange.

He disembarked and asked directions, then headed up the road indicated. He soon found out why the men he questioned seemed amused: every way out of the port eventually met one broad road, the Via Ostiensis, which led only to Rome.

The journey took him much longer than he had supposed, and he was glad that he had bought some provisions. There were plenty of fellow travelers on foot, horse, donkeys, and in carts and in litters. He assumed the danger here was minimal on such a busy road.

As noon approached, he rounded a bend in the road and before him was the city wall of Rome just a short distance away. The size of the wall itself emphasized the difference between Rome and every other city he had ever seen. The gates were set into massive and tall columns, part of the wall, and made of the most elegant marble and stone that were almost blinding in the sunlight. Every detail was finished with an artistic flair. The gate was equally monstrous and ornate. This, he would learn later, was the Aventine Gate, the southern entrance to the city. As he passed through the looming gates, he felt as if he were entering a city of a god. He involuntarily ducked his head in reverence. He felt small and insignificant.

No matter. He had come to Rome.

EPISTOLE ZETA

To Giarri

Peace to you, my dear Giarri. I have not had a good few weeks. The cold is beginning to seep into my bones permanently, I think, and I have contracted a wet cough that will not go away.

But your letters refresh me, indeed. Yes, I do find it ironic that I am here just outside of Rome. When I was here the first time, I had no idea what I was in for. If I could have foreseen this future, I would never have guessed the reason.

On my way here some time ago, we sailed past the Cup, and I was astonished. There is nothing left, Giarri, even after thirty years. As if that huge mountain took back the whole bay with molten rock, fire, and ash.

Someday, I hope you can make it to Rome, Giarri. It is truly the head of the world: the brain, eyes, mouth, and ears of the Empire. Did you know that at the time I first arrived, it had a million inhabitants! I remember staring at the huge temple to Jupiter, Juno, and Minerva on Capitolina Hill, towering over the city, and thinking it proved how powerful those gods must be.

The Forum Romanum was the hub of business, politics, judicial activity, and governance, along with countless shops selling goods and services, which is where I spent a lot of my time.

The sheer number of people was amazing to me and still is: citizens, slaves, freedpeople, poor, gladiators, beggars, shop owners, artisans, thieves, gangs, and prostitutes male and female; Syrians, Egyptians, Asians, Africans, Spanish—even Gauls and Germans!. And there were over 40,000

Jews inside the city walls, though they were on the east side of the Tiber in the slums set up for them. I did not deal with them much when I was here back then, though I heard constant rumors of how they mistreated Paulus. Yet he never let it affect him, despite the fact that they were his own people. And it would be their testimony that ended his life, years later, on the road south of Rome.

Nero was the Emperor then, and a pretty good one until later, as you know. I think Domitian will be turn out to be far worse, in retrospect. At least for us.

Which brings me to your last question. Yes, I did finally meet with the eparch. It is not good news, my brother. He indicated that he will rule soon and that it will not be in my favor. While I pray that it will be an exile, I fear it is more likely to be execution. But I am ready.

Greet everyone there.

23. Roma

Onesimus made his way along the Via Ostiensis, which wound its way into the heart of Rome. He passed shops, squares, tenements, stables, and many public buildings and minor temples. While the homes on the Aventine Hill seemed impressive, the rich and decorous domii on Palatine Hill, overlooking the main forum, put them to shame. That had to be where all the wealth nobles and senators lived.

He came to a road marked "Via Sacra" as he rounded the Palatine hill, revealing, high above, what surely must be the emperor's palace. Onesimus stopped for a moment, his breath taken away at the thought that humans could build such a massive structure. Tearing his gaze away he saw, set below the road, the Forum itself. It was larger than most towns. Even from this distance, he could hear the buzz of the crowd.

He began the slight descent and soon reached the west end of the Forum Romanum. He had felt overwhelmed at the Corinthian agora—this was beyond what his eyes and ears could take in. Massive monuments of every kind stood solemnly, each attempting to outdo the others in size, decoration, and architectural extravagance. Temples, each one more imposing than the next, were on all sides of the Forum. Nearby, a huge monument with a marble crosspiece and tall, thick columns proclaimed Senatus Populus Que Romanus: "the Senate and People of Rome." The public government buildings were no less opulent than the temples, covered in gold, silver, and marble.

The Forum itself was a vast field of green grass in the midst of the blindingly white marble that covered every inch of ground, step, wall, and support. Onesimus guessed it could fit six Colossian forums in it! The descriptions given to him by Marius had only hinted at the nature of this place. Huge columns lined the grass-filled square, and the Rostrum at the far end was like the dais of a king—or perhaps more suited to a god. Monuments were scattered everywhere, some were statues, but others were tall columns with foreign writing—probably Egyptian. At this moment, a purple-robed man was there, speaking and gesticulating wildly to a small crowd gathered before him. The broad thoroughfares surrounding the forum were lined with various-sized stalls, and rooms open to the agora, each with a group of people in front: sellers plying their wares with every food, good, and service. Were there really so many people here that necessitated such a multitude of vendors? He had heard there were a million living in Rome, but that was an unfathomable number to Onesimus, and surely not correct.

And the people! A teaming mass of incredible variety in ethnicity, nationality, dress, status, gender, and size, all weaving through the streets and squares and concourses and porticos and arches. Some were laughing, some talking with one another, while others had their heads down, intent only on their destination. Almost everyone walked: no carts or horses or wheeled contraptions were allowed in Rome during the daylight hours, except for slave-borne litters carrying the wealthy. The space was almost filled with human flesh, filling up the marble-covered container like a thick soup poured into a giant's bowl. Cold eyes, twinkling eyes, curious eyes, fearful eyes...yet almost every set was Roman. If Rome was the most powerful city the world had ever known, then the Romans were the most powerful people.

Onesimus felt small, insecure, and out of place—even more than he did when he was climbing the ladder onto the ship at Lechaeum harbor. There, it had been the physical size of the boat and the harbor. Here, his feeling of irrelevance was born out of cultural, social, and political vastness. Who did he think he was, coming to this place? He would be washed away like a speck of dust in a mighty river.

Without warning he was struck from behind. He stumbled forward, almost falling to his knees.

"Hey, slave!" a gruff voice shouted.

He caught his breath and turned around, flinching. A large man was upon him: a swarthy, dirty face, with muscled arms in a sleeveless tunic. He noticed with relief it was another slave, lugging a large basket that was obviously heavy. The man glared at him and continued past, disappearing into the crowd.

Onesimus moved to one side, shaking. He tried to force himself to relax. He must pay closer attention—remembered what Marius had told him and what Mouse had confirmed: go about your business; act like you know what you are doing; be polite but distant.

Spotting a small food stand, he made his way to it through the crowd. After waiting in line, he ordered bread, strips of goat meat, and asparagus. The food was handed to him without a word. He paid and moved away, sitting near the grass of the forum and tried to act as if he did this all the time.

How was he to find Paulus in this massive city? If he was under house arrest, where would that be? Until he found him, where could he stay? Marius had said the cheapest and most socially appropriate place was among the tenements and taverns in the Subura, northeast of the forum and below the Esqualine Hill. Yet the Subura had the reputation of being seedy and dangerous. Mouse had told him that the road there, the Via Subura, went up over the Esqualine Hill and up to the Necropolis, where dead commoners were burned and their ashes buried.

He should probably try to find Paulus first. After all, he would know Rome and know places to stay. The prison officials would have information on who was under house arrest. Having finished his meal, he stood up and looked around, spotting two slaves sitting nearby, also eating lunch.

"Excuse me, brothers, I am new here and wonder if you could tell me how to get to the prison? I have a message from my master to one being held there."

One of the slaves looked up, mouth full, and said, "Which one?"

"Which one?"

The man swallowed. "Which *prison*?"

"Oh. I didn't know there was more than one. Is there a primary prison?"

The man shook his head and swallowed his considerable bite of food. "Not really. But the closest one is by the river on the other side of the Forum Bovarium. Take that road." He pointed toward an archway.

Onesimus nodded. "Many thanks." He should have guessed there would be more than one. He hitched up his bag and headed toward the archway.

Leaving the forum, he skirted the foot Capitoline Hill, and entered the Forum Bovarium. Most towns had one agora; Corinth had two, but Rome had different agoras for each category of item! This was the cattle market, with its own décor, architecture, and smells. It was also a lot noisier. Onesimus had never seen so many animals together in one place. The crowd appeared much rougher and dirtier than in the main Forum. He made his way through a maze of pens, stalls, and cages to the other side, where one road headed towards the city wall and another headed in the opposite direction.

The slave back in the Forum had not said whether the prison was inside the city walls or outside. He looked about for someone to ask. He spotted an old door slave sitting outside a small building, chained to the doorpost.

"Excuse me, brother, but is there a prison nearby?"

The slave looked up at him mournfully. "Eh?" His voice was barely a croak.

He was old; perhaps he had lost his hearing. Onesimus asked again, a bit louder.

"Yeh. There." He pointed in the direction of a gate set in the wall. Beside the gate was a plain stone building. A Roman soldier stood in front. Onesimus thanked the slave, approached the prison, and bowed to the soldier.

"Pardon me, domine, I have been sent by my master, uh, Gaius Titius Justus of Corinth, to deliver a message to a prisoner here in Rome." He thought a nobleman from Corinth might carry more weight than one from Colossae.

The Roman guard peered at him, looking down from his station on the plinth of the building. He was a large, swarthy man. His leather armor, the red cape, the gladus at his side, and his iron helmet were intimidating. It was soldiers such as this, under the rule of Octavian, who brought the Pax Romana to the entire world.

"Name?" the soldier barked.

"I, I am Onesimus."

"Not your name, idiot, the name of the prisoner!"

Onesimus felt his face heat up.

"Oh, yes, my apologies, domine. Paulus of Tarsus. A Jew."

"There are no dirty Jews in this prison."

"Uh, are you sure?"

"Of course I am sure! I know a dirty Jew when I see one! Even if he has a Greek name! Off with you!" He turned his attention away from Onesimus, and back to staring across the road.

Onesimus turned away, feeling small and ashamed. He retraced his steps through the Forum Bovarium. Maybe he should go to the Subura and find a place to stay. He could start anew in the morning to find Paulus, with a whole day ahead of him. Glancing up at the sky, he estimated that he still had a few hours of light remaining.

He entered into the Forum again and mustered the courage to ask someone for the location of the Subura area—it was to the northeast and not too far. He was becoming tired and thirsty, for he had walked many hours today. He stopped at a stand for a cup of honeyed water laced with a bit of vinegar. Finding a spot on the grass, out of the way of the traffic, he leaned against one of the large columns to rest and drink.

The encounter with the soldier had unsettled him. He took a deep breath. He had made it across three seas from the Asian Province to Rome itself! He was now navigating his way around the monstrous city of Rome. He was resourceful and intelligent. It would be okay.

He would find a place to stay for tonight; then, tomorrow, he would find Paulus and tell him the story of the money at Philemon's villa. Would he tell him the whole truth? That he had been stealing money, got caught, and ran away to see if Paulus would act as an arbitrator? A repentant slave, ready to resume his rightful place in the household?

However, the fact that he had been stealing the money from his master—for a long time—might be a problem. What if Paulus saw him as a permanently flawed slave? He would need to play the role of a sorry, humble, repentant slave to perfection.

Or, he could turn the tables and blame Turia. She had put him up to it, and the wiles of women—which were well-known—had caused him to do something he would never have done otherwise. That should work quite well, and if it came down to the word of a female slave and the word of Paulus, there was no doubt who Philemon would believe.

Then, he would go back to work, focusing single-mindedly on being the best slave Philemon ever had. Perhaps he could rise to vilici at an early age, and then, after twelve years, Philemon would free him at age thirty—with citizenship!

He could play the penitent and humble himself. After all, he *was* sorry that he had run away. If he had known about the custom of releasing loyal slaves at age thirty, he would not have stolen the money in the first place. Philemon should have told him and saved them both a lot of trouble!

He returned the cup to the food stand, then headed out of the Forum along the Via Sacra. The crowd moving was still dense, though thinning. The Esqualine Hill stood in the distance to his left; shadows lay between the rolling hills dotted with buildings.

Maybe he could figure a way to implicate Turia. He could say that stealing the money had been her idea…he been taken in by a scheming woman who had made him fall in love with her. When they were caught, he could say that he was so in love with her that he the blame. He was a just a betrayed lover, taken in by a woman's deception, sorely hurt, who panicked and ran away.

He came to a branch in the road, the left of which seems to climb up towards the Esqualine Hill and the city wall beyond. But the proprietor had told him "take the left branch; the Subura lay between the Esqualine and Viminalus hills." So the road probably went up and then veered back down beyond the first hill.

He took the road to the left and returned to his scheme. He smiled to himself. It explained everything. He would take the blame for not reporting his lover's crime. He could see himself now, shaking his head in shame. "I should have known not to trust a slave woman from the East…but I was so in love for the first time." Who could fail to be moved by this story of slaves, love, and betrayal? It was almost a Greek tragedy!

He would be restored and Turia would have the tables turned on her.

He strolled along, trying to spot holes in his logic or problems in the details. The testimony of Giton and Claudia? Their evidence did not change Onesimus' version of the story—they had only discovered that money was being stolen, and Onesimus and Turia were involved. The story contained enough truth to make it easy to tell, but left out enough to turn it in his favor.

He was feeling quite pleased with himself when he came to a four-way crossing. With dismay, he realized that he had not been paying attention. It was considerably darker than when he had set out from the Forum. The crowd was sparse. The buildings around were shuttered up and quiet. To the left the road appeared to lead back down to the Forum in a different way. The path ahead was a dark road. The road to the right went up, and around a curve, beyond which, high in the air, he saw wisps of smoke. His heart began to beat faster.

Where am I?

He ran up the road to his right and around the curve. Before him was the gate, set in the city wall, shut tight.

The sign beside the gate said "Necropolis."

He was at the far side of the city, and would never reach the Subura before nightfall.

24. Nox

Sweating with fear, he turned and ran back to the four-way crossing and looked back over the city. He must have ascended up the back of the Esqualine Hill, not the front. He must have turned left too late—he missed the proper branch! That meant the Viminalus Hill was farther on, so the road that went left would head down to the Subura from here. He set off, his heart racing.

A few minutes along, he stopped to breathe and saw a cart ahead of him, being dragged out of a shed-like building by two slaves. They were struggling to turn it. He drew near.

"Excuse me, brothers, how far along this road is the Subura?"

"Half a mile," one slave grunted. Onesimus saw that the cart they were pulling held several shroud-wrapped bodies, evidently bound for the Necropolis. It was a bit early for a cart to be out on the road, but close enough to the gate where no one would be likely to complain.

If he hurried, he could make it to the Subura in ten minutes. He picked up his pace, almost running. He passed a few people on the road, now mostly slaves and some carts. He could see the Forum far below in the distance, in deep darkness. His heart sank, because the Subura lay as low as the Forum, nestled in another saddle of land among the seven hills of Rome.

A few moments more and the road leveled out. It was dark and quiet. After the noise of the day, the silence seemed ominous. Occasionally, he heard the creaking wheels of a wagon or a shout, which only made the silence worse. Frantically, he began scanning the buildings on either side for a tavern or other lodging place. If he got desperate, he could stay at a brothel, though that would use up a lot of his money.

Down an alley to his left, a burning torch caught his eye —a tavern, perhaps! The narrow alley, canyon-like with tall buildings on either side, was deserted, but it was only a few hundred feet to the torch. When he arrived, he saw it was not a tavern: there was no sign above the entrance, and the doors and windows were boarded shut. The torch was probably a signal for private guests. He swore and turned, and his eye caught sight of another light down another alley. He squinted. The light was from two torches. He ran down the alley and could hear the noise of a crowd before he reached the door. He breathed a sigh of relief.

He slowed to a walk as he came the front of the building, which was indeed a tavern. Through the open door, he saw a brightly lit room with a large fireplace. It was crowded, and the buzz of voices and the clinking of metal and pottery cut through the silence of the street.

He stepped inside where it was quite warm. He was already sweating from his hurried journey downhill, and the heat made him dizzy. He scanned the room for an owner or slave. Spotting a man in a citizen's tunic who was setting a jug of wine on a table surrounded five or six revelers, he approached.

"Excuse me, *domine*."

The man turned. "Yes?" he said as he continued walking towards a counter at the back. Onesimus followed.

"I need a room for—"

"Sorry, boy, all filled up." He disappeared through an opening in the counter and out a door. Onesimus waited for him to come back. Surely there was *something*. Even the stable, if need be. Slaves often slept with a master's horses to protect them. Or maybe he knew of another place—close by. As he waited, he had to move first one way and another as both patrons and serving slaves brushed by to and from the busy room. A loud commotion in one corner caught his attention; either a group of off-duty soldiers or some gladiators, at a table with a few women. Two brutish men were yelling at one another while the rest laughed.

The owner came back out, and Onesimus managed to blurt out, "—is there another tavern nearby?" before the man zoomed past bearing a large pitcher and a cup, holding up an index finger to Onesimus. Onesimus waited again. As he hurried by on his way by again, the man shouted, "Try the *Black Swan*, over two streets to the left." And he was gone.

Onesimus sighed and headed back out into the street. Now it was truly dark. Two streets over? To the left or the right? The proprietor must have meant former—there were no other cross streets to the right. He began a rapid walk; running would risk tripping over a loose cobblestone or wheel rut. He thought he saw movement in every dark shadow. His heart pounded. His mind replayed the words of Marius and Mouse: don't be out after dark. Yet here he was. He uttered a brief prayer to the gods as he came to the second street and turned left into an alley even narrower than the last. He could hardly see anything. It was eerily quiet. He went a few steps, paused, then stepped slowly forward, peering ahead for any light. After about twenty steps, he realized this could not be the right alley. He should go back to the main street. Surely it would be safer than these back alleys. He turned and started back.

As he drew near to the first cross street, still straining to see, he heard scuffling sounds and grunts, like a group of people wrestling. A cry rang out, and shadows appeared before him writhing and flailing. Curses were shouted, and the shadows resolved into four or five figures that were obviously fighting. Onesimus stumbled to the side and shrank against the wall. One man grabbed another by his arms from behind, and the restrained man pleaded something Onesimus did not understand. Another man passed right in front of Onesimus: a thin, grimacing countenance with a large nose. The man lunged with an outstretched arm, coming up into the belly of the man who was held fast. Onesimus heard a sickening squelch and a grating sound. A horrible scream tore through the night, echoing down the alley, covering Onesimus' own gasp. The man raised his arm and struck the man again in the chest and the scream cut off with a wet gurgle.

Another form stumbled against the wall beside Onesimus and fell to the ground. Onesimus crouched down, trying to be invisible in the shadows. He could barely make out a man—a slave in a plain tunic. He froze, but the man had already seen him. He grabbed Onesimus' arm.

"Come on!" he hissed, and pulled him away down the alley and around a corner. As they turned, he stumbled, and both went down in a heap. They untangled themselves and leaned against a wall.

"You saw!" The slave said. "They killed my master! You saw!" The poor man was sobbing. "I told him it was not safe to go! But you saw! You can testify!"

Onesimus pulled away, staring at the man. He knew what he meant: he wanted Onesimus to testify as a witness. Justice in the Roman Empire was brutal and swift—but there were proper law courts, with evidence presented, plots revealed, and motives surmised. Onesimus could offer his eyewitness account of the murder of the dead master. Along with the other slave's knowledge and testimony, a good orator and counselor could have the men punished for the murder of a citizen. However, it was Roman law that a slave's testimony was only valid under torture, because it was believed that a slave would never tell the truth unless under physical duress.

The loyal slave before Onesimus was perfectly willing to undergo torture to ensure justice for his master. Onesimus had no reason to suffer.

"No...I saw nothing...I was just coming along..."

The slave reached out and grabbed his arm, holding him tight. "Yes, you did! With my testimony, it will be enough. Mine alone is not enough!"

Onesimus twisted out of the slave's grip and shoved him away. He turned to flee and ran smack against an enormous, burly, leather-clad hulk. Large, strong hands grasped Onesimus. He looked up into the face of a soldier. Or perhaps a hired gladiator. He could not move.

"You got the other one, Rufus?" his captor barked. Another large figure appeared out of the gloom holding the other slave. The men searched him and relieved him of his bag and the small pouch he wore inside his cloak.

"Domine, I...I..." Onesimus began. "I don't belong here!"

"You sure don't. This is the quartierre of Decorones Philodomus, and you are guilty of the murder of a nobleman."

25. Carcerum

Onesimus protested again, but it only earned him a cuff to the side of the head. His ears ringing, the two guards dragged the slaves back around the corner. The guard holding Onesimus spoke.

"Sergius! Where are you?"

A voice came from the darkness. "Here!"

"Go check the body. Make sure no one else is about. Wrap the body up and bring it along. Meet you back at the place."

Onesimus was in shock. Were these someone's personal guards? Off-duty soldiers trying to keep the peace?

They scurried along through a series of alleyways, the grip on Onesimus arm as strong as irons. After a while, they came to a stop before a large wooden door with a single torch burning beside it. The guard rapped on the door with his foot, and it opened without delay. They hurried inside and made their way down a stone hallway. Onesimus became aware of a stench: a mixture of body odor, urine, feces, and rotting food.

"Domine," he tried again, "I didn't do anything. I was just—"

"Shut up, slave! You were out after dark looking to rob noblemen, and you killed one!"

"No, I did—"

"Shut up!" He yelled and shoved him through a narrow doorway. Onesimus fell, sliding on knees and palms on a dirt floor. The other slave tumbled in beside him. A loud crash signaled a heavy door closing behind them, and a metallic clank confirmed they were locked in the dank room.

Onesimus dropped down and rolled onto his back, breathing heavily. He was hardly able to believe it. After the warnings of Mouse, Marius, and Justus, here he was. He had stayed out after dark, in a sinister part of Rome, and now he was in a dark, damp cell, accused of the murder of a nobleman. To even *witness* the murder was a horror, but to be accused of it…

Surely he could not be found guilty. He was a slave, but he didn't murder the man, he was just in the wrong place at the wrong time. The other slave didn't commit murder either.

He was a slave, far from home, and knew no one here. Who could vouch for him? The tavern-keeper he spoke to? He probably wouldn't remember him. Mouse? Even if he could find him, he was just another slave who didn't really know Onesimus.

He rolled over and brushed up against a cold dark wall. He sat up, back against the bricks. He put his hands to his face.

It was not long ago that he was basking in freedom, sure that Artemis was shining goodwill upon him. Now, he was in the depths of despair, and Artemis had deserted him.

"Are you okay?"

Onesimus looked over but could not see the other slave in the darkness. He heard rustling of dry rushes on the ground.

"Yes." He took a breath. "Who are those men? Why are they accusing us of murder? I know you didn't do it. And you know I didn't—"

"It doesn't matter."

"How can it not matter? I know we're slaves, but don't they need some other proof? There are laws in Rome—"

"Yes," the slave said. "There are laws. But they won't help us." He sounded unnervingly calm.

"Because we are slaves? Not admissible evidence? But that goes for prosecution, too, doesn't it?"

"Not in this case." His tone was not some much calm as resigned.

"What is your name, brother?" Onesimus asked.

"It matters not."

Onesimus wanted to strangle him. What was all this mysterious talk? This was no Greek play—this was life and death! "What is going to happen to us?!"

The man sighed. "We'll be taken out tomorrow before a tribunal in the forum and accused of murder. Witnesses will testify, and then they will kill us by scourging and then a sword. Or send us to the Arena."

"But there *were* no witnesses—except us."

"Nevertheless, there will be witnesses."

"I saw no one."

"When Decorones Philodomus needs witnesses, they appear. With greased palms and purses full."

Onesimus said nothing. He had heard of such things, but didn't really believe them. Rome was *known* for law and order.

His companion sighed again. "The men who brought us here are the men who murdered my master. They work for Decorones Philodomus, who runs this whole sector."

They sat in silence. Onesimus didn't know how much time passed. It was all so unreal. He had the perfect plan, it was all going to be good, and then, it was all over.

"Why did they kill him?"

The man did not answer for so long that Onesimus thought he had fallen asleep.

"It's an old story. Decorones was a partner with my master in business, running everything in this sector—all the shops, brothels, lending, security, everything. After many years, Decorones wanted his own business, so my master set him up in part of the sector. But he wanted more, and began growing stronger and richer than was possible from just his subsector. My master suspected he was using bribes and doing illegal trading to take business away from my master. After some investigations, we were able to find evidence of the crimes: he had also been cheating with taxes and using government funds. He was censored and fined. His reputation was damaged, of course."

"But if he murdered your master and then accuses his slave, it will be obvious to everyone that it is a falsehood for revenge. He has a clear motive! No one will believe him!"

"I can tell by your accent that you're not from here. Decorones' brother-in-law is an Equestrian. He'll use his influence. Somehow, they will concoct a story that will pin it on me. My master's only survivor is a young daughter. After I am put to death, Decorones will buy the business and then pay off his brother-in-law. Both will become rich. My master is dead—nothing can bring him back. No one else will care enough to go up against an Equestrian.

"But…but…there must be *something* that can be done. Surely there are laws against politicians using such influence."

"Who do you think makes the laws and makes sure how they are carried out? Nothing can be done. It's over."

Onesimus was speechless.

"Best to accept it, brother. It is what Fortunas has given us."

26. Intercessio

He was startled awake by the door opening and slamming shut again. He sat up, blinking. There was a faint light coming from a small grill, high up on one wall, about a foot square. An airshaft perhaps. Was it dawn? Had he slept that long?

The cell was about ten feet square, with stone walls and a dirt floor strewn with dried rushes. His companion was sitting in a corner, arms crossed over his raised knees, head down. Beside the door was a board and a bucket. The board held a hunk of black bread and two cups of water sitting on the board. The bucket was empty—obviously intended for their toiletry.

He tore the bread in half and took one of the cups and sat down against a wall.

The other man didn't move. Onesimus shrugged and ate. The sustenance revived him, and the memories of last night began to clarify. He felt sick and set the rest of the bread down beside him.

He was far from home, in a strange city with strange customs. A dangerous city. It was bad enough to contemplate torture. But to be accused of murder and executed…how did this happen?

He prayed to Artemis. "Please, O great Artemis, hear me and deliver me. I will find a way to repay you. I will go back to Philemon and take whatever punishment comes. Even if it means being a stable slave for the rest of my life. I will give up any hope of freedom. Please deliver me."

He ate the rest of the bread and drank a little water. He tried again to get the other slave to speak, but he did not even get an acknowledgment. Onesimus spoke a few prayers to Jupiter, Juno, and Minerva, too, because he had heard that they were important in Rome. For good measure, he also prayed to the god of the Way, and then to his holy man, Iesous. He tried Mithras, too, for good luck, since these brigands were former soldiers or gladiators.

Time dragged on. He knew it was still the day after his arrival. He tried twice more to elicit discussion, or at least a word or two, to no avail. His thoughts cycled through abject fear, bargaining with the gods, anger and resentment, followed by brief periods of a strange sort of calm.

Eventually, the cell darkened. He could not see his hand in front of his face. How long would this misery last? Part of him wished it would just end. The anticipation was agony.

He was dozing when he was startled once again by the opening of the bolt. The door slammed open against the wall. A bright torch moved about, illuminating the cell, casting spastic shadows. As his eyes adjusted, he saw that the man holding the light was a well-dressed nobleman. Behind him at the door were two guards. The man stood before the slave in the corner.

"Well," the man barked. "I finally have you, you slave of a worm! Who is your companion?"

The slave uncurled himself from his position in the corner, pushed himself up, and looked at the speaker without expression.

The slave spoke. "He is no one. A chance passerby. You have me now, Thallus Dionysus. Do as you will."

The man laughed. "Oh, we will, we will. And you will suffer for your treachery."

"And you, someday, will pay for yours as a minion of Decorones Philodemus."

Onesimus cringed at the boldness of the slave, wondering if the man would strike him.

"Probably so." He smiled, an arrogant grimace. "But not today. Or any time soon."

The slave nodded with composure. "As for this man, he is not a companion. Just a poor slave who happened to be in the wrong place at the wrong time."

The man with the torch raised his eyebrows and looked at Onesimus, then back to the slave. "Indeed? I suspect he is an accomplice you are trying to protect? Why should I believe you?"

"Because it is true. I have never seen him before. He is a foreign slave on a mission for his master, visiting an Equestrian here who is his master's cousin."

None of that was true. They had not talked of why Onesimus was here.

The man's eyes turned on Onesimus. "What is your name, slave?"

Onesimus ducked his head. "Onesimus, domine. From…Ephesus, on an errand for my master."

The man snorted. "Well, your accent certainly shows you are no Roman. What's worse than a conniving Roman slave? A conniving barbarian slave! Who is the Senator?"

"Let him go, Thallus," the other slave repeated. "He is innocent. I will confess to the murder of my master. I am ready to end this story."

Onesimus was shocked. Why did he admit to something he did not do? More than that, why would he try to save Onesimus?

"No. He saw the whole thing."

"He didn't see anything except a scuffle, he doesn't know any of us, and he is a single slave."

Thallus stood, considering the slave before him. He turned once more to look at Onesimus. "Why were you out in the sector, and what did you see?"

"I saw nothing, domine. I—I was lost, it's my first time here. Was trying to find the Subura and got lost. I saw some men fighting, then this slave came upon me, and then we were brought here."

Thallus narrowed his eyes. "Rufus?"

One of the guards behind him spoke. "We chased after the slave. When we found him, this one was with him. He had a bag and a pouch with a good amount of coins."

"When you first encountered our enemy, who was with him?"

"Just his slave, Thallus."

The slave spoke again. "Thallus, if you keep him, then you have two slaves to deal with as witnesses. You know what that means. Let him go, you have one. Who will confess."

Thallus laughed. "Ha! You were always a clever one, if a troublemaker. One slave makes things easier. But why do you want to save him? Quite suspicious."

The slave shrugged. "A last act on my part for a fellow slave, hoping that Artemis will take note and grant me strength and peace at the end."

"Hm." Thallus stood, thinking. "Rufus?" he said again.

"The slave is obviously from the Provinces. And if there is a connection with another Equestrian…"

"I'm inclined to kill him and dump his body in the Tiber. Who would care?"

The slave spoke again. "Because when you put me on the stand to confess, I will also tell of this slave and the Equestrian. And you can't stop me once I am on the stand. If you don't use me as a witness, then your case is weak—and you have motive."

Thallus laughed. "Such boldness in the face of your coming torture. I will relish the world without you and your worm of a master in it."

Onesimus held his breath.

"Maybe I shall free this inopportune slave," Thallus said. "Perhaps a bit of mercy on my part will encourage the gods to be gentle with me when it is my turn."

He turned on Onesimus fiercely. "I do not have to tell you that if you even mention any of this to anyone, I will find you, and you will die an excruciating death.

Onesimus did not doubt it. "I...have no reason...I'm a visitor and just want to finish my—"

"Very well." He turned to the guards. "Throw this nobody out on the streets."

One of the guards brushed past Thallus and yanked Onesimus up by the arm, pulled him out the door and down the hall. The large wooden door was flung open, and Onesimus was shoved, with more violence than necessary, out the door and into the street. Onesimus fell to his hands and knees as the door slammed shut behind him.

He could hardly believe his fortune. Artemis had saved him.

He rose to his feet, lightheaded from lack of sleep and food. He looked around, and his elation turned to fear. Here he was again, in a dark alley, in Rome, at night.

A nobody, just as Thallus had said.

EPISTOLE ETA

To Giarri

Peace to you. I pray for your well-being every day and look forward to each letter.

My cough has remained the same, and the winter has turned even colder; this cell holds no warmth. Our brother, the guard, brought me a small candle to use for heat, but he warned me not to use it unless he was on duty.

Your questions have caused me to ponder our human ability to deceive ourselves. True, like many young men, I alternated between being arrogant and feeling worthless. When things went well, I felt important and intelligent. When bad things happened, I felt useless (no, my humor has not left me yet). So many are buffeted to and fro upon the earth by the winds of chance! All the while chalking it up to whether the gods were paying attention to us or not; whether they were happy with us, or not.

I had never told you any of these details about my first Rome odyssey. I never spoke to anyone about it, except in a general way to explain how I came to be what I am. I never discussed the things I did and the pain I experienced—and the pain I caused others.

Why? Because I was ashamed. I know that should not have mattered, but it did. I am sure that comes as a surprise to you. So I will share that story, in all its ugliness, and you shall finally know the distance I have traveled.

For now, though, it is getting dark, and I can hardly see to sign this letter.

My great joy lies in you, my brother, and all those with you. Greet them all for me.

27. Paulus

He began to run, despite the risk of tripping. His heart was pounding. He was covered in sweat. Why had he not found a place to stay as soon as he arrived in Rome? How foolish he was to try to find Paulus before securing a place to stay. This is not the little town of Colossae. This is Rome. Someone could murder him for his money and no one would blink an eye. Thallus wasn't even worried he might try to tell someone about the murder. Who would believe a "barbarian slave"?

At a crossing with a larger road, he stopped. He had no idea where he had run to. Panting, he squinted in the dark. It appeared that the road went uphill to the left. His eyes adjusted a little more, and he saw that it was not completely dark yet—it was probably not long after dusk, though he had seen no one on the roads.

The road to his right went downhill in the direction that had to be towards the Subura. He began walking. As he proceeded, he tried praying to Romulus, wondering if one of the founding gods of Rome would hear him as a foreigner. He praised his great power and the beauty and splendor and might that he had given to Rome. He told the god that he also wanted to be a Roman citizen, and that he would offer a sacrifice and bring some small measure of glory to Romulus as he could, if only Romulus would help him.

He trailed off in the middle of his words. Why would the god of Rome listen to an insignificant slave from a faraway land? A nobody.

Two men were approaching him, and he tensed up. He stopped, unsure what to do. As they drew closer, he saw they were slaves. One called out to him.

"Brother, are you lost? It's not good to be out at dark alone."

He did not seem unfriendly, though Onesimus was still wary. "I was headed to the *Black Swan*, but I am new here, and yes, I'm lost."

"The *Black Swan*? Well, you've most surely taken a wrong path. It is not near, and the path back is not safe." He pointed back the way Onesimus had come. "Go back until you reach a curve in the road, next to a—"

"Your pardon, but I'm merely looking for a place to stay. It doesn't have to be the *Black Swan*."

"Well, we can help with that! We're headed back to our master's tavern, *The Phoenix*, and you're welcome to come along. The master will appreciate the business, and there's safety in numbers."

Onesimus heaved a sigh of relief. Finally, something encouraging. He joined the two and learned that the small tavern was located in the Subura, and had a reputation of being one of the quieter taverns. Their master was an older man, with grown children who had left for other parts of Italia. He and his wife, along with three slaves, ran the place. They had two rooms for rent, and both were empty this night. Onesimus told them he was on a journey from Corinth, on a mission for his master.

Fifteen minutes more brought them to an inconspicuous entrance set in the wall between two large tenement buildings. Inside, the tavern had six tables in the main room, but there were only three patrons at the moment. The master seemed happy to see Onesimus—not surprising considering his sparse business.

With dismay, Onesimus realized that his bag and pouch were gone. The money, the change of clothes, and a bit of food from yesterday afternoon: gone. All he had were the clothes he was wearing and the coins hidden in his cloak as Mouse had suggested. It would be enough for a couple of nights, but that was it. He felt a sickening in his stomach. Now he *had* to find Paulus, and hope it went well, or he would be in a serious predicament.

He bartered with the proprietor for a meal and lodging, ate a quick dinner of fish soup, bread, and watered wine. It tasted like a noble feast. Sated and relaxed, he retired to one of the small, plain rooms and fell into a deep asleep.

*

He woke to light streaming in through an uncovered opening that served as a window, and the noise of people talking, laughing, and shouting in the street below. The city had come back alive: teachers were beginning their classes, merchants were starting to ply their wares, freedpersons were hurrying to their businesses, and slaves were running errands.

Onesimus dressed and went downstairs. He ate a plain breakfast of bread and honeycomb served by a sleepy-eyed female slave. He asked for directions to the main jail, which turned out to be not too far from the Forum, along the city wall to the northeast. With the events of the last two days fading, he set off with a light heart—though a bit chastened, he had to admit.

Even at this early hour, the Forum was a beehive of activity. Threading his way through the crowds, he marveled anew at this pinnacle of civilization as it played out among the architectural finery. Crossing through the crowds, he trudged up the Via Flaminia and to the northeast slope of the Capitoline Hill. He easily located a cluster of official-looking buildings that housed the prison. Approaching a guard, he asked about the Jew, Paulus of Tarsus. Once again, he was given the same gruff, unhelpful answer: the soldier did not know about any "dirty Jew." However, the guards stood aside to allow him to enter and check with a clerk, if he wished.

The clerk—a slave—was more friendly. After looking through some scrolls and tablets, he found information that had to be about Paulus: a Jewish man, under house arrest, awaiting an audience with the Emperor. Onesimus was relieved that he was still in Rome—prisoners did not stay in prisons for long. But if Paulus had appealed his case to the Emperor, he could be waiting a long time. Every Roman citizen had the right of appeal, but every case was heard at the Emperor's pleasure. It could be years.

After more research through the records, the clerk gave him the location and directions to the house, which was located in the Jewish sector. Onesimus was out on the streets again, headed to an area called the Trastevere. It was not too far, he was assured.

He went back past the Forum, curved around the base of the Capitoline Hill, then out of the city gate and crossed the bridge over the River. Following the road east and then south, he arrived at a neighborhood that had no marbled edifices and no temples. In fact, there seemed to be no public buildings of any kind. Most structures were made of wood that seemed thrown together. Some looked quite unsafe.

There were people in the streets, but they looked and dressed differently than the other Romans. Still, there were smiles, conversations, and boys in the street playing trigon. Following the directions given to him, he found his way into a quiet, small piazza, surrounded by dun-colored buildings of wood and daub. Flowers in pots sat in front of the doors. A small, old, wooden domus, with yellow trim and a large door, caught his attention. A Roman soldier sat outside, looking bored and sleepy in the warming day.

"Excuse me, domine, I have a message from my master, a nobleman in Corinth, for Paulus. Is this where he stays?"

"Go on," the soldier drawled, jerking his thumb towards the large door.

Onesimus went to the door and knocked. After a few moments, a man appeared at the door. He did not look Jewish: he was far older than Onesimus had pictured. "Yes?"

"Paulus?"

"Upstairs." He pointed behind him to a narrow flight. He opened the door all the way and stood aside to allow Onesimus to pass. The musty odor of an ancient house met his nostrils. The narrow stairs creaked as if in protest. At the top was a small landing and a door. The door looked new—a recent addition. The building had probably been a single family domus in the past, which had been turned into a tenement by adding doors and partitions, hastily and poorly constructed for a bare minimum of privacy.

Onesimus stood before the small door. He had rehearsed this first speech many times. He had to find a way into the good graces of Paulus and get him to agree to act as his advocate. Without money, his other options had faded.

He tapped on the thin wooden door.

"Come." A muffled voice. Onesimus opened the door slowly and peered into a small, dim room. There was only one window, which was partly shuttered. The smell of soot was strong. As his eyes adjusted, he saw a plain bed, a small desk, and a single chair. Another door, partially open, led to another room that seemed even smaller.

The desk held a bowl of bread, three or four oil lamps, and many rolls of parchment. Sitting at the desk, with a stilus in hand, was a small, stocky man with a black and grey beard. His hair was the same color and texture as his beard, though it was thinning on top. He appeared somewhat unkempt. The face gazing at him was olive-colored, with a large nose, a full mouth, and piercing eyes. The lines on the face and the creasing of the brow lent an air of sadness and suffering. But the man was smiling.

"Are you going to stand in the doorway or come in?"

"Oh, uh, yes, domine." He stepped in and closed the door behind him. Now that he was here, in front of Paulus, he was stricken dumb. Despite the man's stature, his presence filled the room. He was scared and did not know why.

Paulus set the stilus down carefully.

"Are you mute? What is it? Does the guard want to use the latrine again and continues to insist I accompany him, so I do not escape?"

Onesimus laughed nervously. "No, no, domine…no…I—I have come a long way."

Paulus sat back in his chair. "Have you? That makes two of us." He tilted his head to one side. "Who sent you?"

"My master is Quintus, Philemon Scaptius, and he—"

Paulus raised his eyebrows and sat up straight. "Philemon? Indeed?"

"Yes, domine."

"You have come from Colossae?"

"Yes. My name is Onesimus."

Paulus laughed. "Of course it is. I have been expecting you."

28. Servus

"You…were expecting me?" Onesimus' mind was racing. Could a message from Philemon have gotten here this quickly? Why would Philemon even suspect he'd go to Paulus? Did Justus send a message? How could it have arrived before him?

Paulus was still smiling at him, as if he had a secret joke. "Well, I didn't know for sure. But I suspected that someone from one of the ekklesia in Asian Minor would send someone to help me, once they heard I was in prison." He spread his hands wide. "I am not surprised it is Philemon who sent me a 'useful' servant to assist my work." He laughed a dry crackle at his pun. Onesimus forced a smiled and relaxed.

Paulus believed Philemon had sent Onesimus, as a loan, to help Paulus while he was in prison.

"Yes," Onesimus replied. "Here I am."

Perhaps he should see where this leads.

"I would offer you a seat," Paulus continued, "but, as you can see, the accommodations provided by the Empire are quite sparse." He indicated the small room. "How was your journey?"

"It was uneventful, domine," Onesimus said, shifting his feet. "I came by way of Corinth. Gaius Titius Justus sends his greetings, and offers any help you might need."

"Justus?! It is good to hear that name. He is well?"

"Yes, domine, he is well."

Paulus leaned forward. "First things first, my boy: stop calling me domine—there is only one domine, blessed be his name, and I am certainly no earthly domine—I don't own a single pebble of land nor a single slave!" He laughed and stood up. He was a bit taller than Onesimus had thought, though still a short man. One of his eyes was rather cloudy. Still, the unique presence about him made him seem bigger. Like when Onesimus had seen that proconsul from Rome who had traveled through Colossae, speaking at the rostrum. Maybe it was his demeanor; so full of confidence and gravitas. Yet he did not display the dismissive and superior attitude of so many nobles. He was charismatic, and Onesimus could already see why people were drawn to him.

"Have you eaten, my boy?"

"No, domi—sorry."

"Address me as 'Paulus.' I have not eaten yet, and it's close enough to lunchtime. Would you be so kind as to go down to the shop on the corner, just to the left of the piazza. We can eat and talk. Philip is the proprietor—and a follower of the Way." Paulus stopped and focused his good eye on Onesimus. "You are a follower?"

Onesimus hesitated. He could say yes, but his knowledge of the Way was so slight he feared it would belie him. "No, I am not…Paulus. I have attended the *ekklesia* only a few times, and I learned a good bit at the home of Justus, but I do not know of it as I would like." Tell the truth, but show an interest and openness to this strange religion or philosophy to get on his good side.

"Ah, well, you have come to the right place. That at least, I can do: teach. First, however, lunch." He turned to the desk and began rummaging through the scrolls. "I have some coins here somewhere…"

"Oh, I have money from Philemon for us." It was out of his mouth before he remembered that he had lost almost all of it.

Paulus turned. "Philemon sent money as well? How generous."

Onesimus felt his face redden. "He did. But…but I only have a small amount left. I…I got lost last night and was robbed. All that is left is what was in my cloak."

Paulus' face took on a kind look. "Ah, my boy, what a terror it must have been! Were you hurt?"

"No, no. Just…treated roughly. And afraid. But I am fine." *Tell him!* he said to himself. It might garner more sympathy.

"Well, that is good. Rome can be dangerous. The money is no matter, I have many who supply for my needs." Paulus shook his head. "What a fine brother is Philemon. I do not like taking money for my work, but, on the other hand, it is right for those who have been blessed by riches to help those who labor in the work. Don't muzzle the ox, eh?"

Onesimus didn't know what any of that meant, but he managed a smile and a nod. Paulus told him that Philip served a wonderful fish soup this time of year, so he should purchase two bowls and some bread.

Onesimus took the money and headed out. He was surprised that Paulus would so easily give money to a slave he'd never met. On the other hand, he thought he'd been sent to assist him. Still, rather trusting in this dangerous world. That could work in Onesimus' favor, too.

Deposit the shock of their initial encounter, Onesimus began to feel good. If he just showed up and told Paulus his story, he'd be hearing it cold. Who knows how he would have reacted? This way, Onesimus could let Paulus get to know him, and maybe he'd be more willing to act as an advocate. Likewise, it gave Onesimus time to discern the character of Paulus. If he did not think it would go well, he could easily plan an escape. It would also give him time to figure out how to amass some money.

Yes, Artemis was still leading him, after all.

29. Opus

Onesimus made his way back down the rickety stairs and out into the piazza. He was proud of himself for not just blurting out his practiced story. His plan had been a good one, but the one flaw was that Paulus might immediately have yelled for the guard because a runaway slave—belonging to his friend!—had just shown up.

But this way—thanks to Artemis—will give him more time to determine Paulus' character and person. After a time, it should be easy to know whether he can broach the subject of advocacy, or take off north.

He found Philip's shop and purchased the food. The shop owner seemed eager to help Onesimus once he knew Paulus had sent him. He marveled for a moment at how both Paulus and this shopkeeper treated him more like a freedman than a slave.

Back in Paulus' room, he insisted that Onesimus take his chair as they ate, while Paulus reclined on the bed. Onesimus argued, but Paulus insisted. As they ate, Paulus described the work he was doing in Rome. Onesimus was taken aback, for Paulus was not really "working"—he was offering services free of charge and relying on help and donations of others. This might make it difficult for Onesimus to procure a money cache, should that be necessary. If Paulus allowed him to handle money, he should be able to skim some of the top. If he had to, maybe he could do some work to earn some money.

Paulus had been arrested in Jerusalem for sedition following accusations from Jewish leaders. Since he was a Roman citizen, he appealed to the Emperor and was waiting for an audience. He had to pay for his own lodging and food while under house arrest, and deal with an ever-present soldier out front, but he said it wasn't that bad. People from the Way brought him food, supplied clothing, and delivered messages. Others gave money to pay his rent and expenses.

It became clear, as Paulus spoke that he did not like this arrangement. He did have a skill: he was a worker of leather and canvas, and his method had been to find work at a shop in every town he visited, using his off-time to teach about the Way. Onesimus wondered, he was offering a service by teaching—why did he not like being paid for it?

"Paulus, is this not what traveling philosophers do? They go about, offering to teach, and in return, receive pay and lodging from willing students? Their work is teaching. Isn't that what you do?"

"Exactly right. You are obviously an intelligent and educated slave. Can Philemon really do without you?" He laughed in a short, cackling manner that Onesimus found charming. "That is exactly the problem. Our own writings and Roman society say that those who work in a temple or teaching should be supported by those who benefit from the work. This has been true of the Jews since ancient times, and still today, the priests at the Jerusalem Temple are supported by donations from Jewish people all over the Empire. But, as you say, everyone assumes that I am just one of many traveling teachers of the philosophies. Many of them are charlatans, as I am sure you know. Some of them teach *merely* to make easy money: they don't even subscribe to the beliefs! I cannot abide the thought that people might accuse me of doing this for the money. It is the *message* that matters."

It was clear he passionately believed what he was saying, and felt deeply about what he taught.

He took a bite of bread and chewed before he continued. "So, when I travel about teaching, I avoid being a 'proclaimers-for-hire' by plying my own trade. I refuse to let anything get in the way of the message I have been entrusted with! It is the message that has the power—not me, not the writings, not even my words."

Onesimus was not sure he understood all this, though he would learn that Paulus often talked like this, as if he did not choose his path, but was compelled to follow it. That wasn't particularly unusual—many spoke of the Fates determining their path in life. Yet this was a little different; he talked as if he had been commissioned, and even used the word "ambassador" sometimes. Again, the idea of mixing religion and philosophy, priesthood and politics, ethics and morals was strange.

Paulus sighed. "But, as you see, I have little choice in my present circumstances. So I accept the assistance because it is my task to get the message out, not to control how or what happens with it."

Onesimus frowned. "But you teach the philosophy to convince them and gain adherents, don't you?"

Paulus smiled. "Perhaps it is a subtle distinction. It is a mystery. I am called to proclaim the message, but god alone, blessed be his name, is the one who changes hearts and minds. That is not my doing."

Onesimus did not understand. How does a god change a person's heart and mind? Most gods were busy with their own lives and doings, and rarely became intimate with their followers—though they could be influenced to listen and help.

Paulus had changed the subject, describing his daily work in Rome. Since he believed Onesimus had been sent by Philemon to help him, Onesimus realized he was receiving an orientation to the work. Paulus had arrived many months ago and had asked all the Jewish leaders to meet with him. They had come to visit in groups and singly. At one time, it seemed, he had held importance or status among the Jews, but that his belief in the Way had caused him to lose his gravitas. That fit with Onesimus' encounter with Justus' neighbor in Corinth.

Paulus used words and titles that Onesimus had never heard: they sounded foreign. In any case, it seemed that Jewish leaders were willing to listen to Paulus' message, at first, maybe because of his past status. Some even wanted to hear more about the Way, and many eventually joined a local ekklesia.

"However," Paulus continued, "most of the Jewish leaders rejected me and my message, even calling me a troublemaker." This rejection seemed to hurt Paulus deeply, which made sense if he was once part of their religious leadership.

He also met with non-Jewish groups. The guards allowed Paulus freedom to invite anyone he wished to his domus. The meetings sounded like they consisted of Paulus teaching and argument about philosophy, beliefs, and religion. His eyes lit up when he described it, and Onesimus saw that he loved the debate.

He also mentioned that he worked in concert with the ekklesiai in town. Apparently, there were many ekklesiai in Rome, not just one, which should not have surprised Onesimus, considering the size of Rome.

Paulus' taught to gain new adherents, worked with the ekklesia for the same, and organizing assistance for people who needed food, money, work, shelter, and medical aid. He needed someone to help coordinate between the groups and individuals: Onesimus.

Despite his reservations, Onesimus found himself interested. He had always enjoyed organizing, setting goals, and working on projects, and this would involve that. Paulus' own enthusiasm was infectious. He had to remind himself that he was not here to serve Paulus, despite the fiction that had presented itself. He was a runaway slave trying to find a way to either get back to a better life, or run away for a better life.

Paulus told him that a man here in Rome, Epaenetus, had a slave called Philodemus who was arriving soon to bring a letter. He could take Onesimus with him on errands around the city, show him the domii where the ekklesiai met, as well as other locations that Onesimus would need know in order to assist Paulus.

"I assume you have been taught to write?"

"Yes, I have been trained to write in Greek and some Latin, and have performed that skill for Philemon for some years."

"Excellent! You are a god-send! I always have to borrow a scribe from someone, and they are not always available."

Onesimus was feeling good. He had a place to stay, food, and work. He would appear as a legitimate slave working in Rome. He could bide his time, take stock of Paulus, and keep his eyes and ears open. He could not take *too* long, for eventually some contact—a letter perhaps—between Paulus and Philemon might take place. Ultimately, he was sure, Artemis would show him the best path.

He felt a twinge of guilt for taking advantage of this passionate, well-meaning, and intelligent man. But, he told himself, he *was* helping him in return for food and shelter. They would both gain from the arrangement.

Paulus was still speaking. "There is an extra room next door that I sometimes use for meetings. You can sleep there. We'll arrange to have someone furnish a mattress and blanket. Will that serve?"

What a question to ask a slave! Onesimus was amused at this man, who seemed to have little regard for social distinctions and apparently moved among the wealthy, poor, slaves, and free with equal ease. When Paulus finally faced the powerful Emperor Nero, Onesimus could imagine him being just at ease as when he sat in this sparse room talking with Onesimus the slave.

By then, Onesimus would be long gone. One way or another.

30. PHILODEMUS

Philodemus soon arrived. He appeared to be about ten years older than Onesimus, looking like the typical Roman slave, except that his tunic was of a costly fabric. His master was obviously well-off and dressed his slaves accordingly. Not all masters did so, but Onesimus' experience, the ones who did were showing off: "Look! I am so rich, even my slaves dressed better than common people!"

Onesimus figured that the crowd of followers that Paulus had attracted were wealthy. That could help Onesimus' prospects. However, he mentioned that to Paulus a few days later and found out he was wrong. "Oh, no, my boy. Most of the Way, like most Jews, are from the lowest class, freedpersons, or slaves. Very few are of noble birth. But I see how you could be confused, since usually in the homes of the wealthy we meet. Those are the only homes with a large enough gathering areas. And they are most happy to provide." That seemed strange to Onesimus—the wealthy did not have the poor in their homes except for business. Though Philemon did, he reminded himself.

Paulus asked Philodemus if he would be willing to take Onesimus to see the shops of Demophilus, Valens, Lucius, and the home of Tryphena and Tryphosa, who had an ekklesia in their home. "And the villa of Valeria—if there is time," he added.

"Happy to do so! I have to run errands to Valen's shop in the Forum, and then deliver a scroll from Apion's house back to Epaenetus. We'll have a fine tour!" Philodemus was gregarious and open, though Onesimus detected a quite intelligence behind it all, as well as a highly-educated mind.

The two slaves left the small domus and headed north along the Tiber to the bridge. Onesimus felt like his head was spinning—so much had happened in so short a time. Here he was, working for Paulus and getting a tour of Rome! He needed time to sit and think about his plan, his steps, and his 'story.' It must be sound, especially as he spent more and more time with Paulus.

But for now, he was going to enjoy his first real day in Rome. As they crossed the Tiber, flowing with heavy foot traffic, Onesimus spotted an island in the middle of the river. Philodemus saw him looking.

"The island is called the Insula Inter-Duos-Pontes. It's a place of healing; that building is a temple to Asklepius. It's been there for two hundred years, I think. Maybe longer."

Onesimus nodded. "There was a large temple to Asklepius in Corinth."

"Yes, yes. Idols everywhere. False idols, false hopes."

Onesimus was still a bit shocked that these followers of the Way were atheists, just like the Jews. How could someone reject *all* the gods: Roman, Greek, and foreign?

Philodemus chuckled. "I see from your expression you are shocked. Which makes me think you are either not a follower of the Way, or are new to it."

"I am not a follower, though I attended Philemon's ekklesia." Only once, but there was no need to share that. "I don't really know a lot."

"Well, you probably know we focus on one god. Some of our number think that the other gods *do* exist, but as lesser creatures, and therefore not worthy of worship. Others say they do not exist at all."

So not all of the Way were atheists. "What of Iesous? At first, I thought he was a god, too, but it seems he's more of a high priest?"

"Not exactly. Perhaps in some ways."

"But why do you pray to a high priest then? Is it like some who pray to Gaius Julius as a god?"

"Not really. Our god sent Iesous as a teacher, but more than that, as his representative. An anointed representative. God in the flesh."

"Like Hercules?"

"Again, similar, but different. I can't say I understand it fully. Paulus can explain it best. He has a mind for those things."

"Well, what does Paulus think about the other gods?"

"I'm not sure." Philodemus tilted his head, thinking. "I've heard him mention them. My guess is that he thinks they might exist. But I can't say for sure."

"But if they do exist, why should they not be worshiped since they are greater than humans?"

"Because the one god created and sustains everything. When I began to understand that, I realized the other gods were worthless: they are petty, childish, revengeful, and selfish." Philodemus turned and looked at Onesimus. "I hope I don't offend you. I imagine you worship Artemis, at least."

Of course I do. She's the reason I am here.

"It's a bit shocking to hear someone say that the gods and goddesses do not exist. To say you won't worship them is one thing, but—"

"I know, I know. To suggest that the very gods who built and protect Rome are mere fictions—yes, it is quite a statement." Philodemus seemed to enjoy being provocative. Onesimus enjoyed his forthrightness.

They had reached the opposite shore of the Tiber, where Philodemus turned them towards the Forum.

Philodemus continued, now with a bit softer tone. "I was quite disturbed when I first began listening to the message of the Way. My parents worshiped the gods. Almost everyone I knew did. But as I learned more, and experienced more, I came to understand. It rang true."

"Rang true?"

"Yes. It made more sense of life than anything else I had heard."

"How can you just reject what everyone else says is the truth? Doesn't that tell you it must not be true?"

"It's not everyone. The Jews have never believed in those gods; it was always the same god."

"The Jews and the Way are the same?"

"No, but there are a lot of similarities. We worship the same god, believe the same things about the world. Worship him in similar ways."

"Ok, but everyone knows how strange the Jews are."

"Perhaps. But they are not the only ones who have a different view. The Egyptians worship *different* gods. Even the barbarians, I am told, worship in a different way. Have you read Gaius Julius' writings about the barbarian tribes he encountered in Gaul?"

Onesimus had not, though he'd heard of *Commentarii de Bello Gallico*. Anyone who was educated did.

"He described their gods, but then found similarities with our gods and just assumed they were the same as ours. I asked a Gallic slave I knew who used to work in the Forum. He told me that his people worshiped only one god as the source of all things, those other 'gods' were merely manifestations of their one god—or one source, as he called him."

"Okay, but how is that different than the Greek gods being the same as the Roman gods with different names. Jupiter is Zeus; Artemis is Diana. They're the same."

"Are they? Or did the Romans just assimilate them to what they already knew?"

Onesimus did not know what to say to that. How did anyone know about the gods?

"Britannia, as Gaius Julius called it, has people that he named the Keltoi. They believed in an afterlife for all people, more similar to the Jews and the people of the Way than Greek and Romans."

They had reached the Forum now, and Philodemus waved his hand at the all the structures. "So you see, the gods in all these Temples are not the final word."

Onesimus nodded. He had always thought of himself as well-educated because of the training Philemon had given him, but this man—this *slave*—talked like a scholar or a philosopher. Onesimus asked him about it, and Philodemus said it was not uncommon in Rome. Philodemus had been a city slave for the government of Rome before he was sold to Epaenetus. He had worked for one of the city *aediles* and then for a consul. Not only had they educated him so that he could perform the functions required, but he learned a great deal during his time working for the government officials.

"Ah, here we are," Philodemus said. "Valen's shop."

The shop was a tiny cubicle, squeezed between a large bakery and a butcher's shop. As they waited for the proprietor to finish with a customer, Onesimus learned that Valens was a freedman who made and repaired leather goods. Philodemus introduced Onesimus, then they began to deal with the business at hand. As they talked, Onesimus wondered about Valens' past. How had he become free? How did he choose leatherworking as a profession—was that the skill he did for his master? Onesimus didn't have any such manual skills, of course, but were his skills something could translate into the work of a freedman?

Once finished with Valens, Philodemus took Onesimus past the Circus Maximus to the Aventine Hill. Located on the lower slopes was a fine domus that belonged to Demophilus, another tradesman. After a brief visit with his vilici, they headed up and over to the Via Ostiensis and along the Via Sacra, away from the Forum. Onesimus wanted to pinch himself—he had heard the names of these streets and dreamed of walking them for so long.

Here, in between the Esquiline Hill and the Caelian Hill, sat a cluster of lower class domii, tenements, and shops. Philodemus pointed out a small food shop, now shuttered up, that he said belonged to Lucius. For now, they would head back down past the Forum and up to the Quirinal Hill. There, Philodemus said, was the fine home of Apion, a city consul, and one of the wealthiest and most noble of the Way here in Rome.

Once they arrived, high above the city at the top of the hill, Onesimus waited in the street as Philodemus went inside to obtain a document from one of Apion's numerous slaves. The domus was magnificent, but what caught Onesimus' eye was the view. He could see across the top of the city wall to a large, flat area surrounded on three sides by a bend in the Tiber River, beyond which was a bridge.

Philedomus returned. "Ah, yes, quite a view. That flat area is the Campus Martius. The city holds elections there."

"And that huge bridge?"

"That's the Via Triumphalis, and part of the route taken into the city by the heroes of Rome deemed worthy of an honored procession and parade."

Onesimus tried to imagine the great Julius returning in triumph across that bridge, a massive Roman force behind him.

They left the Quirinal area and walked down towards the Forum. It was now late afternoon, and they stopped and bought some food at a stand. As they sat near a public fountain eating and talking, Onesimus asked Philodemus when he had become a follower of the Way. It might be useful information. Philodemus told him that it was not not long after his master did, which was about five years ago. He briefly related how his master had heard Paulus speaking somewhere.

After they finished eating, Philodemus took him to his master's house. It was near the Subura, and just hearing the name made Onesimus' stomach knot up. As they walked, Philodemus continued his story. His master had not required them to become adherents of the Way, as some masters do when they convert to a religion. He had invited them to the ekklesia and explained the religion and allowed discussion.

Philodemus' beliefs were strong, and Onesimus found his unbending commitment a bit disconcerting. He would have to be careful not to offend him, because Philodemus could be a valuable asset with his connections and knowledge of the city.

Once Onesimus knew the location of Epaenetus' domus, Philodemus offered to accompany him back to Paulus.

"I think I can find my way." He would have preferred the company and the guide, but he needed to know his way around—and not only to help Paulus.

"Tell me," Philodemus said.

Onesimus recited the directions without error. He thanked Philodemus and headed back to the Forum, across the bridge and south, walking rapidly.

He was determined that he would never be out after dusk again in Rome.

31. ERUDIOTIO

During the next few months, Onesimus became more comfortable with Rome, Paulus, and his work. At first, he experienced some trepidation. If something went wrong or someone suspected anything, he'd have to leave Rome quickly. But the work was enjoyable, and no one seemed to think anything about him was suspicious. It was not long before he quit thinking about it.

He found working with Paulus and Philodemus quite stimulating, and it seemed he was learning more than he ever had in his life. From Philodemus, he had found a friend (he must admit) who accepted him fully even though he did not follow the Way. In fact, Onesimus was hard-pressed to think of anyone in his life who had seen his value as Philodemus did. He appreciated and complimented his writing and reading skills, his knowledge of geography and the Empire, and even his cursory knowledge of philosophy and history. He did this despite the fact that Philodemus was more sophisticated than Onesimus. There was no ego, none of the rivalry among slaves of similar station. Onesimus found their friendship a true joy.

From Paulus, he learned about the history of the Jewish people, of which he had known nothing but scuttlebutt, which turned out was often wrong. The Jews were still an odd people with their one god, strange rituals, and food restrictions. But Onesimus also found them somewhat endearing.

He was surprised to learn that a lot of their strange rituals and actions of both the Jews and the people of the Way were not so different from those of the Roman religions and philosophies: fellowship meals, prayers, and some of the ethics and morals. The most confusing thing for him was that the Way could not seem to make up its mind whether it was a religion or a philosophy. The gods did not care much about the actions or deeds of a follower unless it affected the deities directly. They were powerful and didn't need humans, but would work with them (or against them) for a myriad of reasons. Therefore, it was worthwhile to stay on their good side. On the other hand, everyone knew that the philosophies discussed how one should live. Different philosophies had different approaches, but they were concerned with morals and ethics: "right living" as the Stoics called it.

Yet this god of the Way seemed to be concerned about how his followers lived, and his followers discussed morals and ethics like philosophers, but worshipped him like any other deity.

Onesimus could not make sense of it. Nor of how the people of the Way (and the Jews) focused *only* on their own god. Of course, a lot of people devoted themselves to a particular god or goddess, but they didn't ignore the others. Onesimus wondered if he got lonely since he did not consort with other gods or goddesses. Paulus told him that that was why this god created humans. He wanted something to nurture and share with, like a father wants a child or a whole family.

Paulus was fond of repeating that characteristic, but it was a weakness in Onesimus' mind. If he was so powerful, then why did he bother with humans? Zeus mostly stayed off by himself and rarely interfered, dealing only, for the most part, with other deities. Not this god of Paulus: he was like Zeus in his power, yet like a minor god in his interest in humans.

He was also still confused about Iesous. According to Paulus, the god himself had entered into our world *as a human*, which might have made sense had he come as a king or other powerful leader. But he'd been a poor man, traveling and teaching like an itinerant philosopher! The crux of it, though, was that he had been arrested and crucified. It was this that Onesimus thought was ridiculous. How could a god die? Why would he even allow his own arrest?! And where was the honor in following a god who had been humiliated and executed?

Still, Onesimus found these people engaging, and Paulus encouraged his questions and reactions. He enjoyed the intellectual stimulation and the patient manner in which Paulus taught. It appeared that the people of the Way enjoyed debating their beliefs, doctrines, and practices together with great passion—again, more like philosophy than religion. Onesimus asked Paulus if he thought the ideas became stronger through debate or weaker through questioning. Paulus told him that the Jewish scholars of the law had always engaged in such debates.

"It still sounds to me like a confusion between religion and philosophy."

Paulus smiled. "Think of it this way: our morals and ethics are based on god's nature and behavior. He is loyal, so we should practice loyalty; he keeps his word, so we should keep ours."

Onesimus had heard some of that from Justus, and he was educated enough to know that the gods often demanded certain actions from their followers, but it was almost always done to benefit the god or goddess.

"Okay, but what does the god gain from his follower being 'like' him?"

"He doesn't gain anything," Paulus said. "Since he is the creator and sustainer of everything, he is the best source of knowledge for how we *should* live."

Onesimus frowned. "Creator of all things" sounded like Zeus again. But Zeus wouldn't care if anyone acted "like" him or not.

Paulus continued. "If you wanted to know how the aqueducts bring water to Rome from the mountains, you'd ask a Roman engineer who works on them. He would tell you how it works, how it is supposed to work, and what to do if it isn't working."

"Okay," Onesimus replied, "I get that, it is not unlike many of the philosophers who argue that because the universe operates in a certain manner, humans would be well-advised to live by those rules."

Paulus nodded. "Yes."

"But why? Being so powerful, the creator of all, why does he care? Leave it to our philosophers to figure out."

"This is a good question," Paulus said, leaning forward in his chair. "Because god, blessed be his name, wants us to have a good life. And you say again, 'why?' Because we are more than just an aqueduct or a work of art. We are his children. And a true father loves, protects, disciplines, and wants the best for his children."

Paulus made sense, but Onesimus always left thinking that maybe these people were just confused. Which was often said about foreign religions.

Still, these people believed so fervently that they were willing to put up with ridicule, or even, in the case of Paulus, imprisonment and suffering. There was something attractive about that—standing boldly for what you believe.

Onesimus enjoyed being a scribe for Paulus. It was usually letters, dictated to Onesimus, to be sent to other believers around the Empire, or to ekklesia in some city or town. Paulus seemed to have been everywhere and know someone in each place. He even knew people in places he had never been!

Onesimus had always enjoyed writing, whether in Greek or Latin. He found pleasure preparing the papyri, sharpening the stilus, mixing of the ink, the careful manner in which one must dip the ink and form the letters, and the beauty of a finished product well done. Though he had studied some rhetoric under Philemon, he was learning more here. Paulus was quite a master at using techniques and structure in letters.

Rarely did Paulus ask someone solely to carry a letter and deliver it. The Romans had no postal system like the Persians had, except for government communications. Most of the scrolls of Paulus were delivered by someone traveling on business to the town of the recipient. Sometimes it was a slave on an errand. Back in Colossae, writers had to wait weeks or even a month to find someone to take a letter, but not in Rome! Rarely did Paulus have to wait more than a few days. The volume of traffic coming to and from the city was astonishing.

Thinking of Philemon gave him a twinge of anxiety. If anyone found out he had run away…

He wondered if he'd made a mistake in not telling Paulus the truth when he first arrived. Knowing him better now, he thought he might have been willing to be his advocate. Maybe not, though. He was already in trouble with the Empire, and he probably wouldn't want to risk getting entangled in any further legal issues.

He had plenty of time, though he realized that the longer he waited, the worse it made him look: he was deceiving everyone here, in a manner of speaking.

No matter. This was a good situation, and he was even earning a little money here and there when Paulus lent him out. Once he had enough saved up, he could always go north as he had planned. But no one here knew that he was a runaway, and no one in Colossae would ever suspect he was in Rome.

For now, this was perfect. He was almost living the life of a freedman, with the way Paulus treated him.

Artemis had truly smiled upon him, and there was no reason to think it would ever change.

32. PHILIPPIANS

Onesimus had been in Rome almost four months, but it felt like years. He had done so many errands for Paulus and others, and spent both work and leisure time with Philodemus, that he felt like he knew the city like the back of his hand. Sometimes he marveled at it. He had always dreamed of visiting Rome, and here he was, a resident! The reality was as good as the dream had been.

On a bright and sunny day in August—a sweltering day —Paulus told Onesimus he wanted his help on writing a lengthy and important letter. He had been thinking about it for a few days after he had received a communication from an ekklesia. He often worked that way: he would ponder and think and structure the letter in his head, then dictate it to Onesimus. Sometimes he spoke so fast that Onesimus had trouble keeping up. Onesimus had heard that many writers and poets did that, but it was impressive to behold. Rarely did Paulus ask him to change anything when he read it back—which made Onesimus happy, because it was a chore to scrape the papyrus and rewrite over the spot. Sometimes, though, Paulus had him write the first draft on a wax tablet, then, after Paulus had edited it, Onesimus would transfer it to a scroll.

This letter was to be long, and Paulus wanted to spend the afternoon working on it. Onesimus did some morning errands (mostly taking care of some personal needs for Paulus), then returned to their domus where they shared a brief meal of bread, cheese, and olives. Onesimus prepared the papyrus, ink, and the stilus. Paulus usually sat on his bed and dictated, but this time he stood, pacing as he spoke, a sign that this was an important letter for Paulus.

The first words revealed that the letter was to an ekklesia in the city of Philippi on the coast of Macedonia. Typical of all letter-writers, Paulus began with a thanksgiving, but Onesimus marveled at the length of it—it was as long as a standard letter! Most people just wrote, "I thank the gods for you." Not Paulus. He added prayers for the recipients, hints about what was coming in the letter, and his thoughts about the recipients and their god. It was almost poetic.

Paulus described the conditions of his imprisonment, and (as he often said), how being in prison actually helped him to further the message of his faith. Onesimus didn't understand that.

As he continued writing, now into the body of the letter, it struck Onesimus how joyful Paulus sounded. In spite of his restrictions, in spite of the fact that he might be put to death or sent into exile after the Emperor heard his case, and in spite of the constant Roman guard outside his home, he was so happy that he had been given this role by his god.

It was typical for freedpersons and citizens to act and speak a certain way to further their gravitas and honor. It was a sort of accepted manipulation. And, at first, that is what Onesimus thought Paulus was doing. But the more he worked for him, he saw that Paulus' motivation was sincerely for the honor of his god. He really didn't care for his own status—an unusual thing for a Roman! His attitude was more like some slaves he had known, the ones who truly wished to please their masters. Not the slaves who fawned over his master for their own gain, but a sincere slaves who gave of themselves because they truly loved their master. Onesimus had never understood that, either. But that was Paulus in relation to his god.

When Paulus paused to drink some watered wine, Onesimus asked him if he gained anything, beyond the satisfaction of a job well-done, for his dedication. Did he expect a reward?

Paulus laughed. "Oh, I suppose I do think of that on occasion—perhaps an award in the afterlife. But remember, my child, faith is not about running a race for a prize; it is about finishing the race, having run it to the best of one's ability."

"So that's why you work so hard? For a prize at the end?"

"Not primarily. We do not love and serve god because we hope to gain something. We love and serve Him because god is."

Onesimus had heard this language before. A strange grammatical construction, but it only meant "god exists." He pursed his lips. "I have heard you and others say that. But *all* the gods exist."

"Ah, but our god is the very *definition* of existence. He is the beginning and end. He is not just an 'example' of truth or the 'definer' of truth, he *is* truth. He made everything and sustains everything. If his attention drifted away for a mere moment, the entire cosmos would cease to exist."

This sounded like something a Greek or Roman philosopher might say, though they would not say it about any god, nor precisely in those terms. It was mysterious.

"Deep thoughts, eh, my child?" Paulus smiled. "Difficult to understand? So they should be. For, if this god is as we understand, then we should not be able to define him completely. The best we can do is approximate, trust that he knows all else, and follow."

This was another element of confusion for Onesimus, because *that* sounded like one of the mystery religions. The Way encompassed elements of religious piety, philosophic thought and ethics, and of the mysteries of the universe and being. Despite the oddness of it, Onesimus began to wonder if bringing everything together like that didn't make some sense. To weave all those disparate elements together.

"So you see?" Paul continued. "I worship god because he is god. Even if he allows me to be beheaded at the hand of the Romans. It matters not. He is the potter. I am a vessel of clay created by him. Can the potter not do whatever he wishes with the vessel he makes? Put it up on display, use it to hold his food or his excrement? Or smash it into pieces? Whatever, the vessel rejoices. Do you know why?"

Onesimus hesitated. The image of a clay pot, rejoicing because it gets used as a bedpan made him laugh. An interesting analogy. "Because…because the pot is happy to have a purpose in his creator's life? In his art?"

Paulus beamed. "Yes, my child. Very good. And this is not just any potter or even the greatest potter. He is the only potter. Therefore I say: I am happy to rejoice in doing his work…because god is. Now, let's get back to this letter."

As Onesimus continued writing, Paulus spoke, setting up the exposition of his argument. The members of this ekklesia were arguing about something. It was not clear to Onesimus what the argument was about, since he had not read the letter that Paulus had received from them. Paulus used his own circumstances to encourage them to live and think like he did—almost exactly what he had been saying to Onesimus a few moments earlier—so they would get along better.

Paulus had Onesimus read back the last section, then continued, now turning his focus on the anointed one, Iesous. Onesimus listened closely, because he was still confused about the role of Iesous.

Paulus described how every one of the Way in Philippi should think of themselves with humility. They should act together for the good of all the *ekklesia*. He dictated what seemed like a poem, or a song, though Onesimus had never heard it. He wondered if Paulus had composed it himself.

> *Think like this about yourselves,*
> *which was how the anointed Iesous thought:*
> *Though in the nature of God,*
> *He did not regard equality with God*
> *as something to be grasped and used for himself,*
>
> *But he emptied himself,*
> *taking on the nature of a slave,*
> *Becoming in the likeness of humans,*
> *He came in the form of a man.*
> *He humbled himself*
> *and became obedient to the point of death,*
> *even a death on a cross.*

Iesous took the form of a slave? A slave like himself? Onesimus knew that this Iesous had not been a slave, but a freedman. Yet, in some manner, he acted like a slave? Had an attitude of a slave through his service to others?

Artemis cared about slaves, but Onesimus was sure that the god would never take on the *role* of a slave. The idea seemed scandalous and improper. But it also moved him. A god who knew how it felt to be him?

If, as Paulus had said, people of the Way were to imitate Iesous, then did that mean that they also humbled themselves? Like a slave?

That made sense of why Paulus treated Onesimus—and everyone else—like he did. And why the other members of the Way treated Onesimus more like a brother than a slave.

Onesimus didn't like this idea. To be honest, he had become more and more drawn to this god and his ways: genuine, wise, and caring, yet also firm and powerful. And it did makes sense to bring together creation and the gods and life—but this was crazy—

"Onesimus? Is there a problem?" Onesimus realized that he had stopped listening and writing. He was staring at the papyrus in front of him, the stilus slack in his hand.

Philemon. Philippus. Justus. Marius. Mouse. The innocent slave in the prison, falsely accused of murder. All helping him. All serving him.

"My child, what is wrong?"

Onesimus turned to Paulus. "I…I don't feel too well… the heat…I need some air."

He dropped the stilus, and, rushed from the room. His heart was pounding. He was in a cold sweat. He felt trapped.

He stumbled down the stairs. Out into the piazza. Past the guard, who did not even glance at him. Onesimus looked back as he turned the corner to make sure he was not being followed.

He was going to be found out. A runaway slave. It would do no good to say, "I was going to ask Paulus to be my advocate." He hadn't, and two months had passed. He was a runaway.

Arrested. Tortured. Sent back to Philemon in total disgrace. Punished again—maybe even sold to the mines or to a galley.

He kept going, glancing behind him as he went. Almost running, he barely saw the buildings, streets, and the flowing crowds.

Feeling safer now, he stopped and caught his breath. Looking around, he saw he was on the Via Portuensis along the Tiber. He had gone south and was now on the opposite side of the river.

He told his heart to stop beating. He breathed slowly.

What happened back there?

He wasn't sure. Something was wrong, though. Very wrong.

His time was up. He needed to plan his escape and get out of Rome.

33. Dissonus

Onesimus sat down beside the road. He felt dizzy. He took deep breaths to try to calm his pounding heart. The world was spinning.

After a while—he was not sure how long—he became aware of his surroundings again, as if waking from a dream.

What made him think he needed to leave? Nothing had happened. Nothing had been revealed. What was wrong with him?

He thought back to the letter he had been writing. It had affected him. Was it that Paulus was happy no matter his circumstances, but Onesimus had never been? Paulus was delighted because he believed in this ridiculous god who became a commoner like a slave who sacrificed himself—

That was it. That's what bothered him. The idea of sacrifice.

Sacrificing animals to a god was one thing. Sacrificing your well-being or your life...no god deserves that.

Onesimus stood up, panic rising once again. In his mind, he was back in that dark cell in the Subura on his first night in Rome. The sinister shadows danced, like demons dancing in the fires of hell. A man burst into their cell to accuse them of murder. His life was over.

"Let him go, Thallus." That's what the other slave had said. "He's innocent. I'll confess to the murder."

The slave knew they were both going to die. If he had said nothing, he would have at least had someone with him. A chance—however slim—to plead their innocence. Two was better than one. At the least, he'd have company as he faced his fate.

Yet he had pleaded for Onesimus to be set free and took the blame. Why? Why would someone do that for a stranger?

Onesimus knew he did not deserve such a generous act. He was just a common slave who had stolen from his master and run away. Who lied to a fine Corinthian nobleman to get what he wanted, and was at this moment deceiving a good, sincere Jewish man for his own purposes.

That unknown slave had saved Onesimus' life. And since then, Onesimus had not given one thought to it. He could have tried to do something. He could have told the owner of the *Phoenix*, or, better yet, Paulus. But once saved, he didn't care. All that mattered was his own skin.

Just like Turia.

She cared only about saving herself, and the rest be damned—even her lover.

He sat for some time, paralyzed by this insight. He was selfish, self-focused, and concerned only for his safety, regardless of the effect on others.

Just like Turia—the one he had condemned so forcefully. He was the same.

Now what?

He knew. He needed to go back to Paulus. But what could he say?

He sighed, wiped a tear from his eye, and stood up. He turned and began to walk back to the domus.

*

"I…I'm not sure, Paulus. It wasn't the heat. I was confused. I had to go…think."

Paulus cocked his head. "Yes?"

Onesimus took a deep breath. Walking back to the domus, he began to feel better. He could not leave Rome yet; he had not stashed enough money. Moreover, he didn't need to go now. But he owed Paulus an explanation. An honest one.

Still, there was danger here. It would do no good to get himself thrown back in prison, sent to the mines, or put to death. That would not bring the other slave back.

"I had a thought that stunned me. And made me feel... terrible."

"Go on."

"How is it that...I mean, what..." Onesimus sat for a moment and collected thoughts. "When I first arrived in Rome, I got caught outside at night, trying to find where you were. I...I saw a murder in an alley in the Subura."

"Yes, I remember. Surely it was traumatic."

"Yes, but I have seen plenty of deaths. I did not tell you the entire story. The murdered man's slave was there, too, and he asked me to go with him, he...he wanted me to testify with him against the murderers. But we were captured by them and put in a cell. They accused us of the murders and were going to have us brought up before the court."

"Onesimus, my child! That must have been terrifying."

"But the slave told them I had nothing to do with it, and told them that he would confess if they would let me go. Because I was innocent."

Paulus sat back on the bed and nodded. "But he did not commit this murder?"

"No. I am sure of it."

"And you knew, in order to testify, you would be tortured, as the Roman law holds."

Onesimus nodded.

"And? What happened?"

"I...I don't know. They let me go and I...I ran away. I was afraid. I never did anything about it or told anyone."

Paulus face softened. "Ah. And now you are ashamed that you did not stay to testify or at least, later, try to help save the slave?"

Onesimus sighed. "Yes, but—"

Paulus interrupted gently. "A perfectly natural response, and one that surely saved you. I think the Roman practice is barbaric. Many slaves, under torture, would say anything to make it stop."

"I…know. But—" Onesimus was at a loss as to what else to say.

"Do you think it would have been noble to come forward and testify? Perhaps, but you really don't know anything about facts or the people involved. Maybe the slave *was* lying. Maybe he arranged to have his master killed. I would believe anything in this city. Even if he was truthful, who knows? He was going to die either way, as tragic as it is."

"I understand. I…I can forgive myself for running in the heat of the moment, for wanting to never think of it again. But…"

Paulus waited. Onesimus took a few breaths. "You spoke earlier how you—the followers of the Way—how you look to your god, your god and Iesous, as an example of how to live."

"Yes, true."

"When you were dictating the letter, you said that Iesous was willing to sacrifice himself for others, even to the point of dying on a cross, despite the fact that he was innocent of the charges of insurrection. Doesn't that mean that I should be willing to be tortured if it would help someone else?"

Paulus smiled, and Onesimus saw a face filled with both love and amusement. "Well. If you were a believer of the Way, you would be called upon to sacrifice for others should the situation arise. Self-sacrifice is part of the character of the followers of the Way, because it is a characteristic of our god."

Onesimus was silent, and sat for a moment before Paulus continued.

"But, my child, believing what is right and having the strength to do it are two different things. We might know what is right, but are too weak to do it. But god's grace is ours even when we fail. *Especially* when we fail, for he knows how difficult it can be for us at times. He was tortured and suffering himself!"

Self-sacrifice was a Roman virtue, too, in the right circumstances. For a Roman to give himself up in a noble cause was praised. But self-humiliation and humbleness were *not* Roman virtues, yet the people of the Way seemed to revel in it. Like the humility a proper slave would feel, to submit himself to his master's work and well-being.

He knew that the ideal Roman slave was the one who loved his master and whose goals were his master's goals. The slave who would give his life for his master was the noblest slave!

Onesimus had never been that kind of slave. Which might be understandable, but Onesimus had not acted with any more honor than a master of slaves. He was *not* innocent. He stole money, ran away, and lied to Justus, Marius, Philodemus, and Paulus. Just like Turia had used him and then betrayed him.

He could not tell Paulus the truth now. In fact, by opening up to Paulus now he had endeared himself to the dear man all the more. Which was good for his plans.

Did that make him even worse than Turia? Turia betrayed another thief. Onesimus was betraying good, kind people.

Onesimus took up the stilus. "Yes. That makes sense. Thank you. I'm ready to continue writing. I am sorry."

"No need for apologies. These struggles we have are important. It is why I delight in my calling. Know that I forgive you. And I will pray for god to forgive you, too. If that matters to you."

It made him feel worse.

EPISTOLE THETA

To Giarri

Peace to you, my brother. What little news I have of the Empire and the Provinces does not sound good. I hope you and the rest are safe. You are always in my prayers, of course.

I had a bout with a terrible illness, about three days if I remember right. I could not eat, and I got quite weak. However, some good did come of it: they brought me a new, thick blanket. I suppose they do not want me to die before they put me to death. Yes, I jest, and perhaps they only intend to exile me. I still do not know when I will appear again before Tertillus. I do believe it will be to hear my fate, and not just another interrogation.

My illness has left me confused as to what I told you in my last few letters about my time in Rome. It was such a mix of joy, revelation, and shame.

Now, so many are dead. The purge during Nero was terrible, though nothing compared to Domitian's reign. And the earthquake in 61—or was it 64? I cannot recall—took the life of my dear, dear friend. We had such a good time working together, attending the races, discussing philosophies, and sharing stories of our lives. Hearing of his death was almost as painful as that of my only child.

A shameful time for me, but also a time of tremendous growth. It changed my life, yet my actions and internal torment stay with me to this day. Ah, if I had only been less blind.

But, of course, regrets are unnecessary and ungrateful. I cannot change the past, but more than that, striking bottom is often the only thing that gets our attention.

That part of the story will have to wait until later. I must sleep now—I am still quite weak.

As always, greet everyone there for me. Especially little Terentia, who I imagine is growing up quickly.

34. Circus

The winter came and the new year began. As winter began to wane, Rome became unusually warm. Not as bad as it had been in August, but the public fountains were mobbed. Paulus was a kind master and only sent Onesimus out on errands in the morning and late afternoon.

As time wore on, his fondness had grown for Paulus, Philodemus, and the others—both slave and free. They were an unusual group of people. Though they ate, lived, worked, and enjoyed life like other Romans, there was something intriguing about them. They had a passion and an excitement about life, and, as much as Onesimus wanted to deny it, it was because of their philosophy-religion. It did not seem to matter whether they were a citizen, a freedperson, a slave, or a prisoner.

This attitude was similar to some Romans who lived for "the spirit of Rome." These people proclaimed that the meaning and purpose of the Roman Empire was something unique in history, and it was exciting to be part of it. Yet Paulus and the others told him that, someday, the Roman Empire would end. Onesimus found that difficult to believe: what force could ever defeat something so powerful and pervasive? But Paulus insisted.

"The only thing that was eternal," he said, "is god, because everything else was created by him."

Maybe so, but Onesimus was sure that Rome would last forever.

Just after the new year his work, Paulus had approached him with another idea.

"Onesimus, you are doing an excellent job, and I am so grateful for your presence and help. I have another need that you could help me with—if you are comfortable doing it."

"Uh, sure, Paulus, if you think I can do it." What would make it uncomfortable?

"As you know, it is difficult for me to get permission to leave the house here. The chain of command takes time, though they rarely say no for anything in the city. One of the things I would do, if my freedom allowed, would be to rotate my visits between all the ekklesia in Rome. I like to be available to them, get to know new people, and answer any questions or needs they have."

Onesimus thought he knew what was coming, and he wasn't sure he liked it.

"What would you think about attending for me? You could go to a different one every week, then began again with the first. Report back to me about the goings-on and questions they might have for me. I could then answer their questions in writing, which you could deliver before the next meeting."

It seemed that he could not avoid these gatherings, whether in Colossae or Rome. There were about ten or twelve of them, he thought. Yet it was a reasonable request and did not require anything difficult for Onesimus. Except—

"I am happy to serve you, Paulus. But how will the ekklesiai respond to someone coming in your name who is not of the Way?"

"A good question. There should not be a problem—you are in my service and being to Philemon! Still, I have thought that I would ask Philodemus ' master if he could accompany you for each first visit to an ekklesia. He could introduce you."

"Ah, I like that idea!"

"I thought you might. I am pleased to see how well you and Philodemus are getting along."

It was true. Onesimus valued his friendship with Philodemus more and more each day. They saw each other frequently at the forum, on work errands, and at the ekklesia meetings. Onesimus pointedly avoided thinking about what might happen in the future to that friendship.

Sometimes Philodemus and Onesimus went on errands together. Usually this involved trips beyond the city of Rome: twice to Tusculum, once to Aquinum, and once they even took a ship to Cumae and Neopolis. Onesimus found this exciting and educational. He was living in Rome, traveling about the capital on daily errands!

When the two slaves had some free time, they explored the city or attend one of the numerous events that Emperor Nero held for the people. Onesimus didn't much care for the theater, but he loved the chariot races. Whether at the Circus Maximus, the Campus Martius, or any of the other smaller tracks, he enjoyed the excitement of the crowd, the cheering for the teams, the skill involved, and, he had to admit, the danger to the charioteers.

He always cheered for Blue, but Philodemus rooted for Green, which made for a friendly rivalry. One day, while attending the races, Philodemus asked Onesimus why he rooted for Blue.

"Same reason you support Green," Onesimus replied, fanning himself with a cloth. "It's my master's team."

Philodemus frowned. "Paulus follows the races?"

Onesimus blanched. "Uh, no, I mean my master back in Asia Minor. The…the one who sent me to Paulus."

"Oh, yes. I forgot you have two masters. In a way." He shook his head. "I guess we have no other reason to cheer any other team. Our master's loves are our loves."

Onesimus nodded self-consciously. They were waiting for the third singles race to begin.

"I have noticed, Onesimus, that you rarely speak of your household, or of your master, or your home. Ephesus, is it?"

"Colossae. Near Ephesus." Onesimus hoped the race would hurry and start.

They sat for a few moments.

"So," Philodemus continued, "Tell me something about your home."

Onesimus took a deep breath. "My master's a good master. The villa is not big. But it is nice, and there's a fairly good-sized farm. There are about twenty slaves. We grow most of our own food, as well as a decent supply of meat and eggs. We even have our own mill."

"A mill? Wow, that's a master who is well-off!"

"It's not. The mill was already there when Philemon bought it a few decades ago. We can't grind enough to sell, but it's enough to provide the household."

He nodded. "Sounds pleasant. A farm, outside the bustle of the city. Quiet."

"It is. But Colossae is a speck compared with Rome. I laugh when I remember that I used to complain about the crowds on market day!"

Philodemus chuckled. "Yes. Rome changes your perspective. In so many ways."

The third race began, but now Onesimus was distracted by thoughts of home, which brought up thoughts of Turia. He could feel himself entering a black mood. The Red team won, to loud cheering and booing.

When the noise subsided, Philodemus spoke again. "Do you have any family there, or are you a lone slave?"

"No. I don't know where any of my family are, or even if I had any brothers or sisters."

"It's the same for me. But Epaenetus provides me a good home. They are my family."

Onesimus nodded.

Philodemus touched his arm. "My brother, you appear to be morose. Is there some problem with your home? If it is none of my business, tell me."

Onesimus paused. He could not tell him, even though he had become a good friend in many ways. It was nice to have a friend, but he also worried about getting too close. Not with the decisions he would have to make in the future.

He could tell him *some* of the story, though. "There is a girl there. Another slave."

"Ah! A girl. I should have known. You miss her."

"No, that's not it. We *were* close. We even planned on marrying, if the master would ever allow it. We even had dreams of saving money and becoming freedpersons. She was the only person I have ever loved and who loved me."

"So…what happened? Did your master not allow you to marry?"

"We never asked. She…she betrayed me." Immediately he realized he was getting too close to the truth.

"Onesimus, my brother, I am sorry. How did she betray you?"

Precisely the question he didn't want. He would have to play it off as too painful to discuss until he could come up with a story.

"I don't really want to talk about it. It's too painful. It happened just before my master sent me to Paulus. Though I am grateful to be away from her."

"Oh, of course, I understand. Betrayal from a loved one is terrible."

"Yes, it is."

"Well, the pain will heal, as unlikely as that may sound now. And you will find another. But the first time is painful, I know."

Onesimus felt a sudden surge of anger towards Turia. "When I have my revenge on her, I'll be healed." Onesimus turned away and sat back, abashed at his own vehemence.

After a few moments, Philodemus said, "I understand those feelings." An awkward silence ensued.

Finally, Onesimus spoke. "Sorry. It is still more painful than I realized, I suppose."

"It's okay. I understand. I wonder, though…"

Onesimus looked at him.

Philodemus took on a wry smile. "Are we friends enough for me to rebuke you a bit?"

Onesimus wanted to say "no," but the truth was "yes." They had become close enough over the last couple of months. He grimaced and nodded.

"Okay. Revenge is a bitter cup. It will gain you nothing and will eat you up. Even if you attain it, it will not satisfy. You won't get back anything you lost, and those who hurt you will learn nothing. It may just precipitate more pain."

Onesimus shrugged. "It feels good to think of it."

"Yes, it does feel good to imagine revenge. But consider this: revenge destroys rather than builds and hurts rather than heals."

"Perhaps, but it is justice. Repayment for what she did."

"Does it repay? Or just cause more damage? I don't know what you intend to do, but is it possible your actions would cause pain to innocent bystanders—perhaps your master or other slaves? Or even to yourself? In my experience, that is exactly what happens when people pursue revenge."

Onesimus didn't like where this conversation was going. Philodemus was an excellent debater. "Perhaps. So I have to plan carefully to ensure that the revenge is proper and commensurate."

"Can you be sure of that? Can you control how everyone involved will react?"

Onesimus sighed. "I should know better than to debate with you, Philodemus."

He laughed. "Thank you for the compliment—I think. But I am not engaging in a mock debate. I believe that good comes from *creating*, and evil comes from destruction. Good creates; evil destroys."

Onesimus perked up. "You believe? Is this part of your faith in the Way?"

"Yes, Paulus talks like this. I remember a story he told about one of the Jewish prophets. God took him out to a desert, where a vast army had been slaughtered many years before. The valley was filled with bones, desiccated in the heat of the desert and time. Yet god made Flesh and muscle grew and attached to the bone, skin covered them all, and the soldiers came alive—wet, living, and breathing. Paulus said the story was a symbol of how god brought the Jews back to life after it seemed like they had been destroyed by their enemy many centuries ago."

"How does that relate to revenge? I know this isn't the end of the world. A slave betrayed by a lover—how many times has that happened?" He laughed a little. "But it's a catastrophic event for me. It's the only life I have."

"True. And no one with any compassion would minimize your pain. She committed a destructive act. Which makes it an evil act."

"Okay. So she did evil: destruction. But how can I possibly create good out of that?"

"I'm not sure you can. But god can. That's what he does. He creates."

"And how does he do that?"

"You forgive her."

Onesimus snorted. "Right. Just let her off the hook."

"That's not what I said."

"That's one thing I don't get about you people. You say that once someone hears your message and becomes part of the Way, your god forgives that person. I get that. But how do I forgive something like this? She surely doesn't even feel remorse."

"Well, you don't know that for certain. But regardless, you have put up a barrier: a wall built of anger, resentment, and pride."

"Pride? How am I prideful? I was the one betrayed!"

"Because you are saying that no one should dare treat Onesimus like that. Maybe some other slave. But not you! Yet you yourself said this has happened countless times in history. Are you better than all those?"

Now Onesimus was angry at Philemon. "What in the cosmos do you mean? I most certainly did *not* say I was better than all others."

"But you believe it. How *dare* she betray you, of all people! She deserves punishment. But have you never betrayed someone, or hurt someone, even a little?"

Onesimus stood. "How dare you accuse me?! *I* was wronged!"

"Brother, I am not accusing you. Please sit." He placed his hand on Onesimus arm once more. Onesimus shrugged it off. He became aware that people were staring at them. He did not care.

"Yes, you are! I thought you were a friend. But you accused me like all the rest!"

Philodemus frowned. "Onesimus, who has—"

"You all constantly discuss how your god wants justice. But not for me, right?! 'Cause I'm an outsider! Well, fine, Philodemus. I don't need you or anybody!"

He turned and stormed down the steps and out of the circus.

35. Reconciliatio

As he fled the stadium and out onto the street, his mind raced. What did Philodemus know? Did he find out something, or just suspect?

He had to do something. He had been here too long—almost eight months! He was sweating profusely, and his heart felt like it would pound through his chest. He couldn't breathe.

Stumbling to the side of the road, he sat on a curb. He tried to breathe deeply and slowly. *I need to think. Think!*

What exactly did Philodemus say? That he should forgive Turia. Stupid. But not a sign that Philodemus knew the truth.

He had then accused him of pride. Why? Because he would not forgive? Well, if he knew the whole story, *he* wouldn't forgive either.

But that still didn't explain Onesimus' anger and then fear. What had triggered his anger?

He'd said Onesimus believed he was better than everyone else.

Onesimus went over the conversation in his head. Yes, Philodemus had said some insulting things. But he never said anything hinting that Onesimus was hiding something, or was here under pretenses.

He dropped his head into his hands. *What is wrong with me?* Maybe Philemon was merely engaging in discussion about forgiveness and revenge. The two of them often debated ideas and philosophy.

This was more personal, though. It was about Onesimus. And Turia. Is that why he reacted so strongly? Philodemus had said that Onesimus was prideful because he did not believe anyone should ever treat him like that.

Well, that was true. She shouldn't have.

On the other hand, why not? Was he exempt from being betrayed? Did he deserve it less than all other humans who had been betrayed by—

That was it.

Philemon had said, "She deserves punishment…you never betrayed someone, or hurt someone, even a little."

That wasn't true at all.

He had betrayed Philemon. Philippus. The slave in the cell that first night in Rome. Mouse, crouching in the hatchway, trying to get the courage up to go back out into a storm and help Onesimus—when Onesimus was only thinking of saving himself. Not to mention Paulus, and—

He sighed. He owed Philodemus an apology, though he was still wrong about Turia—because he didn't know the whole story. But he had only been trying to get Onesimus to do some self-examination. In all the months they had spent together, Philodemus had been nothing but a loyal friend.

He stood slowly, ignoring the crowds flowing out of the Circus. He shook his head. What to say to him? He had acted badly for self-centered reasons. In a way, he had even proved Philodemus' point.

Almost everyone had left the circus by now. He stepped back inside and through the tunnel, scanning the seats. Philodemus was not there.

Finding him in Rome would be impossible, his errands could take him to so many different places. Or maybe he was headed home, and Onesimus could catch him there. But it was the opposite direction from Paulus' domus. And Paulus wanted him back after the races.

*

It was almost twenty-four hours before Onesimus had a chance to see Philodemus again. Paulus sent him to his domus to deliver a message. Onesimus found himself both hoping he was there and that he was not. But he had to face him sooner or later.

He delivered the message to the door slave and asked if Philodemus was there. The slave left Onesimus standing, returning shortly and said he would be right now. He shut the door.

Onesimus took a few steps back and waited. Did the fact that he wasn't invited in mean that Philodemus was angry with him? Maybe he was coming out to tell him he would have nothing further to do with him except on business.

He finally sat down on the pavement near the street. He was ashamed.

The door opened, and Philodemus, upon seeing him, strode out and shut the door behind him.

"Brother Onesimus! I was hoping I'd see you. Are you okay?"

Onesimus stood, taken aback.

"I—am I okay? Are you okay? I acted…I acted terribly toward you, for no reason…you have been such a good friend, and I—"

"I appreciate that, but all is forgiven. I said something that caused you pain, and for that I am sorry."

"Philodemus, you have no reason to be sorry, there was nothing—"

"Still, I regret the conversation. But thank you."

"Again, I am so sorry, my dear brother."

"You don't need to keep apologizing. It's a sore subject for you, and I should have been more sensitive. Now, I am heading down to the Forum on an errand. Can you accompany me?"

"Yes, I need to give a message to Lucas at the butcher shop."

"Excellent."

They turned down the road and descended toward the hub of the city.

"You should at least be a little angry—you deserve better."

Philodemus waved his hand. "Ah, what is friendship without give and take? Close relationships mean occasional friction—and the opportunity to grow and learn together.

Onesimus shook his head and smiled. "More of your philosophy of the Way?"

"As a matter of fact, yes. But it's also logic—and it makes for sound relationships."

Onesimus had to admit that was true.

They had reached the bottom of the hill and were now approaching the Forum. Onesimus took a deep breath. "Philodemus, I must admit that you are an unusual case of living what you believe. I mistreated you, and you have forgiven me when you have every right to criticize and condemn."

"Maybe. But what you did is a far cry from being betrayed by a loved one."

"Conceded. Still. If, as you say, forgiveness is freeing and healing, how does one possibly forgive betrayal like that? From the one you trusted above all others?"

"Are you sure you want to talk about this?"

"Yes. It is all I have thought about since yesterday."

"Very well." He smiled. "You just do it. Forgive her."

"You all keep using that word 'forgiveness.' What does it mean? What does it look like?"

"You say, 'I forgive…' whatever her name is. What is her name?"

"Turia," Onesimus said. It took an effort to speak it. It felt strange to say it out loud. And distasteful.

"You say, 'I forgive Turia for the horrible thing she did to me.'"

"I just say that?"

"It's a start. Say it often. That's the beginning. Later, you may have opportunity to take actions to show you mean it. But for now, say it. If you can, pray it."

They had reached the shop of Lucas, where Onesimus delivered the message. Philodemus' destination was not too far away, at another shop. Onesimus waited while Philodemus went inside, and then returned with a package.

"As I was saying," Philodemus continued, "You begin forgiving by deciding you will. Repeat it to yourself, and work on truly believing it. Act like you have forgiven them. Personally, I always begin with prayer, asking for the heart to forgive."

What Philodemus didn't know, and what Onesimus was embarrassed to say, is that he had been praying to this god. Not about Turia, of course, but about other things. In fact, for about two weeks, he had not prayed to Artemis or any other gods. It hadn't been intentional; he had just started praying less and less to other gods until he didn't pray to them any longer.

"Eventually," Philodemus said, "you decide that her actions will not determine your mood, actions, or life. You refuse to be part of the destructive cycle. You will not repay evil for evil. Are you finished with your errands?"

"Yes."

"I'll walk with you back to the bridge. So, as I was saying, you just decide that you will not be part of the destructive cycle. For you *and* for her."

"Even if I did believe that was the right thing to do, and did it, isn't there the matter of justice? If she did evil, shouldn't she be punished? Even if not by me?"

"Maybe. Righting a wrong is justice. But maybe she deserves grace and mercy because that is the way of healing. Do you desire grace for wrongs you have done? Or would you prefer justice?"

Onesimus stopped short. Philodemus knew nothing of his wrongs; he was sure of that now. Philodemus stopped with him, but remained silent, perhaps to allow Onesimus ponder the question.

He had taken money—he had *stolen* money—from his master. He took—*stole*—a horse. He lied to Justus in Corinth. And Marius. He was currently deceiving Paulus, Philodemus, and the others. Did he want justice for all of that, or would he prefer understanding and mercy?

"I guess we all want justice meted out to others, but we want grace to be offered to us."

Philodemus laughed. "Yes, indeed! Rather weak and selfish of us, isn't it? But we are called to more. To offer grace where needed."

Onesimus frowned. "Like your god does?"

"Like my god delights in doing."

A god whose *preference* was to offer grace? Strange. As for Turia: he did not want to forgive her. It did not seem right just to let it go. As if he would be saying to her "it's okay what you did."

"As for justice," Philodemus said, "I believe in letting god handle that. Practice forgiveness, and let him handle any punishments he deems necessary. It might be different if you had some authority over her as a parent or a leader. Maybe some punishment or consequences—but even that should be tempered by mercy when possible."

Onesimus thought of the punishment doled out to him by Philemon. He shook his head. "Still, revenge—or at least justice—sounds right to me. But I would be lying if I did not admit that being rid of this pain and anger would be a relief. And to let the gods—to let god—handle it…" He paused for a moment, and swallowed. Perhaps he was just tired and overly emotional, but this was an insight that touched him. "There is something…something to that."

"Something creative and positive?" Philodemus said with a smile.

Onesimus reluctantly offered a smile in return. "Yes. Creative and positive."

By now, they were nearing the bridge where Onesimus would cross the river towards Paulus' domus, and Philodemus would turn in the opposite direction.

"Shall we stop to get a bite to eat and some wine? I have a little while before I have some errands in the Forum."

"I can't," Onesimus replied. "Paulus asked me to be back by late afternoon. He wants to write a letter. I guess Timotheos is preparing for a trip and he wants him to take it."

"Oh, yes. I heard he is going to visit the ekklesia to the east." He stopped. "You know, this is fortuitous, perhaps! He'll probably visit your master's ekklesia!"

Onesimus stared. "What?!"

36. QUADRIVIUM

Onesimus hurried back across the bridge and south toward the domus. His heart was pounding. Just as he had begun to think everything was okay, another shock had come. This was real, not a product of his emotional state.

When Timotheos arrived in Colossae and met with Philemon, all would be revealed. Onesimus could imagine the conversation. Timotheos would say, "Paulus appreciates your gift of Onesimus." The look on Philemon's face would be priceless. Philemon would tell Timotheos what really happened, and Timotheos would come back and tell Paulus that his beloved slave had stolen money and a horse from his master and had run away. Philemon would probably send someone immediately to fetch him. In chains.

Scenes of punishment flashed through his mind. He recalled the punishment of two runaway slaves he had witnessed many years ago in Colossae. They had stolen from their master and attempted to sneak out of the town gate after dark. They were tortured and maimed for life.

Philemon was a kinder master than most—and a master who followed the Way—but a slave who stole and ran was a serious societal issue. Even a merciful punishment would be more than Onesimus could take.

He had become complacent; he had let these people of the Way lull him into a false sense of comfort. He should have known better than to stay this long.

He burst into Paulus' flat with a bit more force than he intended, causing Paulus to jump in his chair and drop a wax tablet he was writing on.

"Onesimus, you startled me!" He picked the tablet back up. "Timotheos is leaving for Ephesus and is to deliver a letter for me. I have asked him also to visit Colossae and our dear Philemon." He looked at Onesimus with a large smile. "I want to thank him for you and to tell him about the fine job you are doing. He could not have made a better choice had he asked me himself."

Onesimus struggled to say something. "Thank…you. Thank you, Paulus." Did he suspect something? Maybe he had already heard from Philemon, and he was playing with him.

Paulus turned back to the desk and picked up the tablet.

"I have been making some notes for a brief letter to your master. I am ready to dictate it, and you can take it over to Timotheos tomorrow."

"Yes…yes…."

Paulus looked up. "Are you okay, my child?"

"Yes. Just a long trip from the track and it is hot."

"Yes. I opened the window earlier, trying to get some air, but it was no help. I may have to go out and sit with the guard in the piazza to see if there is any breeze!"

The small talk irritated Onesimus.

"Maybe—maybe I could go get some fresh water and wine for us before we begin."

"That's a good idea. I don't really have anything else for you to do today, except this letter. We could even wait until evening when it will be cooler. I was just anxious."

"I'll go down to Philip's shop, and then perhaps go pick us up some food?"

"Are you sure you're okay? You appear agitated."

Was he goading him? Make him confess?

No, that's crazy. What to say? Onesimus' ability for quick prevarication seemed to have dissipated in the Roman heat. "Yes, yes, just hot."

"Are you worried that Philemon will recall you? I know how much you enjoy it here. I have seen you grow. You have become confident and content. I would not be surprised if you did not want to leave."

Paulus was correct. He liked Paulus; his friendship with Philodemus was precious, and he enjoyed the work. It was not much different than what he did for Philemon, yet it seemed more…meaningful.

Paulus was right. He enjoyed it here. He loved it. It felt like…home.

But to stay would bring shame, torture, and maybe death. He should have approached Paulus as an arbitrator from the beginning, but it was too late now. What Onesimus had done was not just a dispute between a master and a slave anymore. It was something which Romans and Greek abhorred: the unfaithful and deceptive slave. Roman society offered no mercy for such behavior. The revolt of Spartakos and the others—just south of here—was the prime example of what happens when slaves are allowed to get away with too much.

"Onesimus?"

"Yes, Paulus…uh, it is true. I have—I do enjoy my work here. I do not want to go back."

Paulus smiled. "I thought as much. Well, do not fret. One never knows what god might have in mind for you." Paulus leaned forward and pointed a crooked finger at him. "You, my child, are an answer to my prayers. And not just mine, but many others who prayed that a helper would be sent to me in my imprisonment."

Onesimus was cut to the heart. Onesimus was no answer to prayer. He was a liar and a thief. He was a con artist with a scam. He was not "useful"—he was useless. In the language of these people of the Way, he was a serpent in the garden.

The fact that he now cared so much about these people made the anguish even worse.

"And you are in good historical company!" Paulus shouted in his jocular and easy manner. "Many fine slaves have been named 'Onesimus.' Even Julius Gaius had a personal slave named Onesimus, whom he promised to free when he died." Paulus sat back, abashed. "Of course, that Onesimus is not an apt example, as you probably know. He tried to poison the Caesar, didn't he?" He laughed.

Onesimus tried to laugh, but the story hit too close to home. *That* Onesimus was put to death—though not tortured because Caesar deemed him a faithful slave before the enemies of Caesar had corrupted him. The current Onesimus had no such alibi.

"In any case, Onesimus, we shall see what our god might do. In the meantime, go find us some fresh water, wine, and food. And do not hurry in this heat."

Onesimus swallowed. "Thank you, Paulus. I will be back before dusk. I'll get my bag." He went to the next room and retrieved his money pouch and put it in his larger bag. He stuffed his cloak in, too, but did not take his bedroll or extra clothes. If Paulus happened to look in the room later, he would not suspect. When Onesimus didn't return, and after they had all searched for a few days, Paulus would probably believe he had been robbed and murdered.

Until Timotheos returned, that is. Then he'd know the truth.

Onesimus felt a pain in his heart at that thought.

37. Vale

Though it was the hottest part of the day, there were a lot of people crossing the bridge over the Tiber. He did not want to think too much about what he was leaving behind, so he forced his mind to plan. He would leave the city through one of the northern gates—the Fontinal Gate—then make his way up the Via Flaminia, and then perhaps across to Ravenna. From there he could head north. Or he could turn to the east and towards Macedonia and then up into Moesian lands, as he had initially planned when he left Colossae. He needed to get to the edge of the Empire, where he could start all over and never be discovered.

The Fontinal Gate was just a little to the northwest of the Forum. He tried to pass through the Forum with haste, but the crowd made it difficult. He was surprised at the number of people out at this time of day. Once, he thought he heard his name called out, but attributed it to his panic. Weaving his way across the cobbled stones and marbled steps, he finally left the Forum to travel the road close along the foot of the Capitoline Hill. Soon the city wall came in to view.

As he approached the gate, he slowed. Something didn't feel right. In his emotional state, he feared he was not thinking clearly. Had he missed something?

He realized he felt guilty. He was torn. He chastised himself—he didn't have any reservations or feelings when he left Colossae. He *had* to save himself. This wasn't any different. He had come to Rome with a plan. He'd stayed longer because it worked to his benefit. Now, his past had caught up with him, and he had to go. It was time—

"Onesimus!" Someone grabbed his arm. He spun around, startled.

It was Philodemus.

"I've been following you since the Forum! Where are you going in such a hurry?" He laughed.

"I—I am on an errand for Paulus, up north. Uh, just outside the gates."

"Oh, okay. Well, I just wanted to see what you were doing tomorrow." Philodemus looked at him closely. "Are you okay? Is something wrong?"

"Just out of breath; the heat." That excuse is wearing thin, he thought.

Why was Philodemus here? The chance of him being in the Forum seemed unlikely. Then Onesimus remembered that he had said he'd be at the Forum this afternoon. Onesimus cursed inwardly. He should have remembered that and taken an alternate route. More evidence he was not thinking clearly.

"Yes, it's hot. Do you want some company? I had just finished my errand, and I am free until evening. Is it a far trip?"

"Uh, yes, it—it is...best for me to go alone...thanks anyway."

"Very well." Philodemus was frowning.

There was an awkward silence between them. Onesimus was doing his best to appear relaxed and nonchalant, but he knew he was not doing a good job. He was fortunate it was so hot—otherwise, the sweat on his brow would be further evidence of his panic.

"You seem out of sorts."

Onesimus hesitated. Philodemus was the closest friend that he had ever had—except for Turia, which had turned out to be a fiction.

The conflict in him was raging. Could he—should he—confide in Philodemus? How would he respond if he told him the truth?

No. Philodemus was a model slave. He would be appalled if he knew the truth. He might even turn him in. Philodemus held strong convictions.

"I just have some problems I need to work out. Thanks for asking." That was certainly true.

"Of course. Can I help?"

"Um, no, not right now. Maybe later. Just working through some personal stuff."

Philodemus nodded. "About Turia."

"Yeah. Yes." This was true, too. Sort of.

"Well, I understand. If you allow me, I'll say one thing and then take your leave. Forgiveness and grace can heal anything. And who knows? Perhaps it will have such an effect on her that she will want to redeem herself. She might just end up being the person you thought she was. Wrongdoing and deception can make a person unrecognizable from who they really are."

Though Philodemus was speaking about Turia, Onesimus could not help but apply his words to himself. "You—you believe that? That wrongdoing changes us?"

"I know so—because I have experienced it myself. I'll tell you about it someday. To unburden oneself of all the extraneous dirt of life is liberating. And to receive absolution is...well, it is freedom."

Onesimus thought he saw the beginning of tears in Philodemus' eyes. Philodemus took a deep breath and stepped back. "It is true, my brother. You need to forgive her. Imagine that she confessed it all and *asked* you to forgive."

"That would never happen."

"Maybe not. Maybe it would. But imagine it."

"But...what if she confessed all her wrongs and asks for forgiveness but...I cannot...forgive her?"

"I think you could."

"I don't know if I could forgive a terrible betrayal."

"I know you are not of the Way, but this is the core of who we are. It's true that a confession unburdens the confessor and begins the healing, starts to make whole." He nodded slowly. "The unburdened soul is a free soul."

Onesimus had to get out now. He was near to revealing everything. He had let Philodemus become too close. That would be a disaster—just like getting too close to Turia.

"I understand. Thank you, Philodemus. I will think about what you said. But I must go now."

Philodemus reached out and grabbed his forearms. "Of course. Sorry for delaying you. I will see you later."

Onesimus nodded, and Philodemus took his forearms and squeezed them in farewell. Onesimus turned away before he could see tears starting to well up in his own eyes.

The idea of becoming unburdened…

No. No.

It would only bring more pain, suffering, and betrayal.

Time to go.

38. Libertas

"The unburdened soul is a free soul." Did Philodemus come up with that himself? Probably not—the people of the Way were fond of pithy sayings gathered from many sources. This one was rather noble-sounding. Still, it was just a saying. If Onesimus unburdened himself, he might feel free, but then he would be punished, tortured, or even executed. That was not freedom.

Unburdening himself would cause Paulus pain, too. Onesimus knew Paulus pretty well by now. He would not be angry; he would be deeply hurt and disappointed. Onesimus couldn't do that to him. He had to protect him and the others. This was best for everyone.

He had reached the huge gates, which stood wide open for the day. Some traffic was passing through—mostly merchants with their ox-driven wagons. The lifeblood of Rome. Goods flowing through the capillaries and veins of the Empire: the roads, winding and snaking their way from the extremities to the head, all moving with a purpose. A purpose. It would be freedom to have a purpose.

Onesimus passed through the gates. There were still a few edifices and buildings beyond, but most were only used during the day and shut up tight just before sundown. Ahead, the road curved to the right between the hills. Pine trees dotted the land beside the way.

"The unburdened soul is a free soul." The parallelism of the concise phrase was nicely crafted.

His thoughts turned to Justus of Corinth. He would be angry at the deception wrought by Onesimus. He had quickly perceived that Onesimus' was not being entirely honest. Onesimus wondered if Justus had believed the story he told him. Such a wise, educated, and powerful man. He would surely be angry. This was best for him, too. Not that it was likely he'd ever find out.

He was coming up on a corner around the hill. He had an urge to look back at the city, but restrained himself. If he looked back, he might be lured in.

How superstitious of me. A follower of the Way would not think like that. As if a mere look behind could change the course of history.

"The unburdened soul is a free soul."

The fact that Onesimus had used Philemon's name to get room, board, and travel only added to the litany of crimes against his master. Even Philippus, who was as close to a friend as Onesimus had in Colossae, would be incensed at the way his master had been mistreated by an ungrateful slave.

The road began a slight incline. The ox-carts, headed in the same direction as Onesimus, were now laboring up the slope. He could hear the wheezing and snorting of the oxen, the creaking of the wheels, the calls of the drivers, and the crack of whips.

No, there would be no freedom if he unburdened his soul. Just a lot of pain and suffering for everyone, with the worse of it reserved for Onesimus. He had to protect himself. He had to protect his friends in Rome—they had been too kind to him.

He reached the top of the rise and stopped to rest. No longer able to resist, he turned and looked back. He could not see much because of the trees, but the palace on top of Capitoline Hill was clearly visible. Now there lived a free soul! The Emperor of Rome, Lucius Domitius Ahenobarbus, was popular with the people. He was responsible for the increase in entertainment in the city—races, gladiator contests, and plays. Why, he even engaged in some of the athletic events himself! Everyone loved him. What freedom!

Well, perhaps not everyone loved him. Onesimus had heard some nobles publicly denounce all the entertainment as decadence. He had heard other rumors which, if true, would say that Nero was a burdened soul.

But at least he made a difference in the world. He had a purpose, and he played his part. Onesimus was no one. A mere slave among millions—and a bad one at that. A "nemo" rather than a "Nero."

Onesimus could hear Paulus saying, "you might not matter among the machinations of humankind, but you matter to god." The workings of men and women came and went, he would say, but the plans of god are timeless. Onesimus was not sure what that meant. But he had to admit it made him feel better to think that, at least to a deity, he mattered. In fact, Paulus would say that to god, Onesimus was just as important as Nero. A bit incredulous, but Paulus seemed to believe it.

A raucous noise below caught his attention. Back down the slopes, an ox-cart coming at break-neck speed up the hill. The cart must be empty for the oxen to be able to pull it at that clip. It was passing the other carts, weaving in and out among them, and eliciting shouts from the drivers. The man driving was having a bit of fun in spite of his recklessness. Onesimus smiled at the man's joy at such a simple pleasure. Soon, the man and his cart reached Onesimus, and, as he flew by, the driver gave a cheery wave. His empty cart rattled by, bouncing in its unburdened state. The sounds faded as the cart trundled down the hill behind Onesimus.

"The unburdened soul is a free soul."

It would be nice to be free. If only the story he had lived in Rome had been true. To be working for Paulus and these people of the Way, legitimately. With no burden on his mind.

He stood for a moment more, looking through the trees at the great city. A city he would never see again. But he had to do this, didn't he? To protect them. To save himself. Anyone would do the same.

With a sinking heart, Onesimus realized that Paulus would not run. In fact, Paulus intentionally had himself arrested so that he could appeal to the Emperor, and therefore be brought to Rome. A free ride to Rome so he could teach the Way in the capital city of the Empire. What a crazy plan. To intentionally put yourself in danger for a goal.

A great goal. A purpose.

Onesimus realized with a start that this was Paulus' philosophy: to do all things for the message, no matter the cost to himself. Living for something more significant than oneself. Sacrificing for others. Sacrificing for the greater good. It did sound noble.

Still, his situation was different than that of Paulus. A lot of people hurt if he confessed. Didn't Onesimus have an obligation to protect them?

"You aren't protecting them—you're protecting yourself." The sound of his own voice startled him. He had not intended to speak aloud.

True, he was protecting himself. But wasn't he protecting them, too, from disappointment and hurt and anger?

The words of Philodemus came to him. He—they—believed that confession of wrongdoing was always the right thing to do, regardless of the consequences. Because it was truth. Because it was real.

That's ridiculous.

His heart began pounding. He didn't want to believe it. Yet he could not deny that it made sense of suffering, made sense of the world, made sense of love. If you cheated and manipulated and stole and deceived, you would never be part of something meaningful. Never have the opportunity for friendship. Or love.

"The unburdened soul is a free soul."

They would say that even if confession meant death, one could die a healed man. A whole man, clean and transparent to all, to love or hate. Free from the constant fear of being found out. Free from the worry of having to keep up the façade.

That *would* be freedom.

Onesimus surprised himself. It was as Philodemus said: if he unburdened himself, he would be free, he would be healed, and he would be on the way to being a whole human. And a complete human was free to accomplish much, rather than cowering and sneaking about out of fear and bitterness.

Even if that freedom resulted in punishment or death.

Onesimus laughed, in spite of his predicament. "These people of the Way have really done their work on me."

He might lose every friend he ever had. He would probably lose everything he wanted. He could lose his life.

A dangerous and hidden life on the edges of the Empire, or shame and punishment in the land he knows—but with an unburdened soul.

He took a deep breath. He knew what was right. For the first time in his life, he *knew*. He had never acted with nobility and pure honesty in his life. Especially not if it meant punishment.

Once, he had asked Paulus if he was afraid of being executed after the Emperor heard his case. Paulus had said, "The race ends for all of us at some point, Onesimus. What matters is *how* we run it, not where we place."

Off in the distance behind him, he heard a faint whoop. He smiled. The driver of the unburdened oxcart was still enjoying himself.

He turned back towards Rome.

Epistole Iota

To Giarri

Peace to you. Your last letter gives me hope that you will all remain safe during the troubles. I pray for you daily.

I have bad news. I was brought before Tertillus. He did allow me to plead my case, but did not seem too interested in anything I had to say. I did the best I could, but all I achieved was that he would seek advisement. His inclination is for me to be executed. I suspect his concern is not justice, but politics.

Telling you the story of my time in Rome in these letters has done me good. It amuses me that, back then, I was so fearful of punishment or death. So much so that I would say and do anything to avoid it. Now, here I am, again outside of Rome, facing death, yet my only fear is for other people. Your last letter was filled with such pain. Trust your faith, my brother. All is as it should be. I have run a good race—perhaps not better than anyone else, but I have run it to the best of my ability. And that is all that is asked of us.

I was hesitant, as you recall, to tell you my story. Now, I hope I have time left to finish it for you. I admit that you were right, it may be a story that can encourage others. At least that is my hope.

Keep the faith, my dear brother. I end this letter as always, asking you to greet everyone there. Tell them I am in good spirits. God willing, I will write again soon. Grace and peace to all.

39. Confessio

Walking back down the Roman road, in a near dream state, he thought that he might vomit. Half of his mind kept trying to talk him out of returning. The other half kept pointing out that freedom of the soul was more important than anything else.

And, for now, that seemed preferable.

Soon he passed through the Fontinal Gate, back through the Forum, and traversed the Bovarium. He crossed the wide Tiber river, then walked down the Via Portuensis. All roads he had walked many times in the last few months, but never with this much importance. They were no longer roads; they were paths to his destiny.

As he walked, a calm resolve descended upon him, replacing the fear. It brought a strange sort of comfort. It was the road he had been so stridently avoiding for so long. Now that he was upon it, he found it was not so difficult.

He entered the familiar piazza. The warm day lay like a blanket over the stone paving. The guard was sitting under his tree, his head lolling to one side. A jug of water sat beside him. The afternoon sun cut sharp shadows on the ground. The only sound was that of Onesimus' sandals as they slapped upon the stone, as if all the world had stopped to watch him.

The door to the *domus* was open, as he had left it. He stepped inside and ascended the stairs. One deliberate step after the other. Though he was headed towards shame, ridicule, rejection, and punishment, he still knew he was doing the right thing. A difficult thing, which made it all the more meaningful. Finally, here at the end, he was acting with integrity.

Philodemus was right. He was anxious about the future, but he already felt lighter.

Paulus turned and looked up from a scroll he was reading. He cocked his head to the side as if he sensed the importance of the moment. True to his character, he let Onesimus define it. For a few moments, Paulus sat and Onesimus stood. Just as they had when Onesimus first arrived. But this Onesimus was quite different from the one that stood back then.

Onesimus finally was able to speak. "Paulus, I need to tell you something of great importance."

Paulus nodded.

Onesimus took a deep breath. "I have not been honest with you. I was not sent here by Philemon to assist you."

Paulus' eyebrows went up. "No?"

"No." He felt as if he was not getting enough oxygen. "May I sit down?"

Paulus stood. "Of course. Take my seat." He moved over to sit on his bed, keeping his eyes on the slave. Onesimus picked up the chair and turned it around to face Paulus. The scraping sound of wood on wood seemed unnaturally loud.

He did not know what words to use, but he knew he must begin.

"He did not send me. I…ran away. I had been stealing money from Philemon, in partnership with another slave, and that slave betrayed me to Philemon, and I ran. I thought to go far north, maybe to Phrygia. Along the way, I learned about the Lex Sentia, and I believe Philemon might have intended to free me under that law some day. By running away, I put any hope of that in jeopardy. I came here to ask you to be an advocate, an arbitrator between us."

Onesimus could not read Paulus' expression. he remained silent. Onesimus went on.

"When I got here, I was afraid. I thought I was naïve for assuming you would do any such thing. I figured I would get to know you first. Then you thought he had sent me…and…before I knew it, that was the story I adopted. It was…the easy way. I told myself it would allow me to judge how you might react. As time went on… I became closer to you…and others…I could not bear to tell you the truth. I started to run away today—and…I could not. I had to come back and tell you the truth I…I am so sorry. As inadequate as those words are. So I am prepared—"

"Why me as arbiter? And how did you know where I was?"

"Philemon spoke highly of you, and often. I knew he would listen to you if you agreed to serve. We had a visitor who came to the ekklesia and told us you were here, in prison, in Rome."

"Hm. And how did a lone slave, on his own, get to Rome? How did you find me in this massive city?" Onesimus could still not read any emotion in his words. No anger, no disappointment, and no surprise. Just the cool questions of a scholar of the law exploring the facts. That was more ominous than an outburst of anger.

"I have some knowledge of geography. I took a horse —I stole a horse. I went to Ephesus, boarded a ship to Corinth, then another to Italia, and then here. I asked and searched until I found you."

"Quite resourceful for a slave from an insignificant town." He must be so disappointed, Onesimus thought. "You told me that you had visited with Justus of Corinth on your way. Was that a fabrication?"

"No, domine. Quite by accident, I ended up at his domus."

"Accident. Interesting. And?"

"He also thought I had been sent by Philemon, whom he did not know—but he knew you. I told him I was on a journey to take a message to you from the ekklesia in Colossae. He was more than willing to help me." Onesimus hung his head. "I have deceived many."

"Yes. Yes, you have, my child." Onesimus looked up. "And yet that is no reason to start calling me 'domine' again. I was 'Paulus' before your confession, I am Paulus during and after it."

Onesimus grimaced. "But I am not the Onesimus I pretended to be. I am a runaway, a deceitful slave, a thief, and—"

Paulus held up his hand and Onesimus fell silent. Paulus stood and walked to the window, looking out. After a moment, he spoke without looking back.

"Yes, it is true you are those things."

Onesimus hung his head. This was more painful than he had even imagined.

"Or, rather," Paulus turned to him, "you were those things. Today, you have decided *not* to be those things." He walked to him and placed his hand on his shoulder.

"To me, that is what matters. I will be happy, my child, to act as arbitrator, though we have the problem of months having passed. I may not have known your story, but I do know your heart. In that, I was never deceived. And I know Philemon, as I was the one who brought the message of the Way to him, and even performed the water rights upon him. I can, and will, act as arbitrator."

Onesimus opened his mouth then closed it. He did not know what to say. He had not even dared hope for this.

"But, Paulus, I deceived you…everything you did for me…and I—"

"Enough. Time enough for a full confession as needed. I need to know the nature of the dispute. Did Philemon mistreat you?"

Onesimus sighed. "No, Paulus. That is the problem, and perhaps why you should not so readily agree. I see now that I was the cause of the problems between us. He was a good master, but I chafed under slavery. I wanted to be my own master. I thought highly of myself—too highly—and saw others as less than human. Pride—I was better than everyone else. So I devised a plan with another slave…to extract small amounts of money from payments I collected for Philemon. Over time, we hoped to amass enough."

"To buy your freedom? Hoping that Philemon would grant it not knowing it was his own money? Or did you just plan to run away?"

Onesimus cringed at the stark description of his own actions. He fought the urge to defend himself. "I…we…we hadn't gotten that far with our plan."

"And this other slave? Where is he?"

"She. We wanted to be married. We…planned…" He stopped. Tears came to his eyes.

Paulus smiled a sad smile. "Ah. More pain. And you got caught?"

"Someone—another slave—discovered the money, and figured out that it was she and I who stole it. So she…the woman I…loved…" He stopped. It was difficult to speak. "She…she told Philemon that I was the thief. That I forced her into helping me."

Onesimus stared at the floor. Telling it all, out loud, made it seem even more horrible.

The room was silent. Not a sound entered through the open window. It reminded Onesimus of the end of a gladiatorial match: as one fighter lay on the ground, spent, the other held his weapon high, ready to bring it down on the neck of the one who was defeated. The crowd held their collective breath.

Paulus broke the heavy silence. "It's an old story. The betrayal of a lover. A story found in Greek literature, Latin literature, and even Jewish literature."

Onesimus was not interested in a historical or literary discussion of his plight. He wanted to get on with whatever he must face. "Philemon was furious, of course. It was when he reprimanded me in private that he said something about freedom being granted to a slave on the thirtieth birthday. I knew nothing of this tradition, and didn't think anything of it."

Paulus nodded. "Yes, it is a common custom to manumit slaves in their thirtieth year in Rome and Italia. I don't know about the Provinces. It became so common that Augustus enacted a law to limit it. But, my boy, the custom is for a 'fidelis servus'—a faithful slave—and you have not been that, have you?"

"No, Paulus, I have not. I did work hard, and I did good work—but I was also lazy when I chose; I got away with things when the opportunities presented themselves. When I learned what Philemon meant, I realized I had destroyed the one thing I wanted."

"What happened after that meeting?"

"He deferred his decision about me until the next day. He told me to go back to my cell and stay there."

"So he trusted you to wait. But you did not."

Again, the harsh, unadulterated assessment of his actions cut his heart. "No. I did not. I left for Ephesus that night."

"Do you think he hired a slave hunter?"

Onesimus shrugged. "I don't know. I think not."

"I concur." Paulus sat back on his bed and took a deep breath. They sat in silence for some time.

Onesimus was the first to break the silence this time. "Paulus, I am so sorry. I know I have disappointed you." The tears began to flow again. "I am so sorry to make you angry. I am so sorry. I…" He lapsed into silence.

Paulus looked up at him. "I know, my child. I know." He paused. "I forgive you."

Onesimus was stunned. Just like that? Just like Philodemus had told him he should do towards Turia?

Those words came too easily. "Paulus, I truly am sorry. If I could make it up—"

"My child," Paulus said firmly, "I know you are sorry. Your decision to confess, instead of running away, demonstrates that. I see your heart. I forgive you. For me, it is as if it never happened." He took a deep breath. "However..."

Here it comes. Forgiveness might come from Paulus, but Roman law demanded an accounting.

"You need forgiveness from more than Paulus of Tarsus, and forgiveness doesn't count for anything under the law. I've been harboring a runaway slave, which is illegal. I could say I am acting as arbitrator, but if so, why did I wait so long? Even the Jewish law, which is much more forgiving than Roman law, allows me to keep a runaway slave only if he has been mistreated. You have not."

He hadn't considered how his actions might reflect on Paulus. Onesimus *endangered* him—all the more so, since he was already under house arrest.

Guilt was piled upon guilt, and he was overwhelmed with the enormity of his wrongdoing.

Paulus took a deep breath, and smiled wearily, "Well, we will have to think on that and determine what options are at our disposal. Allow me another question. Why now?"

"I decided I would rather face punishment than to keep living a false life."

Paulus leaned forward, as he often did when zeroing in on a key point of his argument. "Yes, but why *now*?"

"I don't know...Philodemus told me Timotheos was going Colossae, and I was forced to make a decision." He paused. "I saw Philodemus right before I left. He knew something was wrong. I had told him about the woman betraying me—though not the rest. He explained how grace and forgiveness brought healing and wholeness. And freedom from ones' burdens. I couldn't stop thinking about that."

Paulus shook his head. "A chance conversation with another slave changed your plan? Unlikely."

Onesimus frowned. Paulus enjoyed building up arguments one block at a time, then knocking each one down, until only one inescapable conclusion remained. It often made it difficult to see his whole argument until the end. He enjoyed employing the Socratic method. So where was he leading Onesimus this time?

"I guess I don't know."

Paulus leaned back. He was in teaching mode, despite the crisis before them. "What is different about *this* Onesimus—" he pointed at him with a crooked finger "—from the Onesimus that arrived here at my door in Rome on that first day? What happened to him?"

Onesimus sat, thinking. Where was he going? "A…a lot…but…"

"What events have brought you here, in front of me today, as a new Onesimus?"

In a flash, Onesimus saw where Paulus was leading. The last block was in place, and it stood unassailable.

Philemon mentions the Lex Alia Senta. Two slaves, in a taberna in Ephesus, talk about the traditional freeing of 30-year-old slaves. Another pair of slaves, on the steps of the Artemis temple, mention the same thing. He happens upon the house of Justus in the large city of Corinth. Marius' describes the Way to Onesimus, and what it meant to him, as a slave. Mouse's intention to go out and find him during the storm at sea. The slave in the cell that first night in Rome, pleading for Onesimus' freedom. The ease with which he found Paulus. Paulus assuming that he had been sent by Philemon to help with the work of the Way. A chance meeting of Philodemus, in the massive city of Rome, just as he was running away.

And so many other events and circumstances. Paulus did not think any of those things were mere chance.

And now, neither did Onesimus.

40. Communio

His initiation into the Way took place on the banks of the Tiber, just north of the Port of Rome. It was a strange experience for Onesimus. These actions, this joining of a community, was so foreign from his previous way of life. He hadn't wanted to be part of any community, and his interactions with the gods had been only when he needed something. But God had other ideas for him, it seemed.

Many of the members of the Way in Rome were there. Paulus received permission to leave in order to officiate, which meant the Roman soldier stood on the banks, bored—and perhaps a little offended.

Onesimus had heard of initiation rights, of course—they were not uncommon. The mystery religions had them, and though they were supposed to be secret, details leaked to the public. He had heard that the Mithras initiates bathed in the blood of a bull, which washed them spiritually and prepared them for becoming a full member of the community. He heard that Jews in Colossae practiced washing for ceremonial purposes, and officials of the Roman cults often performed hand washings before religious ceremonies.

This initiation had its own unique elements. Standing waist-deep in the water near the bank, he was lowered under the surface three times, each followed by words spoken by Paulus. When he climbed out, he was handed a new set of clothes, a symbol of the new orientation of his life.

He was self-conscious with the others standing on the banks watching. It comforted him to know that most of them had gone through the same initiation.

As he climbed up the bank out of the river to cheerful shouts and claps on the back, he realized that he had already felt a part of this community—indeed had been accepted by them. But the ritual solemnized it. He was one of them now. A follower of the Way.

What a strange turn of events, Onesimus thought.

Everyone went to the home of Epanaetus and shared a meal together. Onesimus had not eaten this well since he was at Justus' domus in Corinth. The promulsis was a fish and egg dish with cucumbers and radishes. For the prima mensa, they were presented with roast fowl, hot cabbage, and some thrushes stuffed with a breaded vegetable mix. Finally, the secula mensa consisted of a fine selection of stewed apples and cinnamon.

As he sat in a quiet moment, satiated and comfortable, he wondered what would have happened had he not turned back beyond the Fontinal Gate? Whatever the future held, this was better. Ironically, as he faced suffering or even death, he felt more alive than ever.

He had watched gladiators step out into the arena and stride forward with confidence. He used to wonder how they had such calm in the face of such danger? He believed he felt that courage now, though for different reasons. He had cleansed his life; he had people who loved him. He could stride forward with courage. He had stared down the truth. He would face the consequences, and would pray to the God of the Way for strength.

Maybe he would falter at the end. He had never been courageous before. But he never expected to become a follower of the Way, either.

As he and Paulus prepared to return to their domus, Philodemus took him aside. "Onesimus, I am happy to call you a brother now—not just as a fellow slave, but a fellow believer. I don't know all the details of your situation, but if I can do anything to help you, name it."

Onesimus was moved. He was feeling more emotional than usual because of the day's events. (And perhaps because of the robust wine.) He embraced Philodemus. "Thank you, brother. You are a major reason why I am here today. And I think I am ready."

Philodemus withdrew from the embrace and smiled. "Thank God instead. I am merely his servant."

Paulus and Onesimus, with their constant companion, the Roman soldier, headed back to the domus. It was nearing dusk, and the city was quiet. As they crossed the bridge over the Tiber, Paulus paused and turned north, looking upriver. Onesimus joined him. The soldier waited, a short distance away. Before them, the north end of the island of Insula Inter-Duos-Pontes was visible, beyond which the river curved eastward. To the right was Capitoline Hill, and the famous Tarpeian Rock was visible from here. Onesimus wondered how many people had been thrown from that spot over the decades. What a terrible fate.

"Well, my child, it has been quite a week."

"Yes, Paulus, indeed."

"I have decided what needs to be done."

Onesimus had been waiting for this, though he did not think it would be tonight. In the two days since he had confessed, Paulus had not brought up what he intended to do about the situation. Instead, he had told him stories and teachings of Iesous of Nazaret. He spent a good amount of time going over the events of the last week of the life of Iesous. Onesimus had heard much of it before, but this retelling, explicitly aimed at him, gave it new meaning. At first, Onesimus thought Paulus was testing him, making sure he understood the basics of the faith.

Now he wondered if the stories of the betrayal of Iesous by one of his own was intended to have some deeper meaning for Onesimus. Philemon (and Paulus) had been betrayed by one of his own, too: Onesimus. Of course, Onesimus had been betrayed, too—by Turia. But she had betrayed another wrongdoer, not an innocent person. He shook his head at the old Onesimus who was so surprised and offended at her actions.

Onesimus had put Paulus in a terrible position: harboring a runaway slave. And now Onesimus had to face the consequences. At least he was facing them on his terms, unburdened and whole.

He felt some of his courage slip. Paulus was already under arrest, and he was not the kind of person to flout Roman law unless it directly conflicted with his beliefs.

"Onesimus, you are my very own heart. I believe God sent you to me, even under these questionable circumstances." He smiled as he gazed out over the smoothly flowing river. His voice softened. "But to fulfill our obligations—to God and to Rome—we must act. I do not want to do this. I wish to keep you with me. This imprisonment—even though it is house arrest—weighs on me. You bring me joy and encouragement and help." He turned and looked into Onesimus' eyes.

Onesimus knew he did not deserve such praise. He could see that Paulus was pained. Onesimus steeled himself to his fate, but he was afraid.

"I have spent much time in thought and prayer. I have taken counsel with Timotheos and others. And I have decided that I am not going to send Timotheos to Philemon."

Onesimus felt a surge of hope followed by fear. Was Paulus going to defy Roman law for him? He could not let him do that! "Paulus?! You cannot—"

Paulus held up a hand. "Hear me out."

Onesimus nodded and dropped his head.

Paulus turned back to the river, looking down at the blue water. The sunlight sparkled in the wind waves in an unpredictable dance.

"I am sending you."

41. Reditus

Onesimus squinted in the bright sunlight sparkling on the blue water. Being just after the Kalends of Martius, it was a crisp, clear day. The ship swayed slightly as it turned out of the Bay of Neopolis and headed towards the open sea.

Standing on the aft deck, Onesimus could see Puteoli, Neopolis, Herculaneum, and Pompeii lying lazily in the late summer sun. Mount Vesuvius rose majestically behind them all as a dramatic backdrop.

He had come to love this beautiful country, and he felt a deep sadness to be leaving it—perhaps never to return. He even loved the city of Rome, with its crowded streets, decadent neighborhoods, and pagan atmosphere. Mostly, though, he was sad to be leaving Philodemus, Paulus, and all the others.

He was also anxious and a bit scared. How would Philemon respond to his return? The letter from Paulus should help. Though Onesimus did not know what it said, he knew that Paulus would do what he could to protect him. To act as a mediator in some way. Onesimus also hoped that Philemon's belief in the mercy of his God would encourage him to be merciful.

Of course, it could also have the opposite effect. Philemon might feel that Onesimus was trying to manipulate him by running to the man who he held in high esteem, and who held a lot of gravitas among the ekklesiai of the Way.

Onesimus could not deny that punishment would be entirely fair. Most masters would have him tortured. Not only was it seen as a just punishment for betrayal, but also as an important warning to other slaves. There were sixty million slaves in the Empire—in most cities, as in Rome, the slaves outnumbered the freedpersons. Slave revolts in the last century had demonstrated how close slaves could come to overthrowing a town.

Onesimus hoped that his punishment would fall short of physical torture or maiming. He would gladly serve in the stables or clean the latrines of the villa! He laughed at himself out loud. The old, self-centered Onesimus would never have said such a thing!

Philemon could choose to sell him, but no one would buy a defective slave as a servant, so it would be to work in the mines or aboard a galley. Anything like that would not bode well for him, and would probably lead to an early death.

Onesimus hoped—and prayed—that Philemon would not sell him, and that he could eventually be restored to his previous position. That might be a lot to want, at this point. It would all depend on how Philemon responds to Paulus' letter, and how Onesimus comported himself from now on.

He was afraid to hope too much. After all, slaves were property, and disobedient slaves were a cancer. A slave who stole and ran away was just slightly above a slave who murdered a freedperson. It was only Philemon's kind nature, and being a member of the Way, which made Onesimus believe he would not execute him.

But there were no guarantees, and Onesimus did not know of any slave who had treated Philemon this badly.

His emotions swung back and forth between hope and fear.

The ship had turned south and was running parallel to the Italian coast. It felt good to be at sea again—a feeling Onesimus found amusing. He had only been on three ships in his entire life, yet it had a familiar feel to it. Perhaps he could have been a merchant sailor. Until he encountered a heavy storm, that is!

He walked towards the foredeck, his travel bag and the leather cylinder slapping against his side. He recalled Paulus' words to him as he left.

"All things considered, it makes the most sense to send you back to him. I wish I could protect you from suffering, and I do need your help. But integrity and honesty demand otherwise. Even if I did not feel beholden to Roman law, I do have a responsibility to Philemon."

"I understand, Paulus. I truly do. And it offers me more hope than turning me over to the Roman authorities."

"Well, Roman law does not require that. It merely required me not to harbor a fugitive slave. And so, I send you back, with this letter. I hope it does not bother you that I did not have you write it for me."

"Oh, no, of course not. It would not be proper."

Paulus sighed. "I wish I could accompany you back to Colossae. I would not only love to visit again, but I could better ensure that Philemon responds as I hope he does."

Onesimus nodded. That would have given him much comfort were it possible.

"Now, Onesimus, I am not sending anyone else with you." Most people in this situation would do so, either a guard or a trusted friend who was headed that way. "I trust you to deliver yourself."

"I will, Paulus. Please do not think that I would—"

"No words are needed. I am sure you will do as I ask. I am not worried."

Those words deeply moved Onesimus. Onesimus had proven himself unreliable in the past, in many ways, but Paulus was treating him as if he were reliable.

"I do believe that your repentance and desire to be a new person was authentic, but it is not my task to judge it so or now. God knows, and it is up to you to prove it."

Onesimus marveled at the faith Paulus placed in him: and in its genius. If he were now a new person, a person of integrity, how could he possibly do anything other than head straight back to Philemon? To do otherwise would be to be a deceiver thrice over!

Paulus had also written another letter, which was to be delivered to the ekklesia in Laodicea near Colossae. Paulus *had* dictated that one to Onesimus to write. Paulus had then sealed both letters and slid them into a leather document cylinder.

It would be an easy matter for Onesimus to take out the letter to Philemon and unseal it. The wax could be melted in just such a way as to not disturb the top part of the seal. Once read, a bit of new wax could be added carefully to the bottom, melted, and then resealed.

In the past, of course, he would have had no qualms. He would have rationalized that it was about him and he deserved to know. After reading, if he thought the letter would work in his favor, he'd reseal and deliver it. If not, he would throw it overboard and head somewhere other than Colossae.

But not today. He was a new man. Or, at least, he was going to do his best to be a new man. He would let God determine the outcome of his actions. Onesimus did not need to worry about planning and manipulating and controlling any longer. It was in the hands of a being far more capable than he. He was free to live a life of genuineness and integrity. No more fear, manipulation, and hiding.

That, he thought, feels like freedom.

*

The days passed uneventfully. Onesimus slept in his small, narrow bunk, conversed with some of the other slaves on occasion, ate the sparse meals, and spent much time in thought and prayer. He had learned that followers of the Way ought to be in constant prayer as a way of life. All the other gods that Onesimus knew would not appreciate being bothered that much. But Paulus' "father and mother" imagery helped Onesimus understand that a bit better.

The ship turned east and sailed through the southern part of the Adriatic Sea, then set a heading towards the Grecian peninsula. It was near here that the ship had encountered that brief but powerful squall. He recalled his terror. He remembered Mouse—he had never tried to look him up in Rome—and his own fear that the small man had been washed overboard. He remembered that he had been less concerned about Mouse's death than saving himself.

He had made some vows back then, on that deck. Did he pray to Ceres? To Neptune? He didn't remember. But he did recall that he had also made a vow to this new God. He smiled. He had merely prayed to God, among others, to cover all his options. One could never be sure which god was listening, or which one might choose to be favorable. Now he could hear Philodemus ridiculing him. "Dealing with deities is like playing dice? Roll your best hand, and hope for a good one? Doesn't seem like a sound faith to me! And the gods sound rather petty!"

Onesimus furrowed his brow. When he had prayed to this God back then, the storm had begun to abate, and then he saw Mouse was alive.

Even before he believed, it appears this God was listening to him. Onesimus would have to ask Paulus about that. Does God listen and help those who are not followers?

With a shock, he realized that he might never be able to ask Paulus anything again.

42. SATISFACTIO

His ship put in at the port of Lechaion. The little port town appeared much as it had when he left almost nine months ago.

That seemed a distant memory.

He purchased breakfast at a small dockside shop, then began a sweaty trudge up the road to Corinth. He passed the North Market on his right, then, after a curve in the road, passed between the basilica and the smaller market. It all looked familiar, but like a distant dream.

As he walked down the marble steps into the busy and bright forum, he recalled how large it had seemed on his first visit. Now it seemed small compared to the Roman Forum. He spent an hour walking about, taking in the sounds, the sights, and the smells—and perhaps putting off his true errand. He did not know if he would ever be here again.

Finally, he left the forum and passed through the amphitheater plaza. It was not long before he was knocking on the door of the domus of Gaius Titius Justus.

The door opened within seconds, and the expressions and words of the giant slave were the same as they were the first time Onesimus had appeared at this door. He remained standing as the door slave went to inform the master.

Standing outside the door, he began to worry. For all he knew, Justus, feeling betrayed and humiliated by a common slave, might take matters into his own hands and punish Onesimus.

But that was unlikely. Slave owners did not usually punish slaves belonging to others. Onesimus was more worried about the anger and betrayal Justus might feel, and that he might not be so quick to forgive as others.

"Onesimus, dear boy, how are you?!" Justus actually grasped Onesimus' arms in greeting, as if he were free-born. "Follow me; I will have some wine and food brought. How is Paulus?"

"He's doing well. Still under house arrest, but working hard. The ekklesiai are thriving and growing."

"Excellent, excellent. I have been anxious for news." They had reached the peristyle, and Justus indicated some cushions for him to sit upon. "Have you just arrived? Have you had lunch?"

"Yes and yes."

The ever-mysterious Plotia slipped in, took instructions from Justus and floated out. Onesimus heart jumped a bit. She was as alluring as he remembered. But his destiny lay ahead of him, across the sea.

She returned soon with olives, bread, cheese, and watered wine. Onesimus gave a brief overview of Paulus' work in Rome. As he did, he related his own struggles with the faith of the Way, and of his eventual acceptance. Justus was joyful at that revelation.

"Ah, excellent. I suspected you were being led to the faith!"

Using his new adherence to the Way as a springboard, he began a confession of his misdeeds. He did not think; just talked.

Justus sat silently throughout, only occasionally raising an eyebrow. He finished by telling Justus that Paulus had sent him back to Philemon to deliver a letter—and to confess and await punishment.

Justus sat silently. He had stopped eating and drinking some time back. He was looking out past the columns of the peristyle. Onesimus was afraid, but also crushed that he had hurt this good man so much. The silence was too much.

"Domine, I am so sorry for my deception. You were so kind, so hospitable, and I took advantage of that. There is no excuse. I was not a man of integrity. I understand that an apology does not make up for my selfish acts, and if—"

Justus cut him off with a swipe of his hand through the air.

"I am not a man used to being taken advantage of, especially not by a slave. If you were my slave, you *would* be punished severely." Justus' tone was controlled and even. "My faith would preclude me from torturing you or executing you, of course, but the punishment would not be light."

Onesimus nodded and hung his head. They sat in silence. He had prepared himself for such anger, but this was more difficult than he had expected.

Paulus had exhorted him to be prepared for any reaction from the people he must confront. Despite his repentance, he should expect judgment and condemnation from some. It was not that he did not deserve forgiveness, it was that some people might not be able to offer it. Humans are weak. Paulus quoted a teaching on prayer that Iesous had given his followers: "Forgive others, so that you will be forgiven," and told him a parable. It was about a poor man who owed his domine a ridiculously large sum of money—the man could not raise that much money in his whole life. Eventually, though, his domine demanded repayment. The man begged and pleaded for more time, a silly request. But the domine was gracious, and, knowing that the man could never repay the massive debt, he forgave the entire amount.

The man thanked the domine, and left his master filled with gratitude. Some time later he spotted a neighbor who owed him some money. Not a large amount, but enough to make it a burden. He told the neighbor that if he did not pay him immediately, he would have him thrown in debtor's prison!

Onesimus asked Paulus how the man could act that way after being forgiven so much himself.

"Isn't that what we all sometimes do? We demand more of others than we do of ourselves. Even followers of the Way sometimes fail to make the connection between God's forgiveness of our great debt and the debts owed to us." Paulus urged Onesimus to have patience towards those brothers and sisters.

Justus leaned forward, and Onesimus looked up. "I am angry and hurt. But, Onesimus, it does not mean I do not forgive you." He leaned back. "Besides, if Paulus himself forgives you, can I do less? As for what your master will do," he leaned back, "that is up to him. The fact that you confessed all—to Paulus, no less!—and that you had the courage to come back here and face me…well, that speaks of a sincere heart and great courage."

"I am sincere, domine."

Justus held his eyes for a moment. "Yes, I believe you are." The tension seemed to ebb a bit. "And what of the letter you carry? What does Paulus say to Philemon about all this?"

"I don't know."

"You don't know? You were not the amanuensis?"

"Not for this letter."

A sly smile came to Justus' lips, "And you have not opened the letter to read it? Come now. I know the tricks of slaves and scribes: melting the wax just so, replacing it with skill."

Onesimus shook his head. "No, domine, I have not. I made a vow to God. If Paulus wanted me to know, he would have told me. It's a self-test to do the right thing."

"Well, well." Justus placed an olive in his mouth, chewed, then spit the pit into a wooden bowl nearby. "Impressive. Maybe God will make something of you after all!" He laughed. "And, I am glad—in fact, I rejoice—that you are now a brother! Plotia! More wine!"

They spent a good while talking of Rome, and of the ekklesiai, and of Paulus' doings. Justus was especially interested in the number and size of each ekklesiai in Rome.

After an hour or so, Justus said that he would have Marius make arrangements for passage from Cenchreae as soon as possible. Did he have sufficient funds? Did he want to sail to Ephesus or Miletus? Onesimus smiled to himself as the hospitality of Justus revealed itself once more. He was a man of fierce intimidation, but with a big heart.

After working out the details, Justus dismissed him and told him to feel free to spend time with Marius.

Onesimus excused himself and found Marius. After a joyful greeting, the two of them took a leisurely walk through the city. Once again, Onesimus related his story and his sorrow at the hurt he caused. Marius was surprisingly calm. He was more interested in Onesimus' change of heart.

While that made the aftermath easier, the telling was just as painful and difficult. How many more times would he have to tell this story? Each time, it was like re-opening a severe wound. How would he ever heal?

They walked to Cenchreae to book passage for the next morning. Marius asked about Turia. What would he do?

"I've decided, Marius, that I will tell her that I nurtured a lot of anger and resentment towards her, but I forgive her."

Marius nodded. "Proper, I think. But not easy?"

"I don't know. So much has happened to me now I am not even sure it matters to me as much as it used to. But I wonder what emotions might surface when I see her. My fear of how my master will react far outweighs anything she might say."

While Marius dealt with the travel merchant, Onesimus sat outside in the sun. How would Turia react? Maybe she would think he had come back to condemn her. Maybe she had been feeling guilty and would welcome the chance of forgiveness. He had no way of knowing. Part of him wanted to get angry all over again, march into the villa, plead his case, and condemn her.

*

There was not a ship with an empty berth to Ephesus for two days. Those days were a reprieve, of sorts, though Onesimus knew that the long walk to the judgment bench was approaching.

During the ekklesia meeting at Justus' domus, a traveling visitor told a story that Onesimus found both strange and comforting. It was about three men who had been prisoners in Persia, who refused to worship the king's god during a festival. The King threw them in a furnace to be burned alive. The God of the Way kept them from being burned up. It was interesting, but everyone told miracle stories about the gods. No, what struck him were the words of one of the condemned men. After the King had pronounced the fate of the three men, one said, "We will not bow down to your god, for we worship the One God. And he will save us. But *even if he does not save us*, we will still not bow down."

In his experience—before Rome—one worshipped a god or goddess for what they could do for you. Yet this man said that even if God didn't help them, they would still worship him. It was so counter-intuitive, and yet it made more sense than anything he had ever heard. If the God of the Way only did what Onesimus wanted, he would not be much of an admirable God! But if he was the God of creation and all being, then he deserved loyalty, no matter what.

The morning for him to set sail arrived too soon. He said his goodbyes, and even Plotia deigned to give him a brief embrace. His story had gotten around the domus, of course.

He wondered if the hug wasn't merely a kind gesture to a condemned man.

Marius accompanied him to the ship. Onesimus reflected on a sad irony: now that he was a man of faith and integrity, with many genuine friends, both slave and free, he was probably going to lose it all.

He grasped Marius by the forearms, thanked him for his help and his friendship. He turned and boarded the ship that would take him back to the land he had left so many months before.

To his home.

To his destiny.

43. Rubicon

The docks of Ephesus came into sight as the ship slid into the bay. Onesimus began to feel great trepidation. Since the ship was arriving in mid-afternoon, he intended to find a place to stay for the night. He also wanted to buy a horse to replace the one that belonged to Philemon—one of similar quality and age as Lampros. He should have enough money—some of the wealthier followers of the Way in Rome had insisted on adding to his pouch before he left, despite his protests. Perhaps replacing the horse he had stolen would be taken as a step towards restitution.

He disembarked and made his way up the road past the coliseum. Just as in Corinth, the buildings of Ephesus did not seem imposing. He passed the temple of Artemis and stopped. It was where he first realized that he might have misunderstood Philemon's intentions for him. If he had only been a responsible and loyal slave as he should have, all might have worked out exactly as he wanted. He remembered how he had gone inside to ask Artemis for help on his journey. Now the temple held no meaning for him.

Another thought struck him. If he had not stolen from Philemon and run away, he would never have gone to Rome and met Paulus. He might have never become a follower of the Way had he remained in Colossae, because he had such a negative and selfish attitude back then.

He had no trouble locating a taberna and securing advice to find a horse. It took him until almost dusk to find a suitable beast. After some negotiating, he was able to pay a fair price for a suitable animal.

*

The next morning he arose, paid his bill, and left without eating, too nervous to eat breakfast. He trotted through the city gates upon Aethon (a rather bold name for an ordinary horse). He remembered how worried he had been the last time he was on this road. Afraid of traveling through the night. Awed by Ephesus. Immature, self-centered, and scatter-brained. And certainly without enough courage to face what now lay ahead, but blissfully unaware.

The trip to Colossae was uneventful, and as he topped the hill above the villa of Philemon, he stopped Aethon. He felt the same strange calmness he had felt when he turned back from the Fontinal Gate to face Paulus.

The main gate of the villa stood open, it being almost the ninth hour. He dismounted and led the horse into the compound. He saw no one from here, though he could hear animal noises and some voices coming from the stables. The fountain at the front of the villa was splashing happily. There must have been good rains up in the hills recently. It all looked so familiar, and yet he looked upon it anew.

He secured Aethon to one of the hitching posts and approached the door. He noted the fine wood, the well-worked iron bracings and hinges, and the chiseled stone of the lintel and threshold. "I now cross my Rubicon," he said aloud. He tapped the door with his sandaled foot.

The door opened. Lentulus, the old door slave, stood blinking at him.

"Lentulus, it's me, Onesimus."

Lentulus nodded an croaked an affirmation.

Onesimus shrugged. "Okay, well, I need to see Philemon."

"Philemon is not here."

He let out an exasperated huff. Lentulus was even more obtuse than when he'd left. "Very well, how about Philippus?"

"Yes. A moment."

He shut the door. Onesimus was a bit offended—he *was* still the property of Philemon and belonged here. On the other hand, it had been almost nine months since Lentulus had last seen him. Some surprise might have been nice. Joy. Anger. Something.

The door opened, and Philippus stood there, Lentulus behind him and to the side, waiting. Onesimus realized that Philippus had probably asked him to stay by as a bodyguard or arresting officer, depending on Onesimus' intentions. Lentulus may not be emotionally or mentally alive, but he was big and strong.

"Onesimus!"

"Hello, Philippus."

Philippus was breathing hard. His face became stern. His voice returned. "I am surprised you would show your face after so long! You are in quite a fix, Onesimus! We were all so angry and disappointed in you. Still are! You… you…" Onesimus was not sure he had ever seen Philippus so out of control.

Onesimus dropped to a knee and bowed his head. "As you should be. But I've come to make it right, as best as I can." He looked up.

Philippus was taken aback. He cocked his head to the side as if he was not sure how to respond.

Finally, Philippus broke the silence. "Indeed?"

"Yes."

"No defensiveness? No placing of blame? You have a lot to answer for. The pain you have caused your master—not to mention thievery and running away—demands an accounting."

"That's why I have returned. May I come in? I'm ready to face the consequences." Onesimus was surprised at the calmness in his own voice.

Philippus seemed downright disoriented. He stepped back and opened the door wide. Onesimus stepped in and to the side, waiting, as a guest would do. Philippus shut the door.

"Philemon is not here. He will be back this evening. I don't know what you were expecting, but I am going place you in the lockup until then."

"Absolutely. That is what I expected, Philippus."

The vilici cocked his head. "I am not sure what game you are playing—"

"No games, Philippus. No longer. I'm sorry for my past, but it is *in* the past. I am different now. I don't expect you to believe me, but my actions will prove it, over time."

Philippus's expression showed dubiousness. "And what is that?" He indicated the letter cylinder.

"A letter for Philemon."

"From you?"

"From Paulus of Tarsus."

"What?! Paulus of Tarsus? *The* Paulus?"

"Yes. I ended up in Rome and worked for him."

"For *Paulus*? I must admit, Onesimus, this is all more than I can take in. What does it say?"

"I have no idea. It is sealed, and I was not told I could read it."

"Well…well…then I will take it and hold it sealed for our master. The master." He reached out, and Onesimus lifted the strap from his shoulder and handed it over.

"Very well, follow me."

They walked through the atrium and into the peristyle without a word. Onesimus wondered why he was taking him through the villa and not around it to the slave lockup between the slave quarters and the mill.

"Philippus, I do want to ask for your forgiveness, too. I know you were fond of me, and I deceived you and took advantage of those feelings. I'm sorry. I know that doesn't mean much right now."

"No, it does not. You have a lot to make up for. You did take advantage of me and made me look bad in the master's eyes. For your own selfish purposes."

"Yes, I know. I *am* different, Philippus. Paulus convinced me of the wisdom of the Way."

Philippus stopped and turned to him, fixing him with a hard stare. "My boy, you had better not be lying about this. Philemon will know."

"I know he would."

"And this is exactly the kind of thing you would do—pretend to be part of the Way to manipulate us."

"Yes, yes, I would have. More I have to make up for."

Philippus turned and they continued, past the kitchens, out the back, and down the path, across the bridge. Onesimus figured it was better to stop talking. Actions, not words, would bring him forgiveness. Not that he deserved it.

They passed through the slave quarters, and he panicked at the thought of seeing Turia. But there was no one around. They would all be at work at this time.

He'd needed to face her eventually. Asking for her forgiveness was not going to be easy, especially since he did not expect her to be any different. He'd need to remain humble and not become defensive. As he pondered the event, he realized that he wasn't angry anymore. Not really. After all, she was part of the events that led him to Paulus, to the Way, and to freedom from fear and anxiety.

They had reached the lockup door, an iron-reinforced single cell structure. It had one small window, up high. Philemon unlatched the lock from the outside and opened the door. Onesimus stepped inside. Musty. A simple cot was the only furniture. Dust everywhere.

"I will have some water and bread brought to you."

"Thank you."

"This had better be genuine, boy."

Onesimus nodded. "It is."

Philippus softened, just a bit. "You were really with Paulus?"

"I was."

"And now a member of the Way?"

"I am."

"And what do you expect?"

"I'd like an opportunity to prove myself—prove I am repentant and ready to serve with gratitude. But I expect punishment. I hope I am not sold away, but if so, it would not be unjust. I would be happy to serve in the stables."

Philippus started to laugh but stopped himself. "That is certainly not the old Onesimus. But even if I forgive you —and I am not saying I do, yet—you didn't steal my money or my horse. My anger is prompted by what you did to my good and kind master."

"I understand. This is of my own doing."

The old man stood for a moment, as if he did not want to shut the door.

"Philippus, if I may. At some point, I would like to speak with Turia. I need to ask for her forgiveness. I know that may sound strange, and you don't know the whole story, but—

"Onesimus."

Something in his tone was foreboding. "Yes?"

"She isn't here."

"What?"

"She's dead, Onesimus. She died in childbirth. It—"

A lightning bolt shot through his brain.

"Childbirth? She was pregnant?"

"Yes. About four or five weeks ago. She had a terrible labor, over 20 hours. Philemon even called in a doctor from town. But—"

Onesimus stopped listening. She gave birth four weeks ago? But that meant—

"The baby?"

Philippus stopped speaking. "Yes, there is a baby. A boy. Claudius has been caring for him, and one of Archippus slaves has been his wet nurse, as she just had a child a few months ago. But—"

"A boy?" He had a son? Why did she never tell him? Maybe she didn't know before he left? Oh—

"Onesimus. It's not good. The boy was almost a month premature. The doctor does not think he will make it."

"Make it?"

"He's going to die, Onesimus. I…I am sorry. She never said, but we all suspected it was yours."

Onesimus stepped back and sat heavy on the cot. The room was reeling.

A wash of emotions came over him. Sadness and grief over Turia, to his surprise. Joy—that he had a son. Regret that he did not have the chance to ask for her forgiveness. He had little hope she would respond in kind—but now any hope of forgiveness and reconciliation was gone. But…a son! A new life!

"Are you all right, Onesimus?"

"Yes, yes. I…I am not sure what to say."

Philippus nodded, the old compassion in his eyes that Onesimus had seen before. And not cared. Now it meant a lot.

"I…I shouldn't do this, Onesimus…but come with me."

*

He was scrawny, splotchy, and malnourished-looking. Onesimus held the tiny being in his arms. He was confused by the feelings of protection and love for a creature he had only just met.

"We've been feeding him, but he won't drink much." Claudia had been surprised to see him, by the look on her face, but kept her thoughts to herself in front of Philippus.

"Thank you. Thank you, Claudia. If allowed, I will take full responsibility for him. Whatever it takes. If not, I am in your debt. And I am sorry for my actions in the past."

Claudia looked over at Philippus.

"I have told him that the doctor does not expect him to live."

A dagger stabbed at Onesimus heart. Why did love have to be so painful? Why did Turia have to die? God had given him no chance to—

It didn't matter. He had learned that he did not have to understand everything about God, only be faithful, because he was in control of the universe.

So many loose ends and an unknown future.

44. Utilis

They passed through the atrium and into the tablinum, which was empty. Onesimus had not slept much, unsurprisingly. Philippus offered let Onesimus stay with the baby at his little house, with him and his family. That was he would not get into trouble with Philemon for keeping a watch on Onesimus. But Onesimus, against his desires, said no. He'd stay in the cell as was proper, and not impose on Philemon and his family.

Philippus motioned for him to sit in a chair before the large desk. Onesimus had never sat in this room: he had always stood. Visitors sat, whether slave or free. Household slaves stood.

"I will go inform the master you are here. I have told him all I know. Prepare yourself. His anger has not subsided, as is demonstrated whenever your name is mentioned." He paused. "Stay strong, Onesimus. If what you have told me is true, God be with you."

"Thank you, my friend. I am prepared. He hasn't read the letter yet?" He indicated the cylinder sitting on the desk.

"No." He reached out and squeeze Onesimus shoulder, then left through the archway.

The room looked the same as it did the last time he was here, but he was keenly aware of how different he was. The fountain murmured in the peristyle. At another time he might find it pleasant. For all of his external calm, his heart was still pounding. A cool breeze drifted in from the archway leading to the peristyle. He heard a woman's voice, perhaps two, from the slave rooms that were located beyond the atrium.

"So! You have the gall to return!" Onesimus jumped as Philemon came striding into the room. "I do not confess to understand why you are here. I would have preferred to discover that you had died! Your return gives me the opportunity to deal with you, however!" He was now behind the desk, his face red, not three feet from Onesimus. "As I have imagined doing *many* times!"

"Yes, domine." He must remain calm. An angry master was a dangerous master. "I've returned to confess my wrongdoing. I was a malcontent, I abused my position, and I betrayed you. I confess and offer restitution—such as I can give."

"Confess? Yes, we know what you did! And more…you stole a horse, as if the money wasn't enough!"

He leaned forward and placed the money bag on the desk. "Here is a start to repayment. There is also a horse outside to make up the for loss. I would like the chance to earn the rest of the money back. Even if it means being sold. I will accept whatever punishment you deem appropriate."

Philemon looked down at the bag. "Well…well…I don't know how you expect to do that. A horse?—" He stopped and furrowed his brow, leaning slightly forward. "Repent? Confess? What kind of words are these from you?"

"The words I believe are right. I ask your forgiveness, though I don't think I deserve it. I know my wrongdoing against you was significant."

Philemon straightened up and looked up and down at Onesimus, as if sizing him up. He leaned forward, putting both hands flat on the desk.

"Are you playing on my faith?"

Just what Onesimus feared. How ironic. In the past, he would have used these terms without meaning them, to manipulate—just as Philippus had said. Now he used them with sincerity, and was disbelieved.

"Domine, I know those are the words of your faith. They are also the words of my faith, thanks to Paulus of Tarsus."

"Paulus?! Yes, Philippus told me that was your story." He stood with a force that caused Onesimus to flinch. "Did you fly all the way to Rome like a bird?!"

Remain calm he reminded himself again. From Philemon's point of view, his story would seem fantastic. In fact, Onesimus realized, it was all somewhat improbable. From a human point of view.

"I did travel to Rome, domine. I found Paulus. I worked with him and the ekklesiai. He did not know the true story of my arrival in Rome until the end. I was convicted of my wrongdoing. When I confessed everything to him, he sent me back. And I came willingly."

Philemon slowly lowered himself back down into his chair. "This does not sound like the Onesimus I knew. So smart, so talented, but also shrewdly selfish and manipulative."

Onesimus nodded. "I was all that, domine. I have learned a better way. I have changed…am trying to change…with God's help."

Philemon sat staring off into the distance, his jaw working. Onesimus decided to keep talking, now that he had the chance. "I know this is difficult to believe, domine. I scarcely believe it myself at times. But I do not ask you to take my word for it, I ask for a chance to prove that I have changed."

Philemon took a deep breath. "Yes, Philippus told me as much. And he is inclined to believe your story—all of it. He also said you want to care for your child? You realize the child belongs to me?"

"Of course, domine. You could sell him, of course, but I am willing to do all I can to care for him, even getting extra jobs, if you'd allow it. As a way to show I am different, but also because it is right for me to do as the father."

"Yes, we all suspected it was yours. And—" he tightened his lips "—apart from this situation, I am sorry that the child will probably not live. Matters not that you are a slave—a wayward slave—you are a human, and it is your baby."

Onesimus was touched, but he also knew this was not out of character for Philemon. Tough—but compassionate. Onesimus just didn't see it before—or care to.

"Thank you, domine. I…all of this is the result of my own doings. All of it. I…I would like the opportunity to do right by it all, but I happily bow to your authority and will accept your decisions and do my best."

It was difficult to think that Philemon might sell the child. That's what happened to him, and the first part of his life was miserable. But he had to trust his new faith. Do the right thing, let God handle the rest.

"So…so domine, I do not expect you to believe my words alone."

He pointed to the document cylinder. "Here are two letters from Paulus. One to the ekklesia in Laodicea and one to you. I do not know the contents of your letter, but it will show that I was with him, and that I came here to deliver it—and myself—to you. To do with as you see fit."

They sat, unmoving, for some time. Onesimus could scarcely breathe. It was almost more than he could stand. His son. His future.

Philemon cleared his throat. "This…this is a most unusual turn of events." Onesimus looked up. "I sent people out to find you for days—a week perhaps. Then we waited. And then…we moved on. I thought you a runaway. Perhaps I would never see you again. Perhaps you would be caught and sent back, or maybe murdered as a lone slave out in the world." The voice was now calm and pensive. "But not, in my wildest dreams, would I have envisioned this. And I am still not sure I believe it."

He reached out and took up the cylinder. Breaking the seal, he twisted the end cap and dropped it, allowing it to swing from its tether. He pulled out two short scrolls, set the cylinder on his desk, and examined the seals and the writing beside each. He broke the seal of one and unrolled it.

It was not long. Onesimus had never known Paulus to write such a short letter during the entire time he was his scribe. It was the length of a typical letter. Was that a bad sign?

"Well, this certainly appears to be Paulus' signature. And it is addressed to me as well as my wife and son… and…." He cleared his throat. "He expects me to share this with the ekklesia."

He began reading. Onesimus' heart was pounding as he watched his master's face. He showed interest, then surprise, and even some amusement. When finished reading, a small, sardonic smile came briefly to his lips. He set the scroll down.

"Well, there is no doubt that this is from Paulus." He shook his head. "Rhetorical finery, humor, and a subtle but unmistakable firmness." He looked up at Onesimus. "You have read this?"

"No, domine."

Philemon gave him a twisted smile. "No? You carried this letter, and you never opened it? I know the tricks."

"No. I…I made a vow to myself as a sign of my new faith. Paulus sealed it, and I resolved to leave it as such."

"Hm. So you say."

They sat in silence again. The curiosity of what was in the letter was almost more than he could stand.

Finally, Philemon stood up. "Onesimus, I don't know what to do. You should be punished. The sacred honor of the family demands it; civilized society demands it; Roman law demands it. Such behavior cannot be tolerated. You know that. Yet your conversion, this letter, your son, and my faith, presents a unique challenge." He stood. "I need to think on this and speak with my wife. Wait here."

He walked to the archway. As he passed through, he said, without looking back, "Read it, if you wish."

Onesimus sat unmoving. Everything seemed so unreal. Turia—dead? As angry as he had been, he never thought of her being gone. A son? He never even considered it. Was there any hope? Philemon believed he needed to punish him—and who could disagree?

He leaned over and picked up the scroll and began reading.

From Paulus, a prisoner of the anointed Iesous, and brother Timotheos.

To beloved Philemon, our fellow worker, and our sister Apphia, and Archippus our fellow soldier, and the ekklesia that meets in your domus.

Grace and peace to you from God our father and the anointed domine Iesous. I always give thanks to God when remembering you in my prayers, because I often hear of your faith and love, which you have towards the domine Iesous and all the followers who are dedicated to him. I also pray that the sharing of your faith might result in all the good knowledge we have from the anointed one.

I have had much joy and encouragement from your love, because the hearts of all the followers of God have been, and continue to be, refreshed through you, my brother.

Because of this, and because I have some boldness through the anointed one, I could properly command you to do as I want. But I would rather appeal to you out of love, and out of the fact that I am just old Paulus, and also a prisoner for the anointed Iesous. And so I am appealing to you on behalf of my child, to whom I acted as a father while in chains: Onesimus.

Yes, the one who was formerly useless to you is now 'useful' to you—and to me. I am sending him back to you—this child who is my very own heart. I would have liked to have kept him for myself, but it was proper, on your account, for me to send him back, so that you could decide on your own and without being ordered, to perhaps send him back to assist me (as I am a prisoner on behalf of the Way). Then your good deed would be a willing good deed and without compulsion.

Maybe this was meant to be: that he was separated from you for a time so that you would have him back for eternity, no longer as a slave, but more than a slave—a beloved brother—as he is to me, but how much more to you and to the domine.

So, if we have had any fellowship together, welcome him as if you were welcoming me. If he has wronged you in any way, or owes you anything, charge it to me. I, Paulus, write this with my own hand: I will repay it. (I won't mention that you owe me your very life). Might I have a benefit from you through the domine? Would you refresh my heart through the anointed one?

I am sure of your intent to do what is right, and I write to you, knowing that you are the kind of person who will do even more than I ask. I even hope that, through your prayers, I can come and be with you soon.

Epaphras, my fellow-prisoner because of the anointed Iesous greets you, as well as my fellow-workers Marcus, Aristarchus, Demas, and Lucas. May the grace of the domine Iesous the anointed one be with your spirit.

EPISTOLE KAPPA

To Giarri

Grace to you and peace, my brother. I hope your health is well.

This will be my last letter. The guard, the brother in the Way, has told me that they are coming for me in the morning.

It reminds me of when the bishop of Smyrna visited us in Ephesus many years ago. Remember? He had also been arrested, and was being brought back to Rome to be executed. They stopped in Ephesus, and the Roman guards allowed him to meet with me. He had been meeting with the leaders of ekklesiai the whole way. I was taken aback by his attitude: he was looking forward to being torn apart by the wild beasts in the Arena! He claimed it an honor to die for his faith. He even forbid anyone to try to save him.

Likewise, Paulus was content when they took him away to be beheaded at the orders of Domitian. I cannot say I am as strong in the faith as those two men. But I go where I am lead, and I look to them, as they look to the Domine, as my example.

The world is changing, and being a leader among the Way brings considerable risk. Please be careful. They may even declare the Way illegal at some point, though there is hope that the lengthy writings by Lucas will convince the powers-that-be we are neither a new or foreign religion—and certainly no danger to the Empire.

I have one last request of you, concerning the letters of Paulus that we collected. Keep looking for the one to Laodicea that I delivered to them, but go ahead and start making copies of the collection as it stands and send them to all the ekklesiai you can. Whether the letter he wrote to Philemon is to be included, I am still not sure. It means too much to me to make an unbiased decision. Paulus saved my life with that letter—spiritually and physically. I leave that decision to you.

Now, my friend and brother, farewell. Do not mourn, for I go on to a greater glory, and we shall meet again. Give my love and blessings to all those with you.

It is with a grateful heart that I sign a letter, for the last time:

Onesimus, Bishop of Ephesus.

A Note from the Author

With over a million books published a year, it means a lot that you are reading this one. Online reviews make a big difference, and if you can spare a few moments, please share your thought about the book here:

http://a.co/25QkNac.

Just a few lines is enough to make a difference.

Thank you!

About the Author

Markus McDowell is an author & editor of fiction and nonfiction in multiple genres. He has a Ph.D. from Fuller Theological Seminary and a law degree from the University of London, and has lectured at universities in the US, Europe, and the UK. He is the author of the literary novel, *To and Fro Upon the Earth: A Novel*, a popular series on prayer, *Praying Through the Bible,* and research works such as *Prayers of Jewish Women: Studies of Patterns of Prayer in the Second Temple Period* and *Prayer in the Ancient Stoic Tradition.*

For more, and a free gift from the author, subscribe to the newsletter at
www.markusmcdowell.com/send-gift/

If you enjoyed this book, please consider leaving an online review. The author would appreciate reading your thoughts.

Sulis International Press
Subscribe to the newsletter: https://sulisinternational.com/subscribe/

https://www.facebook.com/SulisInternational
https://twitter.com/Sulis_Intl
https://www.pinterest.com/Sulis_Intl/
https://www.instagram.com/sulis_international/

AUTHOR'S NOTES

I cannot thank Linda and Swantje enough—their tireless reading (and rereading) of my late drafts is invaluable, making my books far better than they could be were I working on them alone. Thank you; you are both a blessings.

*

The idea for *Onesimus* came to me many years ago as I was finishing one of my masters' degrees. J. B. Lightfoot, a scholar of the late 1800s, had written an extensive and detailed philological, historical, and literary analysis (in five volumes) of writings from the second century known as the "Apostolic Fathers." The collection included a series of letters written by the bishop of Smyrna, Ignatius, who was arrested and being escorted to Rome for execution. His entourage of Roman soldiers stopped at various cities along the way, where they allowed him to meet with church leaders. After the meeting, on the next leg of his journey, he wrote letters back to those churches. One of the stops was in Ephesus, where Ignatius met, among others, a bishop named Onesimus. Lightfoot comments that the name "Onesimus" was a common slave name, and also the name of the slave at the center of Paul's Letter to Philemon in the New Testament. The background of that letter was that slave named Onesimus had stolen something and run away from his master, Philemon, only to wind up with Paul in Rome. Paul wrote the letter to the master on behalf of Onesimus, who had been of great help to him in prison. Lightfoot noted that perhaps *that* slave was the same one who became, many decades later, the bishop of Smyrna. If so, he wrote, it would make a great story.

I agreed—it was a good subject for a novel of historical fiction. I researched that letter, the letter of Ignatius, Roman slavery, Roman society, early Christianity, and all I could find on Onesimus the slave and Onesimus the bishop. Once I felt I had a good handle on what *might* have happened, I wrote the story that Dr. Lightfoot had proposed almost 150 years earlier. I put it away for a few years, then returned to rewrite the manuscript and put it into a final form. The book you hold in your hand is the result.

The sources I consulted in research and writing were vast, and most would only interest specialists. I have included a bibliography below of a few of the more useful sources for anyone wanting to know more.

The novel uses a number of transliterated Greek, Latin, and Hebrew words, rather than English translations. I did this for two reasons. First, many of the English translations bring to mind a modern image that would not make sense in the ancient world. For example, the English translation of the word *ekklesia* is "church," but an ancient person would not have thought of a building, or of a collection of people who met in a building for religious purposes. Using a transliteration helps, I hope, avoid such anachronisms. Second, the use of these words helps preserve some of the sense of the culture and time of the story.

A glossary, with pronunciation and definitions, follows the bibliography.

Markus McDowell
May, 2014
Malibu, California

BIBLIOGRAPHY

Abbott, Edwin Abbott. *Onesimus, Memoirs of a Disciple of St. Paul.* 1882.

Barclay, John M.G. *Colossians and Philemon.* New Testament Guides 12. Sheffield: Sheffield Academic Press, 1999.

Bartchy, S. Scott. "Philemon, Epistle to." *Anchor Bible Dictionary.* Volume 5, pages 305–310. Edited by David Noel Freedman. New York: Doubleday, 1992.

Bartchy, S. Scott. "Slavery (Greco-Roman), New Testament." *Anchor Bible Dictionary.* Volume 6, pages 65–73. Edited by David Noel Freedman. New York: Doubleday, 1992.

Barth, Markus. *The Letter to Philemon: A New Translation With Notes and Commentary.* Eerdmans Critical Commentary. Grand Rapids: Eerdmans, 2000.

Bassler, Jouette M. *Pauline Theology: Thessalonians, Philippians, Galatians, Philemon.* Minneapolis: Augsburg Fortress, 1994.

Callahan, Allen Dwight. *Embassy of Onesimus: The Letter of Paul to Philemon.* The New Testament in Context. Trinity Press International, 1997.

Corwin, Charles Edward. *Onesimus: Christ's Freedman: A Tale of the Pauline Epistles.* 1900.

Davies, Philip R. *Yours Faithfully: Virtual Letters From the Bible.* London: Routledge, 2004.

Dunn, James D.G. *The Epistles to the Colossians and to Philemon: A Commentary on the Greek Text.* New International Greek Testament Commentary. Grand Rapids: Eerdmans, 1996.

Evans, Craig A., and Stanley E. Porter. *New Testament Backgrounds.* A Sheffield Reader 43, Sheffield: Sheffield Academic Press, 1997.

Fitzmyer, Joseph A. *The Letter to Philemon: A New Translation With Introduction and Commentary.* New York: Doubleday, 2000.

Hall, George Washington. *Paul's Son in the Gospel: A Story of Onesimus, the Fugitive Bondman.* Boston: Christopher Publishing House,1943.

Harris, Murray J. *Exegetical Guide to the Greek New Testament: Colossians and Philemon.* Exegetical Guide to the Greek New Testament. Grand Rapids: Eerdmans, 1991.

Krentz, Edgar, John Koenig, and Donald H. Juel. *Galatians, Philippians, Philemon, I Thessalonians. Augsburg Commentary on the New Testament.* Minneapolis: Augsburg Fortress Publishers, 1985.

Lampe, Peter. "Philemon, Epistle to." *Anchor Bible Dictionary.* Volume 5, pages 21–22. Edited by David Noel Freedman. New York: Doubleday, 1992.

Lightfoot, J.B. *The Apostolic Fathers.* Part 2, Volume 2: Ignatius and Polycarp. Peabody: Hendrickson Publishers, 1989. Originally published by McMillan, 1889–1890.

Lightfoot, J.B. *Saint Paul's Epistle to the Colossians and to Philemon: A revised text with introductions, notes, and dissertations.* Grand Rapids: Zondervan, 1971.

Lohse, Eduard. *Colossians and Philemon.* Hermeneia: A Critical and Historical Commentary on the Bible. Minneapolis Augsburg Fortress, 1972.

Moule, C.F.D. *The Epistles to the Colossians and to Philemon.* Cambridge Greek Testament Commentaries. Cambridge: Cambridge University Press, 1957.

Martin, Ralph P. *Colossians and Philemon.* New Century Bible Commentary. Grand Rapids: Eerdmans, 1982.

O'Brien, Peter. *Colossians, Philemon.* Word Biblical Commentary 44. Waco: Word Books, 1982.

Thompson, Marianne Meye. *Colossians and Philemon.* Two Horizons Commentary. Grand Rapids: Eerdmans, 2006.

Thurston, Bonnie B., and Judith M. Ryan. *Philippians and Philemon*. Sacra Pagina 10. Collegeville: Liturgical Press, 2003.

GLOSSARY OF TERMS AND NAMES

Aediles. Ay-DEE-laze. Latin. A government official who presided over certain buildings and festivals.

Amenuensis. Uh-men-you-IN-sis. Latin. A slave who acts as a secretary or clerk; educated in preparation of papyrus and writing.

Amphora, amphorai. Am-FOUR-ah, am-FOUR-eye. Greek. A ceramic vessel with a narrow neck or a broad neck, for storing, transporting, or displaying food or liquid.

Bema. BAY-mah. Greek. Literally a step or platform. Usually used to refer to a judge's raised seat in a town square or forum.

Castrata. Cah-STRA-tah. Latin. A male human or animal who has been castrated. Could be used as an insult.

Cauponas. Kow-POE-nas. Latin. A public inn with a dining room.

Chiton. KEY-tawn. Greek. ("ch" as in the Scottish pronunciation of "loch.") A long, sewn garment that connects at one shoulder.

Chlymes. KLY-mace. Latin. ("ch" as in the Scottish pronunciation of "loch.") A dark wool cloak pinned at one shoulder.

Cognomen. Cog-NO-men. Latin. The third part of the name of a Roman citizen, identifying a particular branch of a clan or family.

Domine and *Domina*. DOE-men-ay, DOE-men-ah. Latin. Usually translated as "lord" into English, it was used as an address to a superior: "master" or even "sir." It was also used to refer to gods, including the Jewish and Christian God ("Lord").

Domus, domii. DOE-mas, DOE-me-ee. A house or home, usually smaller than a villa and located inside a city.

Ekklesia, ekklesiai. Eh-klay-SEE-uh, eh-klay-SEE-eye. Greek. A gathering of people who come together for a particular purpose. The modern translation is "church." Our word "ecclesiastical" comes from this word.

Gladus. GLA-doos. Latin. A short Roman broadsword; standard issue to Roman soldiers.

Iesous. YAY-soos. Greek. The Greek form of the Hebrew name "Joshua."

Impluvium. Em-PLU-vee-um. Latin. A square pool in the atrium of Roman homes, filled by rainwater coming through a skylight above.

Keltoi. KELL-toy. Greek. The name that Julius Caesar gave to the Gaelic tribes living on the European continent and the British Isles.

Lupatria. Loo-PAH-tree-ah. Latin. A derogatory name for a woman, akin to "slut" in modern English.

Nomen. NO-men. Latin. The middle name of a Roman citizen, denoting his or her clan or family.

Paedagogos. PAY-da-goe-ghos. Latin. A low slave who acted as a nanny for children, teaching them manners and protecting them.

Peculium. Peh-CUE-lee-um. Latin. Money or property that slaves were legally allowed to earn and save (though it could be revoked by their master).

Peristyle. PEAR-uh-style. Greek and Latin. A rectangular garden in the middle of a typical Roman villa, with a covered walkway around all four sides, supported by columns.

Pilleus. Puh-LAY-us. Latin. A simple, felt cap with no brim, worn by slaves who had been freed.

Popina. Pa-PEE-nuh. Latin. An outdoor Roman wine bar, providing a variety of wines as well as olives, bread, nuts, and other simple foods. Popinas (popinae) were associated with lower classes, as well as gambling and prostitution.

Posca. PAH-ska. Latin. A drink made of sour wine or vinegar, mixed with water and herbs. It was a standard drink of the lower classes and by Roman soldiers.

Prima mensa. PREE-muh MEN-sa. Latin. The primary course of the Roman main meal; the entrée. This would consist of a meat dish, vegetables, and wine, though in some situations it could be much more extravagant.

Promulsis. Prah-MUL-sis. Latin. The first serving of the Roman main meal, intended to whet the appetite. It often consisted of some kind of egg dish, raw vegetables, and/or a small fish or seafood appetizer.

Secula mensa. SEK-you-luh MEN-suh. Latin. The 'second meal;' the dessert course of a Roman main meal. This was usually something sweet, such as pastries and fruit.

Sesterces. Seh-STAIR-sayse. Latin. A Roman coin, made of brass.

Skata. SKA-tah. Greek. A swear word, similar in meaning to *skubalon.*

Skubalon. SKOO-bah-lon. Greek. A vulgar word for excrement that could be used to refer to the actual substance or as a swear word or insult (like the English equivalent; Paul uses this word in Philippians 3.8).

Stilus. STY-lus. Latin. A pointed instrument used for writing.

Stola. STOW-la. Greek and Latin. The traditional garment of Greek and Roman women; corresponding to the toga for men.

Taberna. Ta-BEAR-nah. Latin. An indoor, single room that served as a commercial shop for retail, often serving prepared foods and wine.

Tablinum. Ta-BLI-num. Latin. In a Roman villa, a room usually off one side of the atrium and opening to the peristyle at the rear. It served as the patriarch's office and where he would receive business visitors.

Thea gnu. Thay-uh g'new. Greek. A "divine woman," a female who is part goddess and part human. Compare *theos aner* below.

Theos aner . Greek. A "divine man." A male being who is part god, part human, such as Hercules in Greek mythology.

Triclinium. Try-CLEN-ee-um. Latin. The formal dining room found in a Roman villa. The table was low; diners reclined on cushions or couches around it.

Trigon. TRY-gone. Greek. A ball game involving three players.

Trireme. TRY-reem. Latin. A Roman galley with three banks of oars on each side.

Vilici. Vuh-LEE-chee. Latin. A slave who oversees other slaves. An overseer.

Made in the USA
Las Vegas, NV
02 March 2024